NEW YORK TIMES BESTSELLING AUTHOR

KAYLEE RYAN

Cover Design: Lori Jackson Design
Cover Photography: Golden Czermak
Cover Model: Kevin Lajeunesse
Editing: Hot Tree Editing
Proofreading: Deaton Author Services
Paperback Formatting: Integrity Formatting

CHAPTER
Layla
ONE

GLANCING AT THE clock, I see it's almost closing time. I usually don't mind the late-night weekend shifts. Tonight, however, has been a nonstop flow, and my feet are killing me. I know it's my shoes; they're a couple of years old, and I wear them every day that I work, which with all the extra shifts I take is a lot. Unfortunately, new shoes are not in the budget. Besides, the tips are always better on the weekends and especially at night. The more they drink, the more they tip. I live paycheck to paycheck, so every dollar counts.

"Layla, VIP suite, a party of one," my coworker, Oliver, calls out for me.

I sigh. He knows damn well it's his turn, but I bite my tongue, grabbing a menu and a glass of water and head that way. The VIP suite is always good for tips. It's a small room of only ten tables that are spread out far enough to enjoy private conversations. I've seen more proposals in that room than I can count. My guess is since it's a party of one, Oliver didn't feel it was worth his time.

He's living on Mommy and Daddy's dime while in college. He's only here to appease them. That's not me making things up—he himself will tell you. I, on the other hand, do not have the luxury of being that choosy. I take all the tables I can get.

The VIP suite is empty with the exception of a single man sitting with his head down, staring at the phone in his hands. "Welcome to the Emerald Entrée. My name is Layla. I'll be your server tonight. Can I start you off with something to drink?" I ask him. I set the glass of water on a coaster and place his menu on the table. Grabbing my order pad and pen out of my apron, I wait patiently for him to look up at me.

"What do you suggest?" he asks, still looking at his phone.

His voice is deep and sexy. He's in a business suit, but he's removed his tie and unbuttoned the top two buttons. He looks officially sexy if that's a thing. I open my mouth to give him my usual spiel about the filet mignon or the grilled salmon, but he looks up at me, and all the breath leaves my lungs. I stumble a little and have to brace myself by placing my hand on his table. He's gorgeous. Dark hair, with a thick beard covering his face. Intense blue eyes that I could easily get lost in. I see lots of good-looking guys come in here daily, but this guy… he's hands down the sexiest guy I've ever laid eyes on.

"Layla," he says, his deep timbre giving life to my name.

"I-I'm sorry." I then ramble off a few of our most popular menu items.

"Filet is fine. Well done, salad, no dressing, and broccoli," he says without even opening the menu.

"And to drink?" I manage to ask.

"Water is fine. Thank you, Layla." A smile tilts his lips as he hands me his menu.

"T-Thank you. I'll have your salad right out." I take the menu and rush out of the room. I get his order keyed in and grab a salad, along with a fresh glass of water and head back to his table. This time I'm more composed. "I'll be back with some fresh rolls. They just need a few more minutes," I say when I reach his table.

He nods his acceptance but doesn't say anything. I can feel those blue eyes on me, and it's unnerving. Pushing through, head held high, I manage to set his fresh water and salad on the table without making a fool of myself and spilling or dropping it. Then rush away.

"I'm heading out, you good?" Oliver asks me as soon as I step back into the kitchen.

"You're leaving early?" I don't know why I bother to state the obvious. This is nothing new for Oliver.

"Yep, all cashed out. The only customer left is yours in VIP. Doors lock in fifteen," he says, waving over his shoulder.

My aching feet want me to shove my worn-out size eights up his ass. Instead, I take a seat at a table near the kitchen and start to roll silverware into our cloth napkins. Maybe five minutes have passed, but I feel like I should go check on blue eyes. With an internal groan, I stand and make my way to his table, which is in the back of the restaurant.

"I can take that for you," I say, reaching his table. I grab his now empty salad bowl. "Is there anything else I can get you? Your meal should be right up."

"Did you hurt yourself?" he asks bluntly.

"I'm sorry?" I stand a little taller.

"You're limping." With a nod of his head, he motions toward my feet.

Heat floods my cheeks as embarrassment washes over me. "No, just need some new shoes," I say cheerily. I want to run from his table, but that's unprofessional, and I refuse to let him make me feel as though I'm beneath him. "Would you like steak sauce with your steak?" I ask, changing the subject. My voice is strong, even though my insides are shaking from humiliation.

"Yes, please," he says, his blue eyes lifting to my face.

I nod, turn on my heel and walk at a normal pace to the kitchen, and no matter how hard I try, I can't seem to keep the limp at bay. Damnit. Time to check my credit card and see if I can fit in a cheap pair of shoes. Although, that's part of my problem. The cheap ones wear out faster. Not much I can do about that when it's all that I can afford, and I'm lucky to work that into my budget.

Dropping his salad bowl off in the kitchen, I check with the cook on his steak and go lock the front doors. I can't cash out my register yet, and surprisingly, Oliver actually wiped down his tables and has his closing prep done. I'm thankful we don't have to stick around and clean. The dishwasher does, but he was almost caught up when I dropped off the salad bowl. We have a cleaning crew that comes in each night and scrubs this place spotless. I've helped out a few times when they were shorthanded.

"Layla, order up," the cook calls out for me. I rise from my seat where I was rolling more silverware. "Kitchen's closed. We can do dessert if we need to," he tells me when I place Blue Eyes' meal on a tray.

"Thanks, Ronnie." I give him a kind smile. He's old enough to be my dad and treats me as though I'm his daughter. I'm grateful for that. In my experience, there are not many men out there who can be nice without wanting your body in return.

Walking back to serve him his steak, I don't rush, to try and eliminate my limp as much as possible. "Here you go," I say brightly. I place his plate in front of him. "This plate is really hot," I warn him as I do all of my customers, just as I was trained to do. I set an extra cloth napkin on the table along with a bottle of steak sauce, and another fresh glass of water. "Is there anything else that I can get you?" I ask him.

"No, Layla. I'm good." He addresses me by name. It's the first time the sound of my name has ever sent shivers down my spine. Not in a bad way, but in a "this man affects me" kind of way.

"Great. I'll be back to check on you." I turn and walk away.

I busy myself wrapping silverware, staring at my watch for what feels like every thirty seconds. I don't want to hover, and with it being closing time, that makes it look bad. There is nothing worse than your waitress hounding you a million times when you're trying to eat.

"Thank you, Layla," his deep timbre greets me.

My head pops up to find him standing before me. "I'm sorry." I move to rise from the booth, and he raises his hand to stop me, his eyes dropping to my feet. "I've left money on the table to cover the bill." His eyes wander up my body back to my face.

"T-Thank you. Have a great night." His reply is to nod and walk out the door. Grabbing a tray, I make my way back to his table. Loading up his leftover dishes, I lift his plate and find two crisp one-hundred-dollar bills. I look over my shoulder to see if he's standing there watching me, but he's not. It's just me in the VIP room. His bill could not have been more than fifty dollars. My hands shake as I tuck the money into my apron. I'm embarrassed and grateful all at once. As quickly as I can, I clean off his table and drop the dishes off to the kitchen. Pulling up his bill, I shake my head when I see it was under fifty dollars. Pulling one of the hundreds out of my pocket, I cash out his check and pocket the remaining change. Quickly, yet efficiently, I rush through my closing procedure on the register, lock the money in the safe, and finally, I can head home.

"You ready to head out?" Ronnie asks, appearing beside me.

"Yes, you?" He holds his arm out for me, and I don't hesitate to slip mine through his.

He makes sure that he walks me to my car every night. No matter how many times I tell him I'm fine. He insists. On the nights we're not on the same shift, he always calls to make sure one of the other guys walks me out. He worries when he doesn't need to. "How was it tonight?" he asks.

"Good. It was busy, but that's good for tips."

"Was that last guy bothering you?" he asks, his fatherly concern stirring my already haggard emotions from the night.

"Not at all. He, uh, he noticed my shoes were hurting my feet. He simply saved me a trip," I confess.

"Layla, if you need help," he offers, just as he has so many times before. My heart swells with love for him and the support he's always given me.

"Thank you, Ronnie, but I'm holding my own."

"You'll tell me if you need anything? Linda and I will do anything we can."

"I know you would. I can't tell you how much that means to me, but I'm doing okay. Things are tight, but I live on my own, that's to be expected."

"You deserve better," he says, his jaw clenching. Ronnie and his wife, Linda, invited me to dinner my first Thanksgiving here in Florida. When they found out I was spending the day alone, they refused to take no for an answer. Since then, they've become like family to me. They are the only people here who know of my sordid past. Of the family I was born into, and the reason I'm here in Florida all on my own.

"Hey now..." I lean into him as we approach my beat-up Honda Civic. "What doesn't kill us makes us stronger, right?"

He chuckles. "My wife is rubbing off on you."

"Full of wisdom." I laugh. Linda is the most positive person I know. No matter how hard things get, she has a glass-half-full optimism. I try to pull from her strength. Lord knows my own mother is no kind of role model.

"That she is," he says as I step out of his hold. "You drive safe." He stands back while I climb in and shut the door. With a wave through the windshield, I start my car and lock the doors. Only then does he head to his own vehicle. Once he's settled, and his headlights come on, I pull out, with Ronnie pulling out behind me.

It's nice to know that I have someone out there who cares enough to worry. It's a new concept for me, and it's taken me a while to accept that they're doing it because they do care. When you grow up in a home without love, you don't really recognize it. I was lucky enough to land a job in the kitchen, washing dishes seven years ago. I was eighteen years old and on my own. I fled Indiana the day they handed me my high school diploma, and I've never looked back. Not that I needed to. There is no one following me, wondering where I am.

CHAPTER
Layla
TWO

"LAYLA, YOU HAVE a party of one in VIP," Maria says as I pass her on my way to the kitchen.

"I'm not on VIP tonight," I remind her. We switch off weekends due to the tips, and I had VIP last Friday, and then there's my solo customer I've had every night this week.

She shrugs. "He requested you."

Blue Eyes.

I'm sure it's him. I've worked here for seven years, and he's the first to request me specifically.

"Of course he requested me," I say under my breath, grabbing a menu, silverware, and a glass of water.

"He's hot. Let me tell you, if you're not interested, I am. That man is fine," she says, waving her hands in front of her face as if they would cool her down.

My heart rate spikes, and nerves start to set in. It's been this way every night I've worked for the last week. He comes in late, sits in VIP, and asks for me. I don't know who he is or what he's after, but I'm thankful for him and his generous tips, even though I can't keep accepting them. It's too much. Standing tall, well, as tall as my five-foot-six frame can stand, I head to the VIP section. As soon as I enter the room, I see him. As before, he's staring down at his phone. He's sitting at the same table in the back of the room. Tonight, however, there are two other tables that are occupied.

"Welcome to the Emerald Entrée, my name is Layla. I'll be your server this evening," I say, trying to remain professional, placing his menu, silverware, and glass of water on the table.

"Layla." He looks up, and once again, I'm captivated by those blue eyes.

"Hi." I wave, making the moment even more awkward. Reaching into my apron, I grab my pad and paper. "Would you like an appetizer?" I ask, getting right down to business.

When he doesn't reply, I look up to find him staring at my same pair of worn-out shoes. The same pair of shoes he's looked at every time he's been here, in this exact seat. "We have pretzel bites on special tonight," I continue to ramble on.

"I'll have…" He looks up, and my breath hitches in my throat. I manage to write down his order as he lists the exact same meal— the one I have memorized. His blue eyes are intense, and it makes me wonder what he's thinking about. Well, other than the fact that I still have the same shoes on my feet. I'd love to know what he's thinking. Then again, the way he was just staring at my feet with a scowl on his face, maybe not.

"And to drink?" I ask him.

"Water."

"Of course, I'll get this put in and have your salad right out." I turn and walk away, mindful that his eyes are on me. I can feel his stare. Typing his order into the computer, I go gather his salad and another fresh glass of water. "Here you go," I say, setting it in front of him.

"Tell me, Layla, have you worked here long?" he asks. He's

been making small talk all week. What is there to do in the area? How far to the nearest mall? Questions that surprise me coming from him, but ones we get from tourists all the time. Well, until this one.

I look around and realize the other diners have left, and it's just the two of us. "I have. I just had my seven-year anniversary."

He nods. "Do you like working here?"

He's not giving me the creep vibe, but I'm still uneasy with his questions. "I do. I needed a job, and the Emerald gave me a shot. I've been here ever since." Taking a deep breath, I internally chastise myself. I don't know why I just blabbed all of that.

"I'll go check on your meal. Enjoy," I say, turning away before he can ask another question, and I spill my life story. It's those eyes. He could get me to tell him anything. He should work for the CIA or something. Hell, he might, I know nothing about him. I don't even know his name.

I busy myself with my other tables, and this time when I drop off his meal, he's on the phone having a conversation, so I'm able to drop off his food, along with steak sauce, a refill, extra napkins, and rush off. I don't know what it is, but there is something about him. It's as if his presence alone is commanding. I check on my other tables, then head back to his, hoping that he's still occupied with his call.

When I approach, he lifts his head and watches me. "Did you save room for dessert?" I ask.

"Just the check," he says, tossing his napkin on his now empty plate.

"Great, here you go. I can take it whenever you're ready."

"Wait." He stands, pulls his wallet out of his pocket, grabs a few bills, and hands it to me. "Keep the change, Layla," he says. His fingers slide across mine as he hands me the money, and my hand tingles from his touch.

"Thank you, uh, sir," I say, fumbling with my words and once again making myself look like a fool in front of him. Unlike him, I've not badgered him with questions, including his name. He always pays in cash, so there is no credit card to tell me his name. Hence the nickname, Blue Eyes. It fits him.

"Owen." He holds his hand out for me. My fingers are still tingling, but my manners and blatant curiosity of the magic of his touch—and if it will happen a second time—have me placing my hand in his.

"It's nice to meet you, Owen. Thank you for your generosity." I know I already thanked him for his gracious tips, but there are several bills now shoved in my apron, and I'm certain it more than covers his meal, just as before.

"You work every night?" he asks.

I can see how he would think that. I've been here every night this week. "Most weekends. I don't mind the shifts that no one else wants to work," I say with a shrug. Again, giving him more information than necessary for the conversation.

"Do you ever get a night off?"

"Yeah, usually not on the weekend. This week I picked up some extra shifts." His eyes bore into mine, unnerving me. Shifting my weight from one leg to the other, I look over at the table. "Thank you again. Have a great night."

"Are you dismissing me, Layla?"

"N-No." I clear my throat. "No, just, uh, thank you. You don't have to go." I stumble over my words. I don't know who this guy is, but from a look, you can tell he has money. Just my luck, he's some big wig that could get me fired. I need this job.

Reaching out, his thumb lightly brushes under my eye. "You look tired."

Who is this guy? He's seen me a handful of times, and he thinks he knows I'm tired? What's worse is I am. I haven't been sleeping well. There is no reason for it, but the truth is apparently obvious in my eyes. "Just a long day," I answer him.

"Hmm. I'll see you soon, Layla." With that, he steps around me and walks out of the room.

I stand frozen, my knees locked, and my mind racing. *What just happened?* My hand goes to my cheek. I can still feel his touch. That man is intoxicating and trouble. Nothing but trouble. Shaking myself out of my Owen trance, I get busy clearing his table.

Owen.

It's not a name you hear often, and I have to say it suits him. Then again, so does Blue Eyes, but I can't very well call him that to his face. Something tells me that I've not seen the last of him.

"You ready to lock the doors?" Maria asks me.

Turning my wrist to look at my watch, I see it's past closing time. "Yeah, my last one just left."

"Oh, honey, I noticed. That was the hottie in VIP. Did you get his number?" she asks.

"No."

"Why the hell not? How do you know him anyway? He asked for you by name."

"I don't. He came in last weekend, and Oliver pawned his table off on me. He's been here every night since."

"Has he asked for you every time?"

"Yeah," I say, thinking about how after that first night, I watch for him to come in. I've never been there waiting for him, though. He always has to ask for me.

"He must like what he sees." She hip checks me and goes to lock the doors.

Reaching into my apron, I pull out his ticket to cash him out. I'm not surprised that he's left the same generous tip as he has every day this week. It's too much, and I should give it back to him. I think about how that extra money helped me. It's wrong to keep taking it. I know that. Starting now, I'm going to give it back to him. I appreciate his generosity, and it's helped me more than he will ever know, but I can't keep taking it. I don't know what he's playing at, but I can't keep accepting these huge tips. I can hear my bank account crying as I make plans to keep the tip on me in case I see him again so I can give it back.

"You ladies ready to go?" Oliver asks. Ronnie was off tonight, so he's tasked with taking us to our cars. He sees it as an inconvenience but does it anyway. Secretly, I think he's afraid of

Ronnie. Ronnie doesn't take his shit, and that scares Mr. Spoiled and Privileged.

"Yes," Maria and I say at the same time.

Grabbing our bags, we head out to the lot, following behind Oliver. "Have a good night, ladies," he calls out, throwing his hand in the air for a wave. He doesn't bother to make sure we're in our cars, but he never does.

"You on tomorrow?" Maria asks.

"Yes, I'm on the next two days."

"Bummer. I'll see you next week." She climbs in her car and drives away.

Unlocking my car door, I climb inside, tossing my bag into the passenger seat and locking the doors—something Ronnie insisted I do as soon as I get inside. Key in the ignition, I turn it, and nothing happens. I try again and still nothing.

"Shit." I slam my hands against the steering wheel. "Come on, don't fail me now. Not tonight of all nights." I try yet again and nothing but a clicking sound, no sign that the engine is going to start up and drive my tired ass home. Peering through the front windshield, I watch as Maria's taillights disappear. Oliver is long since gone, which leaves me all alone. I don't have a cell phone—that's an expense that I can't afford. I'm barely keeping a roof over my head and food on the table. Exhaling a deep breath, I grab my bag, the keys, and climb out of the car. I lock the door, even though no one would want to steal it. Ronnie has beat it in my head to keep it locked to keep others from hiding in the back seat. I think he watches too many murder mysteries, but I don't tell him that. I just lock my doors. It's easy enough, and it makes him smile when he sees that I've listened. Linda said she does the same. "Pick your battles," she once told me. I'm lucky to have them both.

The back parking lot where the employees park is dimly lit, so I keep my hand on my bag, keeping it close, and rush around the front of the building and the main entrance of the hotel. Once we shut the door, we're locked out for the night, so I'm going to have to ask the front desk to use their phone.

CHAPTER
Owen
THREE

'VE BEEN STAYING at the Emerald Seaside Resort for a week now. They're struggling financially, which is why I'm here. That's what I do. Jase called in a personal favor, and to be honest, getting out of Nashville for a few days sounded like a damn good plan. A few days has turned into a week. I don't understand where the financial bleed is coming from, but my gut tells me it's someone, not something that's causing them to lose money hand over fist. I called Jase last night to give him my thoughts. He asked me to stick around until he can find out why they're dragging their feet giving me access to the books. It's been seven days. Their time is up.

So far, nothing glaring has jumped out at me. The hotel is clean, with plenty of staff, and filled with guests. The amenities are on point, and I'm struggling to find out why the owner is requesting a buyout. He claims that he can barely keep the place in the red. That just doesn't make sense.

Not interested in being holed up in my suite staring at the four walls, I head down to the lobby. The hotel has a nightclub, and by the brochure provided in my suite, last call is not until two in the morning. That gives me two hours to take in the atmosphere, something I've yet to do during my stay this past week.

The elevator doors slide open, and I step out, taking a look around. There are guests milling around, and again there should be no reason that this place is losing money. My eyes scan again, and that's when I see her.

Layla.

Stunning.

Long blonde hair, tight little body, and striking blue eyes. She's a tiny thing, several inches shorter than my six foot three. She's sitting alone on a bench, her elbows resting on her knees, and her hands buried in her hair. I can't see her face, but I know it's her. It's the golden blonde hair. I can almost guarantee that it's her by her hair alone. I could easily pick her out of a crowd.

"Layla," I say when I reach her. She sucks in a breath and looks up at me. Her eyes are red, and her cheeks wet from tears. "What's wrong?"

"Nothing." She hastily wipes her eyes. Standing, she reaches into her purse and pulls out some cash and holds it out for me. "Thank you for your generosity, but it's too much."

I stare at her hand. "It's yours."

"I can't keep accepting these kinds of tips, Owen," her sweet lips say my name.

"You can." The tips I've given her are nothing for a man like me.

"I-I'm not for sale." She glances at her feet, and I want those blue eyes on me.

"Layla." My voice is strong, causing her head to slowly rise, and those blue eyes to go wide. "I'm not trying to buy you."

"I don't understand." She looks at her hand that's now clutching the cash as if it were her lifeline.

"You provided a service, and I tipped you. End of story."

Her eyes well with more tears. "Thank you," she whispers.

"Now, tell me what's wrong. Who hurt you?"

She shakes her head. "No one. My car won't start, and I couldn't get ahold of Ronnie, and the tow truck said it's going to be a hundred dollars to tow it two miles to the repair shop. My feet hurt, and I'm dreading walking the eight blocks to my apartment, but I don't want to spend the money on an Uber, and I'm tired," she adds. "So, damn tired."

"Who's Ronnie?" Sounds like a real prick for not picking up for her. He's obviously not concerned for her safety. It pisses me off. If you're going to be in a relationship, then you need to be in it. You make the choice. He needs to man the fuck up.

"He works with me. He and his wife, Linda. They helped me when I got to town, and now they're family."

I feel my shoulders relax. "Come with me." I hold my hand out for her. No way can I leave her here like this.

Surprisingly, she doesn't question me. Instead, she places her small hand in my larger one and allows me to guide her to stand from the bench. With her hand in mine, I lead us to the front of the hotel, and motion for a car. That's another perk this place offers, a car service. Sure, they bill it to your room, but it beats having a rental and to pay for parking. Layla is still and quiet beside me. "Climb in," I say when the car pulls up. She bites down on her bottom lip, a few seconds of hesitation before she pulls her hand from mine and slides into the back seat.

"Address?" I ask her.

She rattles it off to the driver. "Thank you, Owen," she says softly.

Giving her a nod, I turn to look out the window, pretending that seeing her upset doesn't affect me. I watch as each block passes, the more rundown the homes look. When we pull up to a rundown apartment complex, I stare at the thugs that are hanging around. "You live here?"

"Yeah, I was lucky to find this place when I moved here seven years ago. It's not much, but it's home."

"Where is your family?"

"Ronnie and Linda," she starts, but I hold my hand up, stopping her.

"Your blood family."

She shrugs. "It's really not that interesting," she tells me.

"Try me."

Taking a deep breath, she slowly exhales. "I never knew my father. Anytime I asked about him, my mom would tell me that he didn't want me and left us. My mom, well, she's only a mom in name. I was cooking and cleaning up after her when I was a kid. My earliest memory is when I was about five. It's fuzzy, but I can remember the bus dropping me off at our apartment of whatever rundown dump we were living in. She'd be passed out on the couch; alcohol, drugs, not really sure. Anyway, I made a peanut butter sandwich, she woke up and swiped it off the counter, stumbling back to the couch. That started our routine. I took care of her."

Jesus. "Where is she now?"

"I'm not sure. I left Indiana the day they handed me my high school diploma. I never looked back."

"Aunts, uncles, grandparents?" Surely, she's not all alone.

"None that I ever met. Mom didn't know her dad, and from what she tells me, her mom wasn't much better." She sits up a little taller in the seat. "I'm sorry. I don't know why I just laid all that on you. Thank you for the ride." She holds out her hand, and the cash is still there.

"I'm not taking that," I tell her. My voice is commanding. I'm expecting an argument, but she surprises me when she leans in and kisses my cheek.

"Thank you, Owen. I'm not sure who sent you to me when I needed you, but I'm grateful. Thank you for your generosity and for the ride." She reaches for the handle and climbs out of the car.

I hear catcalls as she shuts the door, and I'm shouting at the driver to stop, and to wait for me. My door flies open, and I jog around the car to catch up with her. I glare at the men who are calling out to her, placing my hand on the small of her back. She visibly relaxes and allows me to lead her to the main entrance of the apartment building.

"I'm right here." She points to the first door on the left." Her hand trembles as she places the key into the lock and turns the knob. Turning to face me, she says, "Thank you again. For everything."

"Do they bother you?" I ask her.

She shrugs. "They're harmless."

"Until they're not."

"I've lived here on my own for seven years. I can handle myself. Tonight, I had a momentary moment of weakness. I'm sorry you had to see that."

"Pack a bag," I tell her, looking at the flimsy handle and lock on her door.

"What?" She takes a step back and into her apartment.

"Pack a bag. You can't stay here."

"That's not up to you," she says, crossing her arms over her chest.

"Layla, it's not safe."

"This is my home, Owen. And who do you think you are? Telling me where I can and can't stay. You don't know me."

My jaw ticks. "I can't let you stay here. Look at this lock." I reach for the door handle and wiggle it, showing her it's loose.

"Thank you for your generosity." She steps back, reaching for the door, and I place my hand on it to stop her.

"Please."

More tears coat her cheeks, and I hate that I'm upsetting her, but damnit, I can't let her stay here. This place is a dump, and those guys are sitting right outside her window.

"I don't have anywhere to go," she murmurs.

Fuck me. "I'll take care of it. Please, go pack a bag."

"What are you going to do?"

"Get you a room. Hell, I have a suite. You can stay with me."

"Then what, Owen? That's fine for tonight, or even until you go back to wherever you came from, but then what? That still leaves me here, in this ratty old apartment. Look, I appreciate your concern, but this is my life. I've worked hard to keep this shitty roof over my head."

"I'll stay," I say, taking a step forward, putting us toe-to-toe.

"No." Her hands land flat against my chest, holding off my advances to enter her apartment. "I don't even know you. Hell, you just told me your name tonight. This is not happening." She huffs out a breath, blowing the errant hair out of her eyes. "I'm a big girl. I've got this. Thank you again for the ride, and the generous tips. I'll see you around, Owen."

She gives me a shove, and I stumble back, surprised. This gives her enough time to slam the door in my face. "Layla." I pound my fist on the door. Nothing but silence greets me. "Shit." Making my way outside, I take in the five guys who are sitting around drinking and smoking. "Gentlemen," I greet them. "How about a little business proposition?" I ask them.

"What ya got in mind?" one of them asks.

"Hundred bucks for each of you to leave this building and not come back for at least twenty-four hours." They stumble to their feet. Hands held out. I slap a crisp hundred in each of their hands and watch as they blindly walk away from the building. It's not much, but I'll feel better about leaving her here on her own. I bought myself some time, but now I need a plan. I can't let her stay here. I know that. What I don't know is why it bothers me so much.

CHAPTER *Layla* FOUR

I F I THOUGHT I was tired last night, that's nothing compared to today. I didn't sleep at all. I couldn't seem to shut my mind off. One minute I'm worrying about my car and how much it's going to cost to fix it, and the next, my mind is consumed with Owen.

While I appreciate his concern, I barely know the guy. No way am I letting him put me up in a room, or even stay with him. No way. I've served him a week's worth of meals, and we've exchanged small talk. That does not translate to a sleepover, or a hey, let me put you up for the night. Granted, the over-the-top tips he's been leaving are going to go a long way in helping me repair my car. Just when I thought I might be able to get ahead, have a little extra in the bank for an emergency, said emergency rears its ugly head.

Such is my life.

Glancing at the clock, I see I have to be at work in an hour. I need to get my ass in gear. Grabbing my purse and making sure I have my keys to the car that doesn't run, I head out after double-checking that the door is locked. Speaking of, I'm surprised "the gang" as I call them are missing from the front stoop. They're not really a gang; at least, I don't think they are. It's weird that their catcalls don't greet me, as well as the cloud of smoke and fumes of the alcohol on their breath. I shake out of my thoughts with a small smile. I'm worried about a group of men who have more times than not scared the hell out of me, if only Owen could hear my thoughts. I'm sure he would have something to say about missing them.

By the time I make it to work, I'm a sweaty hot mess. Thankfully, I brought my uniform rather than wore it, and some deodorant to freshen up. My first stop is the staff restroom and I do just that, before rushing to the break room to call the repair shop.

Tying my apron around my waist, I make sure I have a pen and my notepad. I'm surprised when I look up into the vibrant blue eyes of Owen.

"Hey." I give him an awkward wave. "I'm, uh… not used to you being here this early."

"What time do you get off?"

Okay, no small talk. Got it. "Closing."

"You closed last night. It's eleven now. That's a twelve-hour shift."

"Can you honestly tell me you've never worked a twelve-hour shift?" I ask, my hands on my hips.

"That's different?"

"Right," I scoff. "Look, Owen, like I said last night, I'm a big girl. I can handle it. Maria needed the day off, and I offered to work for her. I can use the extra money," I say, groaning internally. That last part slipped out. I didn't mean to say it, but as with every time I'm around him, I tend to open my mouth and word vomit just happens.

"Have you heard anything about your car?" he asks, ignoring everything I said.

"No." I sigh. "I had to wait until I got here to call."

"Why?"

"I don't have a home phone or a cell phone."

"What? You can't stay there alone without a phone."

"I've been fine the past seven years without one."

He inhales loudly. "Layla," he says, exasperated.

"Owen, table for one?" I ask him.

"Fine," he says through his teeth. I have to fight back my grin. Owen pissed off is kind of comical, especially since he has no merit. This is my life, and he has no say so. We're not even friends, simply acquaintances. "Same table?" I ask.

"No. Here is fine." He walks to a table not far from the main entrance, that just so happens to be in my section.

"What can I get for you?" I ask, pulling my order pad out of my pocket.

"Grilled chicken sandwich and fries, sweet tea." He hands me the menu. "Where did you have your car towed?"

"Parker's. I'll be right out with your tea." I don't stick around for his reply. "Sexy, infuriating man," I grumble, standing at the computer to enter his order.

"Hey now, what did I do this time?" Oliver asks.

"Not you."

"Come on, Layla. You know you want me." He holds his arms open as if showing off his body.

I will admit he's easy on the eyes. He has shaggy blond hair, big brown eyes, and you can tell he takes care of his body. However, when he opens his mouth, it all goes to hell. He's as conceited as they come, and spoiled. I like my men to have a little more depth. Not that there have been many men in my life. I've dated here and there, but nothing serious. I work all the time to survive, and that's not conducive to a social life. I'm better off. There are some crazy people out there. I've dated a few and luckily dodge further dates.

"Uh-huh." I laugh at his antics. "You keep telling yourself that, buddy."

"Hey." He wraps his arm around my shoulders. "We'd make a good team, you and me."

We've done this dance many times before. "Yep. Just like oil and water," I say, and he throws his head back and laughs.

"I'll wear you down. Just you wait." He grins and strolls toward the kitchen.

Shaking my head, I grab the glass of tea I just made for Owen and head to his table. "Here you go." I set the drink in front of him with a straw. "Your food will be right out."

"He your boyfriend?" he asks.

"Who?"

"Surfer boy." He motions toward the kitchen.

"Definitely not." I laugh.

"He know that?"

"He's very much aware that there is nothing between us other than being coworkers and there never will be. Not that it's any of your business." Turning on my heel, I walk away. I'm half tempted to let Oliver take over his table, but who knows what he would say to him. The lunch rush is slow today, and I'm grateful since I'll be here until closing. Peering through the kitchen door, I see Linda, Ronnie's wife, plating up his meal. They work opposite shifts most days, but it works for them. I grab another glass of tea, a few napkins, and a bottle of ketchup and place them on a tray. When Linda slides the plate through the window, I'm ready for her.

"Thanks, Linda."

"You're welcome, dear." She smiles kindly and goes back to work.

"Can I get you anything else?" I ask, setting everything from my tray on the table in front of him.

"No."

That's it, one word, short and to the point. I don't bother to say anything else, already sensing he's in a bad mood. I walk away and check on my other table. I ignore the fact that I can feel his eyes on me. It's with extreme effort that I don't look in his direction. When I drop off my other table's meal, I walk toward him. "Leave any room for dessert?"

"When is your next day off?" he asks, not bothering to answer my question.

"What day is it?" I ask him.

His brow furrows. "Thursday."

Mentally I pretend to go through my schedule in my head. "Tomorrow," I say, trying to hide my relief. Today is a nine-day stretch for me, and my third double during that time.

"Have dinner with me."

"I don't think that's such a good idea."

He sits back in his chair and crosses his arms over his chest. "Explain."

"Why do I need to give you an explanation? I just don't think it's a good idea."

"Layla."

My name almost sounds like a warning rolling off his lips. "Owen," I counter. I see the corner of his lip twitch.

"I'll be at your place around two."

"Why so early?" I ask, and he grins. *Damn it.*

"I'll be there at two, Layla." He stands and tosses a few bills on the table.

I don't break eye contact when I say, "That's too much."

He leans in close. So close I can smell his spicy cologne, feel his hot breath as it hits my ear. "My money, Layla."

Goose bumps break out on my skin. He's lethal, with those eyes, and that deep voice, and his... commanding attitude. I should hate it. Hate him, but it has the opposite effect on me. It turns me on, and I hate that. I hate that my body betrays me, and I can't seem to resist him. I want to tell him not to bother showing up, that I won't be there, but we both know that would be a lie. I'll be there, and I'll be ready. Call it curiosity.

I watch him until I can no longer see him. He's like a tornado that has stormed into my life. He's stubborn as hell, and his eyes give all new meaning to the phrase panty dropper. My gut tells me he's trouble, but I'm still going to be ready to go with him tomorrow—wherever it is that he's taking me. My life has zero fun, zero excitement. I work too much to have time for much of anything else. But I'm living on my own, have food on the table and a roof over my head. I do that all on my own. I never want to have to depend on anyone else to take care of me. That was how my mother lived her life and me by association. I never want to live that way again.

The rest of my day drags on. I go through the motions, but my mind is on Owen and why he would want to have dinner with me. He's seen where I live, where I work. He's out of my league financially. And he's being cryptic about being at my place at two. Dinner is not until five, at least. I know he's not one to eat early. What could he possibly have planned?

"Hey, Layla. I got a customer at the bar asking for you," Mark, the bartender, tells me.

"What?" What is going on in my life? I went from hiding in the shadows to being requested all the time. Surely, it's not Owen. He's already been here today.

"Some guy asked me to have you stop and see him when you got time."

"Thanks, Mark. Let me get drinks for my table that just got seated, and I'll be over." The restaurant is pretty big. We have the VIP section in the back, our normal tables, and then another bar section. That consists of a long bar and several high-top tables. I never work the bar. I prefer to not deal with the drunk assholes. Give me the families and crying babies any day.

I see him as soon as I turn the corner. He's sitting at the bar, eyes glued to the television watching some sort of fight. Slowly, my feet carry me toward him. "Hey." I place my hand on his shoulder to get his attention.

He turns slightly in his seat, glancing over his shoulder. If I'm not mistaken, his eyes light up when he sees that it's me. "Hey." He sits up straight and turns fully to face me.

"What are you doing here?"

"I'm your ride home."

I fight the urge to roll my eyes. "I had planned on splurging for an Uber. Some crazy guy keeps leaving me these outrageous tips."

He grins. "Yeah, sounds like a good one."

"Meh, the jury's still out," I say, barely containing my own smile.

"I'll be here," he says. "Let me know when you're ready to go."

"Owen," I start, but the look on his face stops me. "Thank you," I say, instead of the arguing. He nods and turns back around, eyes on the television.

"Can I get you anything?" I ask, leaning in close so he can hear me.

He turns his head, which puts us close, too close. Instinct tells me to pull away, but my body craves the way he's looking at me — the way he makes me feel, yearning for his attention. "Just to get you home safe," he says huskily.

Swallowing hard, I nod and back away. Turning on my heel, I get back to work. Thankful that my tables are on the other side of the restaurant tonight. Just his presence alone is distracting; being able to see him as I serve my tables would be an even greater challenge.

CHAPTER
Owen
FIVE

I RENTED A car for today. I could have used the driver from the hotel, but something about spending the day, just the two of us appealed to me more. *She* appeals to me. There's just something about her that pulls me in, makes me want to take care of her. She's so open with her past, with her struggles, yet she has yet to throw herself at me.

She has no idea who I am, and that just makes me want to get to know her even more. She knows I have money. I've been leaving her substantial tips since that first night. Sure, it's a little over the top, but when I saw her limping and the state of her worn-out shoes, I knew she needed it. Then the next night, she was still wearing those tired shoes, but the sincerity in her thank you was profound.

So, here I am, pulling into the parking lot of her rundown apartment building. As promised, the thugs I paid off the second night in a row are nowhere to be seen. I paid them a visit before going back to the hotel restaurant, waiting for her to get off work. My gut twisted as the car pulled away. This place really isn't safe.

"Hey," she says, opening the door before I have a chance to knock.

"Layla," I greet her. "You ready for our day together?"

"Do I look okay?" She looks down at her pink sundress and flip-flops. "I didn't know what we were doing, you said dinner, but you're here now, and I didn't know what to wear, so is this okay?" she asks in a rush.

Placing my index finger under her chin, I lift her gaze to mine. "You look beautiful. You have what you need?" I ask her, dropping my hand. I don't know what's gotten into me. I don't do this. I don't date, not really. Sure, I have a beautiful woman on my arm for charity events and have been known to bring a companion home with me at the end of the night, but this... dinner dates, that's not me.

"Thank you," she says shyly, a blush coating her cheeks. "Where are we going?"

Placing my hand on the small of her back, I guide her to my rental. "We're going shopping."

"Shopping?" she asks when I open the passenger door for her.

"Yep." I don't give her any more information than that. Once she's strapped in, I shut the door and rush around to the driver's side.

"Shopping for what?" she asks.

"I need a few things. My stay has been extended." I have what I need from the resort. However, I have yet to see the numbers. I called my brother Royce and let him know I was extending my stay. He's so blissfully happy with his fiancée, Sawyer, he simply told me to have a good time. She's good for him. It's nice to see him happy again. He deserves it after what his ex did to him. I could have left yesterday like I was scheduled to do, but then I would have been leaving her, and I'm not ready for that just yet. I don't know what this pull is, but I'm sticking around to find out. Besides, another week here on the white sandy beach isn't exactly a hardship.

"You're here on business?" she asks. "I mean, I assumed since I've not seen you around before, but I wasn't sure."

"Yes."

"What is it that you do?"

"I'm a CFO. Chief Financial Officer," I explain. "A friend of mine is looking to buy the hotel, and he asked me to come and check it out."

"Is the Emerald in trouble?" she asks, surprised.

I nod. "They are. That's why I'm here as a guest. Trying to see the flow of things, get an idea for the occupancy and amenities."

"It's always full. We stay busy year-round. I mean, I know I'm in the restaurant, but the hotel is always busy."

"I can see that. What I'm not sure of is the reason for the financial hardship."

"What does that mean, will we be losing our jobs?" she asks hesitantly.

"No. If my friend buys the hotel, it's for an investment, not to shut it down."

"Will you tell me if it gets to that? I've been here for seven years, and it's all I've ever really known."

"Your job is safe." I reach over and give her knee a gentle squeeze, and it's a mistake. The silky softness of her skin against my fingertips is not something I was prepared for. I know I should remove my hand, but I can't seem to find the power to do so. Instead, I leave it there and stroke her soft skin with my thumb.

"Okay," she says softly.

Glancing over, I see her eyes on my hand, and that her breathing is accelerated. She doesn't ask me to move, nor does she try to move me herself. That's all the invitation I need. The rest of the drive is quiet, and I'm thankful since all I can think about is getting her under me, wondering if she's this soft everywhere. My money is on yes.

"I've never been here," she confesses as we pull into the local mall.

"No? Where do you shop?" I ask her.

"Walmart," she says, her cheeks pinking.

I don't reply to that. How can I? Her struggles have me choked up. This beautiful, thoughtful woman deserves so much more than the life she's been given. She meets me at the front of the car, and unable to help myself, I reach out and entwine her fingers with mine. It's as if now that I've touched her soft skin, I need to be in physical contact with her all the time.

"Where to first?" she asks. I can hear the nervousness in her voice. To my surprise, she doesn't pull away.

"We've got all day. You lead the way."

Her eyes light up. "What do you need?"

"Shorts, shirts, shoes, the basics," I tell her. In all honesty, I don't need anything. The hotel has an excellent laundry service, and I've taken full advantage of it. I need to check out those services, so why not?

"Here." She pulls me into American Eagle, and straight to a rack of cargo shorts. She starts sifting through the racks.

"I'll grab a couple of pairs. Why don't you go browse?" She hesitates but nods and walks away. I grab two pairs of khaki shorts in my size and stealthily watch her. She picks up a shirt and smiles, holds it to her, and then she looks at the price tag, and the joy that was once present is now diminished. Little does she know this trip is more for her than me. Originally, it was to just buy her a pair of new shoes, but now... now I want to give her everything.

She walks away, a few racks over. I move quickly, grabbing the shirt and placing it under the shorts in my arms. I watch her closely as she does the same thing with a pair of shorts. She digs through the pile to find her size, holds them up, and then shakes her head when she sees the price tag. Those too end up in my arms and under my shorts.

"Hey, are you following me?" she asks, teasing.

"Busted," I say. No use in denying it. She's going to find out soon enough.

"Get what you needed?" she asks.

"I did. Ready to check out?" She gives me a silent nod. "Why don't you go scope out our next store while I hit this line?"

"Sure," she agrees quickly and walks toward the door.

That was easier than I thought it would be, but I just wonder how long I can keep up the same spiel without her catching on?

By the time we reach the shoe store, I've managed to buy her two pair of shorts, three shirts, a dress, and a necklace. In doing so, I also bought two pair of shorts, five shirts, and two pair of swim trunks for myself—all things I don't need.

"What kind of shoes do you need?" she asks.

"Gym shoes, maybe some flip-flops. I didn't pack any."

She throws her head back and laughs, the sound washing over me, making my body yearn for hers. "How do you travel to Florida and not pack swim trunks or flip-flops?" she asks.

As the day goes on, she has grown more comfortable with me. "It's a work trip," I remind her.

"It's the beach," she counters. "Besides, you're doing this as a favor, right? Are you even getting paid?"

"Hush." I lean my shoulder into hers and reluctantly release her hand. All our bags are in my other hand. Not holding her hand is not something I'm willing to relent on. "Go shop, woman," I tease.

"Yes, sir." She mock salutes me, and my dick is hard as stone.

I grab a pair of men's flip-flops in my size and hurry to pick out a pair of tennis shoes. I drop them off at the counter and go to find her. She's standing looking at rows of black shoes, similar to the ones that she wears to work. "What size are you?" I ask her.

"Eight," she answers, not thinking. "Wait, why?" she asks.

Placing my bags at our feet, I point to the chair. "Sit." I pull out pairs of eights in every style and pile them on the floor in front of her. "What are you waiting for, start trying them on."

"Owen." She bites down on her bottom lip. "I can't."

"Sure, you can. These are on me. This was my plan all along," I confess.

"No. You've done too much for me. I can't let you do that."

"It's not up to you. Now, you can try them on and get a pair that are comfortable and that you like, or I buy them all, and you're stuck."

"All of them?" she gasps.

"That's what I said."

"Owen, you're crazy." She shakes her head, a small smile playing on her lips.

"Maybe. Get busy." I point to the stack of shoe boxes. I study her as she looks at the mountain of boxes before her, then back up at me. I nod, giving her the go-ahead. I didn't realize I was holding my breath until she reaches for the first box and removes the lid. I stand here, vigilant, watching her try on each pair, and walk around in them.

When she places the fourth pair on her feet, I know from the expression on her face, these are the ones she's getting. She bounces a little and looks up at me with a soft smile.

"They feel like clouds."

"Have you walked on clouds?" I tease.

"You know what I mean," she says, rolling those stunning blue eyes at me.

"They look good on you," I tell her. What I don't tell her is that she would look good in a paper bag, or nothing, yeah, she would definitely look good in nothing. Shifting my stance, making room for my growing erection, I turn my focus back to the shoes.

"Owen!" she gasps. "These are eighty dollars."

"Okay."

"That's too much. I can get a pair at Walmart for twenty."

"You could, but we're here, and I want you to have these." I grab the shoe out of her hand and shove it into the box. "You put those up while I go pay."

"Owen," she calls after me, but I wave over my shoulder, not bothering to stop. Swinging past the flip-flops, I grab her a couple of pairs—the ones she has on today are worn out; I've seen her adjust the thong when it popped out twice today. Taking them to the counter, I motion to my shoes as well, and quickly check out.

"Thank you." Her soft voice comes from beside me.

Turning, I see her holding the bags that I left there. "You're welcome. Now, I'm starving. You ready to eat?"

"Yes." A simple answer to a simple question.

Grabbing the bags of shoes, I try to take the others from her, but she insists that she can carry them. Then she surprises me when she reaches out and links her fingers with mine.

Once we have the bags loaded, I spot my cell phone in the cupholder. I chuckle, picking it up to see that I have five missed calls from the office.

"What's so funny?" she inquires.

"I left my phone in the car."

"Ha-ha," she mocks me. "That's funny?" She sounds confused.

I look over at her. "Yes, that's funny. Considering I never forget my phone. Ever."

"Hmm, must be old age," she teases.

I smile at that. "No." I reach over and tuck her hair behind her ear. "It's all you. You are extremely distracting."

"I'm sorry?" She poses it as a question more than apologizing.

"Don't be. You are the best distraction." Fighting the urge to pull her into me and kiss the hell out of her, I turn back to my cell phone. "I have to return a few calls. Won't take me long." She reaches for the door handle. "What are you doing?"

"Giving you some privacy."

"I don't need it. Stay put." Dialing the office, my assistant, and future sister-in-law, Sawyer, answers. "Hey, Sawyer, it's Owen. What's going on?"

"There's a Parker's Garage trying to reach you. They said they're fixing a car for you, and that it's ready. They have the total."

"Did they give it an overhaul as I asked?" I ask her.

"New tires, spark plugs, oil change, filters," she rambles on a long list of things the garage did to Layla's car.

"Great. Call them back and take care of it. I'm on my way there now."

"You got it. Also, Jase called and said that he's still working on getting the numbers together."

"That's fine."

"You feeling okay?" she asks with an unsure laugh.

I glance over at Layla. "Never better," I tell her.

"All right, Owen Riggins, there is something that you're not telling me, but you will," she assures me. She's not wrong. If anyone can get it out of me, it's Sawyer or my brothers. "I'm going to call the garage and get that taken care of. You behave."

"Thank you. I'll be unavailable the remainder of the day."

"I'm liking the way this sounds," she replies, and I hit End on the call and toss my phone back in the cupholder.

"Is everything okay?"

"It is now," I say, placing my hand back on her knee and pulling out of the lot.

"Sounded important."

"It was. Very important. Otherwise, my assistant wouldn't have called."

"You make your assistant handle your personal life?"

"She gets paid very well for her time. Besides, it's two phone calls, one to me and one to the garage. Trust me. She's overly compensated." I don't tell her that she's engaged to my workaholic brother, and that she begs us to give her more to do. She's bored, despite my brother's resistance, she wants more work to fill her time while at the office. Royce is working on an after-hours service to contact us, and each of us takes turns being on call. He doesn't want Sawyer to have to deal with it. Funny, how this is the first assistant he's ever worried about getting after hours calls. He's a new man thanks to Sawyer.

"You should hire some more help. I know what it's like to be overworked. Granted, I bring my overtime all on myself because I need the money, but if she's doing that a lot, you should get her some help."

I think about what she's saying, and that's when an idea starts to form. "You know what? I just might do that. Now, what sounds good to you?" I ask. "I have one quick stop to make, and then we can grab some food."

"I'm up for anything."

"Layla, that's not what I asked you. Tell me," I urge her.

"Honestly, Chick-fil-A."

"Really?"

"Yeah, I don't eat out ever unless you count work, but we get a huge discount. It's been ages since I've eaten there."

"Chick-fil-A, it is."

"We could get it to go and go sit on the beach," she suggests.

"Done." I point my rental in the direction of the garage, and lucky for me, I remember a Chick-fil-A being nearby as well. It's not where I had planned to take her, but the light in her eyes when she talks about the simplest of things such as eating fast food, how can I not take her there? Eating with her on the beach is just the icing on the cake.

CHAPTER
Layla
SIX

"WHAT ARE WE doing here?" I ask Owen when we pull into Parker's Garage. "My car isn't ready yet. It won't be for a while. I have to get some money together," I say, feeling the embarrassment of my words sitting on my shoulders.

"Stay here. I'll be right back," he says, ignoring my question and climbing out of the car.

I open my door and follow him inside. "Owen."

"Layla," he counters. "Do you ever listen to what you're told?"

"Do you ever ask instead of telling?" I fire back, crossing my arms over my chest.

He sighs. "Frustrating beauty," he mumbles under his breath.

"Mr. Riggins." The guy I recognize as the manager who said my car would be okay here until I gathered the money to fix it greets Owen. "We've got you all fixed up. Your assistant just called, so we're all set."

"Wait. What's going on here?" I step around Owen and look at the manager.

"He took care of everything, Ms. Massey. Your car is as good as new."

"Owen?"

"Thank you," he tells the manager. "We'll take the keys now, but we'll be back to pick it up later this evening."

"No problem. Thank you for your business." The manager shakes his hand and disappears down the hall.

Owen turns to face me. "Ready?"

I cross my arms over my chest and glare at him. "What just happened here, Owen?"

"Come on. We can talk about this in the car." He reaches for me, and I step back. "Layla."

"Tell me, did I imagine this, or did you just pay to fix my car? I don't have the money, Owen. I can't pay you back for this."

He exhales loudly. "I don't want you to pay me back. Let's go to the car, and we can talk more privately."

I look around and see that the guys in the garage are watching us through the window. "Fine." Turning on my heel, I stomp out to his rental car. I slam the door harder than needed, but I'm angry, hurt, embarrassed, and hell, I'm so damn confused about what's going on here.

"Layla," he starts, but I turn in my seat, and the look on my face must stop him.

"Why? Why would you do that? I was taking care of it. I needed to work a few more shifts, but I was handling it. Why would you go behind my back and pay to have my car not only fixed, but apparently you had them do an overhaul? You don't even know me, Owen."

"I don't expect you to pay me back. I did it because I can. Because I see how hard you work, and because from what you've told me, you were dealt a shitty hand at life, and I wanted to do something nice for you."

That takes some of the wind out of my sails. "You don't even know me," I say again, this time with less heat.

He reaches out and cradles my face in the palm of his hand. "I do know you. I know you bust your ass for a tiny wage, you work your life away only to feel like a hamster in a spinning wheel. I know you have no one, other than Ronnie and Linda. I know that your feet hurt, but you can't afford new shoes. I know that you give food to the thugs who hang out outside of your apartment building. You are scraping to get by, yet you give what you have to those in need. You're an amazing woman, and no matter how hard I try, I can't stop thinking about you."

My heart flips over in my chest. "How did you—"

"They told me. After I paid them to leave the last two nights so that I knew you would be safe. I didn't find out until after I paid them off the second night that they sort of look out for you."

I nod. "I tried to tell you they were harmless."

"I know you did, but what I saw was this beautiful woman, living on her own in a rough part of town, and a group of guys catcalling and making lewd comments to her."

"It's not your problem," I remind him.

"You know, I tried to tell myself that too, but it seems as though when it comes to you, I'm making it my problem." He leans in closer. "I can't seem to help myself, Layla, not when it comes to you. You captivate me, and you're one of the strongest women I've ever met."

"That doesn't make it okay." My voice is barely a whisper as he leans in closer.

"I know." His lips are now just a breath away from mine. "I'm going to kiss you now," he says, his voice husky.

"Are you asking?" My heart is racing, and my palms are sweating. He's going to kiss me. I'm sure of it, no matter what I say. What I'm even more certain of is that I want him to.

"I'm telling." And with that, he leans in and presses his lips to mine. He's still giving me the chance to back away, but I don't take it. I want to know what it's like to kiss this sexy, overbearing man.

When his tongue traces my lips, I open for him, and he growls. His hand that was once on my cheek slides around to the back of my head, and he holds me close, sliding his tongue past my lips. It's slow, sensual, and sexy. The feel of him holding me to him, the way he tastes, the heat of his body, it's better than I ever could have imagined, and I confess that over the last week, it's been a recurring image in my mind.

He slows the kiss and rests his forehead against mine. "W-What was that?" I ask, trying to catch my breath.

"That was our first kiss."

"That shouldn't have happened." I say the words, but I don't mean them. I want to beg him to do it again.

"The first but not the last," he assures me, ignoring me as usual. With a small peck to the corner of my mouth, he removes his hands from my hair and pulls away. "Now, let's get you some Chick-fil-A." He backs out of the parking lot, reaches over, and entwines his fingers with mine as if it's something we do every single day.

He acts as though it's normal for us, and if I'm being honest, it feels normal. Like I've known him and his hands and lips for a lifetime, when I don't know him at all. It's odd yet comforting at the same time.

"You still want to eat on the beach?" he asks.

"Yes, if that's okay with you?"

"Perfect. What do you want?" he asks, pulling the car around to the drive-thru speaker. I rattle off my order, and he adds a milkshake for both of us. Reaching into my purse, I hand him a ten-dollar bill. "What's that?" He stares at my hand as if I'm offering him a rattlesnake.

"For my food."

"Put it away."

"Please, take it. I can pay for mine."

"I don't care if you have millions of dollars sitting in the bank. You're with me, I pay. Get used to it."

"Why?" I blurt out.

"Why what?"

"Why do I need to get used to it?"

This time he turns his head to look at me. "Because, this"—he points at me then back at himself—"there's something there, and we're going to take the time to find out what it is."

"What if that's not what I want? What if what you're feeling is all on you? What then?"

He hands his credit card to the girl at the window and hands me a bag of food and the milkshakes, which I place in the cupholders. He pulls up, then stops to look at me. "You want it. You want me. This feeling, the spark that charges between us, the current that flows through me when I touch you, you feel it. I can see it in your eyes. This is not all on me, not by a long shot." He turns back around and drives us a few short blocks to the beach.

After finding a spot that's not littered with tourists, we sit on the sand and begin to eat in silence. The sun is starting to set, and I realize we've spent the entire day together when it only feels like minutes.

"I love the ocean," I say, breaking the silence. "Growing up, life was hard. My father, I never knew him, and my mom, well, she blamed me for him leaving. She was hooked on drugs. We moved from one dumpy apartment to the next, following whatever man she'd latched herself onto at the time." I take a break and grab a sip of my milkshake. "I turned eighteen three days before I graduated from high school. Something, I wasn't sure I'd get to do with all the moving around we did."

"That had to be hard." His deep timbre is soft. Soothing.

"Yeah. I wanted better, you know? I knew that I had to graduate. That I had to get that little piece of paper, or I would end up just like her. That wasn't what I wanted. I wanted out. I wanted a new life."

"Where are you from?"

I look over at him and smile. "Indiana." My eyes scan the ocean with the setting sun as its backdrop. "I'd been saving, working after school, and hiding the money. Mom didn't care if I was home or not. On the rare occasion she did ask, I simply told her I was out with friends. I bought a bus ticket for the day of graduation. As soon as they handed me my diploma, I walked off the stage and out the doors. I didn't have close friends, I was always the new girl, and it's not like I could invite anyone over. So I stayed to myself. With just a backpack filled with a few meager items of clothing, I walked onto the bus and never looked back."

I turn to look at him and find him watching me intently. "This is the first place I came to—this beach. I sat here for hours, just looking out at the ocean. It was the first time I'd ever seen it, and I was in awe of its beauty. The way it's never-ending."

"The water, it matches your eyes," he says huskily. "Like you, I could stare at them for hours."

"You are unlike anyone I've ever met, Owen Riggins."

"Good." He leans in and presses his lips to mine. "Now, eat up, and we'll take a walk on the beach."

"Thank you for dinner. It's my favorite, and I don't get it often." I can see the question in his eyes as I gather our trash and place it in the bag. "Eating out isn't a luxury I can afford most days," I say, avoiding eye contact.

"I'm sorry you were dealt such a shitty hand at life."

"I'm doing okay," I say, shrugging. "There are rough times, but all I have to think about is where I came from. How I've gotten where I am on my own, and it gives me the strength to keep pushing through. Even on the days when I let the thought of giving up filter through my mind, I keep fighting my way through life."

Something passes over his features, but I can't describe it. "You ready for that walk?" He doesn't wait for me to answer. He stands, grabs our bag of trash, and walks it to a nearby trash can on the pier. I follow along behind him like the lost soul that I am. When I'm within reaching distance, he offers me his hand, and without hesitation, I take it.

I don't know this man. He could be a serial killer for all I know, but something in my gut tells me he's good. Everything he's done for me, a complete stranger, solidifies that. I've always been one to follow my gut. My gut told me to get out of Indiana as fast as I could. My gut told me Florida was where I needed to be.

"Tell me about you," I say once we're on the beach.

"I grew up in a big family. I have four brothers. One older and three younger."

"Wow. I can't imagine what that's like."

"Chaos." He chuckles. "We were always getting into something growing up. Luckily our parents guided us and kept us on the straight and narrow. We have a lake on our family's property, and we spent every waking moment there growing up."

"You have a lake?" I ask in disbelief.

"Yeah, we would fish, ski, Jet Ski, swim, you name it. We still spend as much time there as we can."

"Sounds beautiful. Where is home?"

"Tennessee."

"I'm picturing something like a postcard, vast trees surrounding the lake."

"That's pretty much it."

"You should send me a picture when you get home," I say without really thinking. This man is just passing through. He's not going to want to keep in touch with me.

"Or I could show you."

It takes me a minute to process what he's saying. "I can't go to Tennessee."

"Why not?" He stops walking and steps in front of me. His hands rest on my hips, and the heat from his body seeps into mine. It's comforting in a way that I can't explain.

"I live here. Besides, I could never afford the travel expenses."

"You would be my guest."

"Owen." I sigh. "Your heart—" I place my hand on his chest.

"—is the kindest I've ever known, but I can't keep letting you take care of me. I need to stand on my own two feet."

"What if I want to take care of you?" he asks, his voice gravelly.

"It's getting late. We should go." The thought of this kind, gentle man wanting to take care of me sets my soul on fire. However, we can't go there. *I* can't go there. I need to be able to take care of myself. Always. I never want to be dependent on someone else ever again.

"Fine," he grumbles, pressing his lips to my forehead. "Let's go get your car."

"I'm paying you back, Owen. It's going to take some time, but I'm going to do it."

"I don't want your money. You want to pay me back, then spend time with me. Anytime you're not working while I'm here, you're with me," he suggests.

"Owen—" I start, and he stops me with his finger pressed to my lips.

"I want to spend time with you." His voice is soft, almost pleading, and it's as if he's speaking the words I want to say. I'm just too afraid.

"I work a lot."

"I know. I'm here for a few more days. Let me have the time you're not working."

I find myself nodding before the word "Yes," slips past my lips.

"That's my girl." He smiles down at me before taking my hand and leading us back to his rental.

CHAPTER *Owen* SEVEN

I TOSSED AND turned all night long. It took every ounce of willpower I had to leave her again. Each day that I leave her, it gets harder and harder. That's why I have a plan. It came to me in the wee hours of the morning. I almost called my brother Royce, but I decided against it. Instead, I lie awake, working out the pitch I was about to give.

"What's up?" Royce answers.

"You got a minute?" I ask.

"Yes." There is no hesitation in his voice. "You okay?"

"Yeah, just want to run something past you."

"Shoot."

"In order to tell you my plan, I need to start from the beginning."

"I'm listening," he says, and by the tone of his voice, I know he's concentrating on nothing but our conversation.

"Jase sent me here to look over the place and look at the

numbers. As you know, the first week I was here, they were dragging their feet, and all I had to do was experience the hotel, and watch things like capacity, cleanliness stuff like that."

"I'm with you," he tells me. "I'm surprised that you didn't come on home and have them send the numbers to you," he adds.

I'm getting there, brother. "During that time, I've had dinner each night in the hotel restaurant." I pause, not really sure how to say this next part. "I met someone," I say, just tossing the words out there. "She's a waitress," I'm quick to add. "I barely know her, except from what I've observed and what she's told me, but I can't stop thinking about her. Hell, it just about tore me to pieces inside to say goodbye to her last night knowing she was staying in her shitty apartment in her even shittier neighborhood."

There's a long pause, and I'm about to keep rambling when Royce finally asks, "What do you need from me?"

His acceptance of my feelings for Layla sends relief washing over me. "I know it's crazy, but I had an idea. She's had a rough life. No family except for a man and a woman who run the restaurant at the hotel who kind of adopted her into theirs. I want better for her."

"It's more than that," Royce calls me out.

I nod even though he can't see me. "It is. I'm not ready to let her go yet." The words come out in a rush as if I'm releasing a secret out into the world.

"I felt like that once."

I swallow hard. "I know."

"Tell me what I can do, Owen."

"I want to give her a job. She's not had any experience, but she's smart, and I know she can learn. I was thinking that maybe she can be a back-up for Sawyer. I know you hate that she works so much now that she's taken on more duties from each of us, not just you. I thought maybe they could job share or something? Or maybe she can be Sawyer's assistant? Fuck, Royce, I don't really know. What I do know is that I've never had this kind of reaction to a woman, and the thought of leaving her here when I come home is tearing me up inside."

"Done. It helps you keep your girl, and it gives mine some breathing room. I want kids, and the way she's been working, she'll never agree. This works in both of our favors. You think that you can convince her to come with you?"

"I don't know."

"Do what you have to do. I'll fill Sawyer and the guys in, and you bring her home. We'll make it happen."

"Thanks," I say, choking up. "I don't know if I can convince her to stay with me, so I'm going to have to maybe find her a place to stay."

"Done. She can stay at Sawyer's apartment. Her lease isn't up for another three months. You can renew, or maybe she'll move in with you by then."

"You sure?"

"Yes. It's just sitting there. I know Sawyer isn't going to care. Hell, she's going to love having another woman around."

"I've got my work cut out for me convincing her."

"Offer her a generous salary, one she can't refuse. You're the numbers guy. You know we can afford to do it. Besides, it sounds like she might be a Riggins soon anyway."

"Whoa, no one is talking marriage here."

"Not yet." He chuckles. "I've been in your shoes recently, and I know that fighting it is useless. Bring her home. I want to meet her. She has a job here as long as she needs it."

"Thanks, Royce."

"It's your company too. This is our legacy, Owen. I know you wouldn't do anything to harm that. You trust her. She's in. That's it."

"You trusted Jennifer."

"Yeah, and I fucked up. I'd like to think that you and those other three loons we call brothers learned something from my mistake. However, if it turns out that this girl—What's her name?"

"Layla." Her name rolls off my tongue like a caress.

"—if Layla turns out to be a mistake like my ex-wife, we'll handle it together. You're not in this alone."

"You make it sound like I'm going to war."

"You are, but the battlefield is your heart. Keep me posted, and I'll get things set up on my end. I think we'll put Sawyer in the small conference room. Turn it into an office. If I thought I could get away with moving her into mine, I would. But we both know my fiancée isn't going to go for that. Anyway, we'll convert the small conference room that we never use into an office and put Layla at the front desk."

"Thank you."

"It's the magic, brother." He laughs and ends the call.

I feel better after talking to Royce, and I know, without a doubt, he will handle things on his end just like he said. There have been times when I've taken for granted the family that I have and the fact that I know they are always there for me. This is one of those times that I'm thankful to have them. I hate that Layla doesn't have that support. I want to give that to her and so much more.

"Hi," Layla greets as she slides up to my table. "You want your usual?" she asks, pen and paper in hand.

"I missed you today." I can tell from the shock on her face that's not what she was expecting me to say. I'm a man of few words, but when I do speak, it's me. It's real. I don't see the point in hiding it or beating around the bush. I missed her, and I wanted her to know.

"Owen." She breathes my name, and I have the mental image of her doing so while I'm pushing inside her.

"The usual is fine, Layla."

"You're later than usual," she says. She's yet to write down my order, which is fine. I'm sure she has it memorized.

"I was working today, and I have a proposition for you. I was hoping we could talk when you get off?"

"I'm off in an hour."

I nod. "We can take a walk on the beach."

"At night?"

"I'll protect you," I tell her with a grin.

"It's not that I'm scared. I've just never done it before."

"You love the ocean."

"Yeah, but a woman alone on a quiet beach sounds like a scenario for something bad to happen. I'm careful, Owen."

"I'm glad that you take precautions. Let me show you the ocean at night," I say, reaching out and running my thumb over her wrist.

She stares at me for several seconds. "I'd like that. I'll get this put in," she says, and rushes away.

I watch as she walks away and see the limp from before is gone. I'm glad to see a new pair of shoes did the trick. A pang of sadness hits me when I think about everything she's sacrificed to try and make a better life for herself. She's doing it all on her own. The exhaustion around her eyes and her too-thin body is a strong indication that she's struggling. Not that I didn't already know that. I want to take the struggle away from her. I want to bring the light to her eyes and knock some of life's bricks from her shoulders.

The next hour passes quickly. I eat dinner alone while my eyes scan the restaurant for a glimpse of Layla. She checks on me a few times, and with each moment she steps away from my table, my craving for her burns brighter. Hotter.

"I can't believe you work this close to the beach and have never taken a walk at night," I say, lacing my fingers through hers.

"My life growing up was rough, Owen. I saw what the world is capable of. What evil could do. Too many nights I stayed awake with my dresser pressed against my bedroom door to keep the creepy men my mother hung out with from sneaking into my room."

"Layla." I stop and turn her to face me. "Did they hurt you?" There is a dark edge to my voice. I don't know what I'll do if she says yes. I already feel as though I could commit murder to defend her honor.

"No. I was smart enough to lock them out. Doesn't mean I didn't cower in the dark of the night afraid that they would." Her voice cracks and I act on instinct.

My arms wrap around her, and I pull her into my chest. She doesn't hesitate to return the embrace. As we stand here in the darkness, nothing but the roaring sea around us, she steals a piece of me, a piece of my heart. "I've got you," I tell her with conviction.

She holds on a little longer before lifting her head. I don't release my hold on her as her eyes find mine. "Thank you, Owen. I'm sorry I broke down like that. I just… I don't feel alone when I'm with you."

"Never again, Layla. You will never be alone again," I assure her. My hand cups her soft cheek. "I promise you." More tears fall from her eyes. "Come on." With my arm around her shoulders, I lead her back to the hotel and to the elevator. She stays snuggled into my side without question. Once we reach my floor, I lead her to my room, pushing the door open for her. She doesn't hesitate to step into my suite.

"What are we doing?" she asks. Her voice is gravelly from her tears, and I hate it.

Ignoring her question, I dig into the dresser, pulling out a T-shirt for her to wear. "You can change into this."

"Owen?"

"I need you with me tonight, Layla. I wish I could explain to you why, but I can't. I don't have the words. All I have is this need to comfort and protect you. I promise you that you're safe with me. I need you here with me."

I watch as her big blue eyes well with tears. My gut twists when I see them, knowing I'm the reason this time. I open my mouth to try and console her, but she beats me to it.

"Okay."

One word softly whispered by the beauty who has enthralled me is all it takes for my shoulders to relax. "Thank you, baby." I take a step forward and lean over until my lips are pressing to her forehead. "I'll be right here," I assure her, stepping back so she can get around me to the bathroom to change.

I let my eyes trail her, following until she disappears behind the bathroom door. The audible click of the door closing and the lock engaging spurs me into action. Going to the nightstand beside the bed, I pick up the phone to call room service. I've already eaten, but I'm sure she hasn't. I order a few random items that I hope she'll like and wait patiently for her to join me.

CHAPTER
Layla
EIGHT

MY LEGS TREMBLE beneath me as I stare at Owen's shirt that I placed on the counter. Reaching out, my hands grip the ledge, offering me the balance my legs are incapable of. He needs me here.

That's what he said. I don't think anyone has ever told me they needed me. My head swims with what it means.

Owen is unlike any man I've ever met. He's this sexy, serious businessman, and he needs me. *Me.* Layla Massey. The girl who grew up moving from one shithole to the next. The same girl who hid in her bedroom with her furniture against the door to ward off the advances of the company her mother kept. That girl. He wants *that* girl. He knows how I grew up. Sure, I skimmed the details, but I gave him enough to understand. He's a smart man.

He wants me to stay here with him, and even though I've only known him a short amount of time, I want to be where he is. I know it's dangerous, and it's crazy, but my gut tells me that Owen is one of the good ones. He's a man of his word, and I know I can trust him. He's done so much for me, a complete stranger, already.

Sucking in a deep breath, I slowly exhale before I begin to strip out of my clothes. I smell like the restaurant, and the shower taunts me. It's bigger than my entire bathroom at my apartment, and the appeal is just too strong.

The hot spray feels incredible against my tired muscles. And the water pressure... I don't think I've ever taken a shower with the pressure this strong. Using the hotel provided bottles from the sink, I take care of business. It's the best shower I've ever had in my entire life, and I have Owen to thank for it. I'll just add it to the list of things I have to repay him for. My hope is that one day I'll be in the position to do so.

I don't know how long I've been in here, but the bathroom is filled with steam, and my hands are pruned. Reluctantly, I turn off the water and climb out. I didn't think this through, as the only clean clothes I have is his T-shirt. I hate the thought of putting on my other clothes, but I don't have much choice.

"Layla," Owen's deep voice greets me through the door.

"Sorry!" I yell back. "I'll be out soon."

"I got you something. I'm going to leave the bag next to the door. I'm going to step out of view while you retrieve it."

"What is it?" I call back.

His deep chuckle, although muffled, filters through the door, and it has me immediately relaxing. "You're going to have to look for yourself. I'm walking away now."

I count to ten slowly, then again just to be safe. With the towel gripped tight and holding it around my body, I unlock the door and peek out to see a shopping bag on the floor. I open the door a little wider and grab it quickly, slamming the door. I don't know why because I've imagined being naked in front of Owen more times than I can count since I met him, but having that be reality and not fantasy is not something I'm sure I'm ready for. I can only imagine the women he's been with. He's sexy and has his shit together. That's intimidating when you're talking about taking your clothes off.

Turning the lock on the door, I set the bag on the counter and begin pulling out the contents. I feel my face heat when I pull out a black silk bra and panty set, and surprisingly in my size. Next is a T-shirt with the hotel's label, and a pair of cotton shorts.

He bought me clothes.

Hot tears prick my eyes. I'm no one to him, yet he continues to take care of me. It's overwhelming the feeling of being seen. Not just being seen, but it makes me feel not so alone in the world.

I slip into the bra and panties that fit perfectly and are nicer than anything I've ever owned. I reach for the shirt and shorts and spy his shirt on the counter. I have a choice to make. I can wear the clothes he got me or his shirt. Indecision plagues me, and I go with my gut. Placing the shorts and the T-shirt back into the bag, I grip his tee in my hands and bring it to my nose, inhaling his scent. Making a quick decision, I slide out of my bra and slip his shirt over my head. It's huge on me, hanging to my knees, but that doesn't bother me. His scent wraps around me just like it did earlier tonight when he held me in his arms.

I place the bra back into the bag and pull out the hairbrush that was sitting in the bottom, and the pack of hair ties, and a toothbrush. *Can he be anymore perfect?* Five minutes later, I'm turning off the bathroom light and stepping into his room.

"Hey." His voice is gruff as he takes in the sight of me in his shirt. He grins, his white teeth shining through his dark beard. "I thought you might be hungry," he says, pointing to the table filled to capacity with food.

"I can't eat all of that," I say, eyes wide as my stomach grumbles loud enough for him to hear.

"I wasn't sure what you would want, so I got a variety. Come on. I'll help you eat it." He motions for me to join him.

"You've already eaten."

"I'm a growing boy," he says, rubbing his stomach. I'm positive his T-shirt is hiding washboard abs from the feel of his body pressed to mine earlier tonight. Such a shame to keep them hidden.

With careful steps, I take the seat next to him at the small dining table and we begin to eat. Together we sample a little of everything. The food is delicious, and the experience is one I will forever remember. "This is a first for me," I confess as I wipe my mouth, tossing my napkin on the table.

"Having dinner with a man in his hotel room?" he asks, his eyes sparkling with mischief.

"That too. It's a first for me staying in a hotel, or to have room service, and like you said, with a man."

"You've never stayed in a hotel?"

"No. My mom and I did stay in a motel once. It was dirty and disgusting. There was a gap in the bottom of the door. I swear I watched it all night long, thinking some kind of critter was going to crawl into our room in the middle of the night."

"How old were you?"

I shrug. "Not sure, I think about six or so."

"Well, I'm glad I can be your first." He winks, and my heart trips over in my chest. His eyes remind me of a blue sky on a warm summer day. It's soothing.

"Me too," I say honestly, as I place my hand over my mouth to cover my yawn.

"All right, beautiful, let's get you to bed."

I watch him as he pushes from the table and stands, offering me his hand. "Owen—" I start, but stop, not able to find the words.

"You're safe with me, Layla. I know you don't know me, but I promise you that you can trust me. I just need you here with me tonight. The bed is huge, and I'll stay on my side if that's what you want."

I nod. My head says that him staying on his side is the best plan, while my heart beats double time at the thought of sleeping with his arms wrapped around me all night long.

"I'm going to lock the door and turn off the lights." He kisses my temple. "Go ahead and get comfortable."

"Um, what side? I mean, do you have a side?" I ask, sounding like every bit of the inexperienced twenty-five-year-old woman that I am.

"I'm used to sleeping alone, Layla. You pick whatever side you want. All I care about is that you're here."

He walks away, and I turn my gaze to the bed. I have a twin in my apartment. I've never slept in anything larger. In fact, it wasn't until I moved out of the structure my mother called our home that I had an actual bed frame. It was left in my apartment when I moved in, and the landlord said it was mine if I wanted it. I remember feeling as though everything was going to be okay. I had a roof over my head, and a real bed to sleep in. I spent some of my savings to buy a new mattress. It was a luxury I didn't plan on, but I was giving myself something I'd always wanted—a bed of my own.

The suite is bathed in darkness when he turns out the lights, and I rush to climb into bed and under the covers. I have to fight back a moan at the softness of the mattress. I feel like I'm lying on a layer of clouds. My body sinks in, and suddenly I can feel the exhaustion of the day starting to set in. The bed dips beside me, and through the darkness, under the covers, his hand finds mine. Something so simple, but meaningful all the same. I've never slept in bed with anyone. Not even my mother. As a kid, I spent a lot of time in my room alone, hiding and being ignored.

As soon as his fingers link with mine, the anxiety of what we're doing melts away. I can't explain it, but I feel connected to him on a level I've never experienced before. He said that he needed me, but at this moment, I realize that I need him. I needed this moment to feel safe lying next to him.

"Owen?" I whisper into the darkness.

"Yeah?"

"How did you know what I needed?"

I feel the bed move as he turns to face me. "What do you mean? What did you need?"

I swallow hard. "You. I needed you, and I needed this," I say, squeezing his hand.

I hear the breath leave his lungs before his whispered request, "Can I hold you?" he asks, his voice soft and gruff. "Nothing else, you can trust me."

"I-I've never done this. I've never slept with anyone else," I confess, giving him a piece of me that no one else has. What he doesn't know is that my statement has a double meaning.

"Come here." He doesn't give me a chance to object as he moves in closer, and I find that I'm drawn to him, and I easily turn to give him my back, letting him wrap his arms around me. "Much better," he says over a yawn.

As each minute passes, my body relaxes further into his. For the first time in my life, I feel safe and protected. Seen. I owe that to the man who slumbers peacefully behind me. He's been asleep for a while, but his hold on me is tight. Even in his sleep, he's keeping me close. It's with that thought I finally let sleep claim me.

There have been many times in my life where I've woken up startled by the feeling that I'm being watched. This time, the feeling is different. I can feel his eyes on me, and his hand that rests on my hip. There is no panic or even regret for sleeping in his bed last night. It's the best night's sleep I've had in my entire life.

"Morning, beautiful," he murmurs as my eyes flutter open.

"Hi," I say, closing my eyes and burrowing into him.

His deep chuckle vibrates his chest. "Do you work today?"

"No. I'm off."

"Good. I want to spend the day with you, and there's something I need to talk to you about."

That has me lifting my head to look at him. "Everything okay?" I ask hesitantly.

"Yes. Everything is perfect. I'm going to order us some room service and grab a shower."

"You don't have to do that—"

"Stop right there," he says before I can continue. "You're mine for the day, Layla. Let me order us some food, and we can talk while we eat."

"Okay." I nod, because when you have a man like Owen who insists on spending the day with you, you don't pass that up. It's something I've quickly learned.

After a swift press of his lips to my forehead, he climbs out of bed. I watch as he calls to order room service, and again he orders way more food than the two of us could possibly eat before he disappears into the bathroom. My mind races with what he could want to talk about. Knowing Owen, it's going to be something he feels like is good for me. Something else that has him helping me. I'm grateful for him, but at the same time, I know that I can't lean on him too much. I can't get used to him being there for me day in and day out. He's only passing through. He's going to be leaving soon, going back home to Nashville, and I'll be here all on my own again.

Distance.

No matter how much I want to spend the day with him today, I just can't. I'm already letting myself get attached to him. I'm getting used to having him to lean on, and I can't do that. Jumping out of bed, I gather my things, and I'm almost to the door when the bathroom door opens.

"Layla."

I freeze at the sound of my name. "Thank you for everything," I say with my back toward him. "I've taken up enough of your time and generosity," I say, hoping my voice sounds strong and confident when I feel anything but.

I feel his hands land on my hips, and the smell of his body wash surround me. "Where are you going, baby?" he asks, his lips next to my ear.

"H-Home. I was going home."

"We have plans." He presses his lips to my cheek, and the scratch of his beard against my skin causes me to melt into him. It's a feeling I will always associate with Owen, long after he's out of my life.

"I've leaned on you enough. Thank you, but it's best if I go."

Before I know what's happening, he's stepping in front of me, and his big hands are cupping my cheeks. "I want you to lean on me, Layla. I want you where I am, and I never want you to leave." His voice is raw, as if his confession took extreme effort.

There's a knock at the door followed by "Room service."

"Go sit down. I promised you breakfast and conversation." His lips press to my forehead, and it's familiar. Forehead kisses are his thing.

My heart tells me to do as I'm told while my head is telling me to run. My heart wins as I turn and walk back to the small table in his suite and take a seat. I don't know what he wants to talk about, but he's adamant. I'll give him his chance to talk and get whatever it is off his chest. Then I'll go back to my small rundown apartment and dream about the best night of my life.

CHAPTER
Owen
NINE

I OPEN THE door to accept the room service, all while my heart is beating like a bass drum in my chest. One more minute and I would have missed her. She would have slipped out quietly, and I would have lost her. Sure, I know where she lives and where she works, but something deep in my gut tells me that if she had walked out of the door, that would have been it. Her walls would be up, and my chances of knocking them down would be slim to none.

"Thank you." I tip the young man delivering our food and close the door. "You hungry?" I ask her.

She nods. "Thank you. I'll never be able to repay you for all that you've done for me."

"Eat," I say, handing her a plate. "Starting now, no more thank yous. No more how will I ever repay you. From this moment forward, you accept that I do what I do because I want to. I'm on your team, Layla."

"I've never had a team," she replies softly.

Fuck. "Now you do." Grabbing a plate, I begin to pile it up. We eat in silence for several long minutes until I can't take it a moment longer. I need to talk to her about this. "So, I have a proposition for you."

"You're not getting my bacon," she says, pointing said strip of bacon at me. It makes me smile to see her happy and indulging.

"I won't take your bacon," I assure her. "It's actually a job opportunity."

"What? Is this some kind of *Pretty Woman* set up? I hang out with you while you're here, and then you leave?" she asks. I can hear not only the pain but the disappointment in her voice.

"Not even close." Reaching across the small table, I cover her hand with mine. "I want you to come and work for me and my brothers at our company."

"What?" she breathes.

"Come work for us. I've already talked to my brother Royce. He's the oldest and the CEO. He's on board. His fiancée, Sawyer, she's taking on more work from me and my other three brothers, and Royce hates that she's working so much. He wants her to slow down not take on more. He wants a family, they both do, and you coming to work for us, taking some of the workload from her shoulders will help everyone out." I pause, letting my words sink in. "And I'll get to see you every day."

"Owen, I can't even process this. You want me to come and work for you? In Nashville? In Tennessee?" she asks.

"Yes."

"You want to see me every day?"

"More than anything." I watch as her eyes widen at my response. "I have plenty of room, you can stay with me, but—" I start when I see her mouth open to object. "If you're not ready for that, you can stay in Sawyer's old apartment. It's still furnished, and it's just sitting empty. It's in a good neighborhood, and it's close to the office."

"A-Are you ready for that?"

"Ready for what, baby?"

"Me moving in?" she croaks.

"Yes."

"How? How are you so sure? You barely know me."

"I know enough, and we have the rest of our lives to discover the rest."

"The rest of our lives? Are you feeling okay?" she asks, her eyebrows raised in concern.

I can't keep the chuckle inside. "I'm fine, Layla. I admit this isn't me. I've never done this, and normally I need my space, but the thought of having you in my space, well, that's a game changer."

"This isn't a game, Owen. This is my life," she says, her voice raised.

"I know it's not a game." I pull my hand back, running my fingers through my hair. "I will give you as much space as you need. However, I do have one request."

"What's that?" she asks hesitantly.

"We date. You give me a chance to show you who I am while I learn more about you. Exclusively," I add.

"You want to date me?"

"Yes."

"You want to give me a job?"

"Yes."

"Who are you?"

"Owen Riggins." I smirk.

"You know what I mean." She rolls those big blue eyes of hers.

"I'm a man who never gives up when there is something he wants. My brothers and I took over my father's company and have watched it grow into more than we ever could have imagined. We wanted it, and we made it happen. I want you, Layla."

"I have a job and an apartment. I can't just pick up and move to Tennessee."

"You have a job making minimum wage and a shitty apartment. You've picked up and moved before. Why not now? Why not with me? This time you're not going to be alone. You have my family and me there to support you."

"Your family?" she asks, shocked. "They don't even know me. *You* don't know me."

"They know that you're important to me, and that's enough. And I do know you, Layla. I know that you're a fighter. That you fought to give yourself a better life, and you're still fighting and struggling. I know that this job alone will change things for you, not to mention a nice clean apartment in a good neighborhood. I know that you and my future sister-in-law will get along great, as she's feisty just like you."

"I'm not feisty. I'm cautious."

"That—" I point at her, not able to hide my grin. "—that's the feistiness coming out in you. I'm going to lay it out for you, baby. If I had my way, we'd be packing up your things and moving you into my place where I could hold you every night, just like I did last night. I know it sounds utterly insane, but that's how I feel. I'm a man of my word. I think I've proven that to you. You can trust me. You can trust my family. Please, come home with me."

"You realize this is crazy, right?" she asks. "I mean, we just met, and you want me to uproot my life for you?"

"Not just for me, Layla. For you." I go on to tell her how much she'll be making as an assistant for Riggins Enterprises and her eyes bulge. "That's not just a special salary for you, that's what the position pays."

"I don't know how to be an assistant, Owen."

"You're smart, and Sawyer is amazing. She'll help you." I love Sawyer like a sister, and I've never been more grateful than I am at this moment that she loves my broody-ass older brother. Well, I guess he's not so broody anymore. Not since Sawyer came into his life. Knowing that she has another woman there other than my mom to support her is a huge selling point.

"I—What if she doesn't like me? What if they don't like me?" Her voice is soft as her insecurities shine through.

Standing from my seat at the table, I offer her my hand. She takes it and follows me to the bed. I sit and pull her into my lap. "They're going to love you. You make me happy, Layla. I want to be with you, and that's all they are going to need to know to like you on the spot." I don't know what I can say to convince her, then an idea hits. Reaching for my phone on the nightstand, I keep my arm tight around her waist and start a video call with Royce.

"Hey, O, what's up?" he asks.

"I have someone I want you to meet. Is Sawyer around?" I ask him. I feel Layla stiffen in my arms, but my hold is tight. No way am I letting her run.

"Babe!" Royce calls out. "Owen's on the phone." I hear footsteps and then see Sawyer's face appear on the screen next to Royce.

"Hey, you. How's Florida?" she asks, her smile genuine.

"Good. I'm heading home in a couple of days. They're still giving me the run around with the reports. Jase says he's working on it. At this point, they can send them to me. I've seen what I need to see," I tell them.

"Hi." Sawyer waves, ignoring me. "I'm Sawyer, Owen's assistant," she greets Layla.

"You're Owen's sister-in-law," Royce corrects her.

"We're not married yet, Riggins."

"Details," he mutters.

"Hi." Layla waves. Her reply is soft.

"Guys, this is Layla. She's the one I was telling you about."

Royce nods, a slow smile tilting his lips. "So, you're the one that finally got my brother to come out of his shell?" he asks.

"Um, I guess so?" Layla asks, looking at me.

I laugh and offer her a reassuring smile. "I told you I was a workaholic. This is all new to me, baby." I don't bother to lower my voice or hide my term of endearment, and the way her eyes widen tell me she noticed.

"So, Layla, did Owen talk to you about our offer?" Royce asks.

I watch as her head slowly turns toward the screen of my phone. "We need the help. This one won't stop taking on projects from my idiot brothers." Royce grins, pulling Sawyer into his lap.

"He just told me."

"Good. Are you joining the Riggins family?" Royce asks.

I don't miss the way his eyes flash to mine. His words have a double meaning, and we all know it. Well, maybe not Layla. She's still uncertain. I know this is all fast, but I know what I want. I want Layla.

"It would be nice to keep my future husband off my back in regard to working too much."

"He used to be the same way before he met you," I tell Sawyer. It's not news to her, but I like seeing the way her eyes soften when she hears the way my big brother has changed his life for her. He's a better man with Sawyer in his world, he knows it too.

"I've never done that kind of work," Layla tells them. Her eyes are still glued to the screen of my phone. "I've only ever been a waitress."

"Pfft." Sawyer waves her hand in the air. "If you can keep up with a bunch of whiny customers, the Riggins brothers will be a breeze." She laughs when Royce tickles her side. "No, really, you can do it. It's nothing crazy, and Royce and I have talked a lot about this. You could take over the reception desk while I continue on with my support projects for each of them. It would be answering phones and taking care of their schedules and other minor tasks. We will eventually train you so that you are more support for me as well."

"You don't know me. How can you just offer me this job so easily?"

Royce and Sawyer give Layla their full attention. Sawyer opens her mouth to speak, but Royce beats her to it. "I know my brother. I know that if you weren't important to him in some way, that he wouldn't be bringing you into our family. We're more than just a corporation. Riggins Enterprises is our family. The five of us have devoted our lives to this company just as our father did before us. If Owen wants you there, if he believes in you, then we believe in you too."

I see the tears as they begin to well in her eyes. "I have a lot to think about. Thank you for your generosity."

"Call me if you want to talk about the job," Sawyer tells her as her eyes flash to me. "Or Owen. I know a little bit about handling the Riggins brothers. Owen, give her my number, will you?" she asks sweetly.

"Yeah." I chuckle. "I'll give her your number."

"You coming home soon?" Royce asks.

"Yeah, day after tomorrow." He nods.

"It was so nice to meet you, Layla. I hope you'll be working with us," Sawyer says, waving at the camera.

"You as well. Thank you again," Layla replies.

"I'll see you two soon," I say with a wave, ending the call, and tossing my phone on the bed.

"They seem really nice," Layla comments.

"They are. So, what do you say, Lay? You coming home with me?"

"Can I think about it?"

"You can. I leave the day after tomorrow. I hope that you're on the plane with me. Hell, we can rent a car and drive back so that we can bring your stuff with us, or we can ship it, whatever you feel like you want to do. I don't care as long as I know you're coming home with me."

"What about Ronnie and Linda? They gave me a job and their time and friendship when I had no one."

"We can come back and visit them as often as you want. They can even come and stay with us in Tennessee. I have five bedrooms in my house. There's plenty of room."

"Five?" She gasps. "Why do you have five bedrooms when you live alone?"

I brush her hair back out of her eyes. "Because I want a family one day. I had almost given up hope that I would find someone I'd want to spend all of my days with, then I found you."

"Those are strong words, Owen Riggins."

I place her hand over my heart. "I know they are. I'm not a man who says things he doesn't mean." Leaning in, I kiss the corner of her mouth and her breath hitches. No matter how badly I want to devour her and have her taste on my tongue, I need to remember to take things slowly. Without a doubt, Layla is worth it.

"I just need to think."

"Can you think while we lounge around in bed all day?"

"We can't stay in bed all day," she scoffs.

"Why the hell not? You're off, and I'm here for you. My job at the hotel is complete until I get the final numbers. I say we order room service all day, and just spend the day together."

"I—Can we really do that?" There's a hint of hope in her voice.

"We can do whatever we want." I kiss her cheek, move her off my lap, and set her on the bed before going to the windows and pulling the curtains.

"What are you doing?"

"Movies are better in the dark."

"We're watching movies?"

"Unless you had something else in mind?" I ask her, raising my eyebrows.

"No. Movies are good. It's been ages since I've watched one."

"How long is ages?"

I can tell she's thinking from the look on her face. "Two years ago. Ronnie and Linda had me over for dinner and invited me to stay for a movie."

"What do you watch when you're at home?"

"Nothing. I have a few books I've read more times than I can count. I don't pay for TV or the internet for streaming. Besides, I work a lot."

"That—" I point at her. "—*that* is why you should accept my offer. I want you to be able to enjoy life, not working yourself to the point of exhaustion for a small wage and nothing to show for it."

"I'll think about it."

I nod, accepting that answer for now.

Grabbing the remote, I climb into bed next to her and scroll through the movies. I choose a chick flick. It's not one I've seen before, and I'm positive she's not seen it either. Putting my arm around her shoulders, I pull her into my side as we settle in to watch the movie. I've never done this before either, and I'm looking forward to it. Anytime I can spend with her is a win in my book.

CHAPTER
Layla
TEN

I'VE BEEN HERE for three hours of my twelve-hour shift, and I couldn't tell you the first thing that's happened. I'm going through the motions as I think about Owen, and our day together yesterday. We watched movies, ate way too much over-priced room service, talked for hours, and stole a lot of kisses. Technically, they're not stolen when given freely. I could spend days doing nothing but kissing him. The scratchiness of his beard, the way his hands cradle my face, I feel protected. And the need he claims to have for me, I feel that too. From my head to my toes, I feel his need, his desire, and I want more.

"Layla, are you even listening to me?" Linda chuckles.

"Sorry, Linda," I say sheepishly.

"What on earth has gotten into you?" she asks.

I bite down on my bottom lip, debating on how much I should tell her. "I met someone," I blurt out.

"Oh, I heard. Rumor has it Mr. Tall, Bearded, and Handsome has been in here a lot on the nights you work." She winks.

My face is hot from embarrassment. "He has. He always asks for me, and well, we've been spending some time together."

"Why the long face?"

"He offered me a job," I confess.

"Order up!" Johnny, one of the cooks, yells.

"That's mine," I tell Linda.

"Tonight, you and I are going to chat, sooner if we can both get a break later. I want all the details." She offers me a warm smile, something I've come to accept with her.

"Okay." I easily agree to her terms, because I need someone to talk to about this. Owen gave me Sawyer's number, but she's too close to him, to the situation. I guess Linda is too, but I trust her to give me her honest feedback to help me make my decision.

He goes home tomorrow. I feel a knot twist in my belly when I think about never seeing him again. Then, there is the home and the life I've made for myself here in Florida. It might not be a sprawling five-bedroom, but I have a place to lay my head at night. Sure, times are tight, but I'm making it on my own.

By the time the lunch rush is over, my feet are begging me for a break. I'm just about to clock out when I hear a familiar sexy voice from behind me at the bar.

"You taking a break?" he asks.

Turning, I see Owen standing at the bar, looking as handsome as ever. "Yes. We just finished the lunch rush. I was going to grab something to eat."

"Mind if I join you?"

"You hungry?" I ask him.

His eyes rake over my body. "Sure. Whatever you're having is fine. Oh, and it's on me."

"I get a discount because I work here. It's my treat this time," I tell him.

"Layla," he warns.

That makes my smile grow. "Go sit." I point to a small corner booth where the staff eats out of the view of customers. "I'll be right over." He shakes his head but does as I ask and heads toward the small corner booth.

"Linda, how about a couple of burgers and a plate of fries?" I ask sweetly.

"Was that him?" she asks, nodding toward the bar where I was just talking with Owen.

"That's him," I confirm.

"He's a looker." She wags her eyebrows.

"Linda!" I pretend to scold her. "What would Ronnie say?"

"I'm married, not dead. Now, help me get this fixed up so you can have lunch with your man."

"He's not my man."

"No? Sure looks that way to me."

"What makes you say that?"

"It's all in the eyes. He didn't take his off you."

"That doesn't mean he's mine."

"Maybe not yet, but you want him to be." I open my mouth to object, but she stops me. "Don't try denying it. You and I are still going to have that chat." She points at me before pulling down three plates.

"I'm going to grab us some drinks. I'll be right back." I rush to the bar area and make us both a glass of sweet tea, and drop it off at the booth. "Our food is almost ready," I tell him, placing our glasses on the table.

"Hey." Reaching out, he grabs my arm. "Come here." He gives my arm a gentle tug so I'm leaning into him and presses his lips to mine. "I missed you."

"You dropped me off this morning, and we spent the day together yesterday."

He shrugs. "I want all your time, Lay." He winks and releases me.

I stumble back to the kitchen on shaking legs. As soon as Linda sees me, a huge grin lights up her face. "He's yours all right." She grabs a serving tray and places two small plates, each holding a juicy burger and another filled with more than one order of fries. "Go on. You only get thirty minutes. You don't want to keep your man waiting."

I roll my eyes at her but don't bother to object. For one, I know Linda, and I know it wouldn't do me a bit of good. For two, I like the way it sounds, Owen being my man. I also like the way it makes me feel. Just the thought of all the things he said to me yesterday about us being together coming true, warms me from the inside out. I want him. I'm just afraid to take that leap.

"Here you go," I say, placing our plates on the table. I slide into the booth and grab the bottle of ketchup, squirting some onto the side of the plate of fries. "I hope you like ketchup." I grin at him, sliding a fry through the condiment and popping into my mouth.

"If I didn't, I would now," he says, his eyes heated as he watches me.

"Eat up, Riggins."

He smiles, shaking his head before repeating my process with a fry.

"Have you thought anymore about my offer?"

"Owen, it's been hours, and I'm working."

"Don't try to make me think that that beautiful mind of yours isn't spinning over our circumstances."

"Fine. Yes, I've thought about it. That's all I've thought about."

"Can I help?"

"Tell me this isn't crazy. We barely know each other, Owen. I can't just move in with you."

He nods, wipes his mouth, and takes a drink of his tea before he replies. "It's crazy," he agrees. "It's soon," he agrees. "However, no one can tell you how you feel, Layla. I know that it's a very short amount of time, but already you've become important to me. I'm a firm believer in when you know, you know. I know that you are the woman for me. Yes, it sounds crazy as fuck, but the feeling here—" He taps his chest, over his heart. "—that feeling is strong, and I know this is the magic."

"Magic?"

He sighs and leans back in the booth. "This is going to sound even crazier. My dad claims that the love of a good woman is magic. He swears that when he first laid eyes on my mom, he felt what he likes to call the 'magic.' That having the right partner changes a person."

"Do you believe that?" I ask softly.

"See, that's the thing. I always used to think it was just something Dad spouted off to my brothers and me. That changed recently. First, when Royce met Sawyer. He was married before, and I could feel it in my gut she wasn't right for him. Hell, we all tried to tell him, but he married her anyway. It ended in disaster, and with my brother's heart broken. It wasn't until Sawyer came into his life that the pain and betrayal from his marriage left his eyes, and he started to live again. To really live. He stopped working sixteen hours a day, and he was the fun-loving guy we all remember before he married the she-devil."

"He changed?"

He nods. "For the better. That was the first time I believed in the magic my dad always talks about."

"And the second?"

"When I met you. I used to be just like Royce, working long hours, throwing all I am at my job. I keep to myself. I'm the quiet Riggins brother." He smiles. "I've never wanted more with a woman, not until you limped into my life." He winks, and I can't help but smile. "I think we owe it to ourselves to see where this goes. I know you feel it, Lay. I can see it in your eyes, in the way your breathing changes when I'm close."

I nod. "What if it doesn't work out? What happens when I give up my steady job to take yours and follow you to Nashville, and you decide it's not the magic, and the feeling is just a bad case of indigestion?"

He throws his head back in laughter. It's a deep rich sound that I could listen to all day. His white teeth shine through his thick beard, and I wish I had a camera, or a cell phone I could use to take a picture of him. I want to remember him this way.

"That's not going to happen. If it makes you feel better, we can draft a contract that ensures your job security."

"I might suck at it."

He nods. "You might at first, but you're a fighter, Lay. I've seen you, and from what you've told me, you fought to be where you are today. I want to give you a better job, a safe place to live, and share my family with you. I want to give you all that I have to give. I just need you to take a leap of faith and trust the magic."

My heart pounds so loud I'm sure he can hear it. My eyes sting with tears from his words. I believe him. He wants to be with me. I don't know why, but I trust him and his words. I just don't know if it's the right choice for me. I knew when I left Indiana that I was going to be on my own. I planned for years. I had a plan. *This* isn't a plan. This is me leaving the safe haven I've made for myself and running off to a land unknown, for all intents and purposes, chasing the fairy tale. That's exactly what he's offering me—a fairy tale. A chance to be a part of a family and have my own in him. Maybe not right away, but he claims that's his end game.

He calls it magic.

"I'll be here to pick you up after your shift," he says. He must see the turmoil his words have caused. I don't know what to do.

"I'd like that," I confess.

He stands and hands me money. "Lunch is on me, and before you say you get a discount, that's fine. You use this to pay and keep the rest for the incredible company."

My legs tremble as I stand and face him. "I'll see you later." There is hope in my voice. I know he'll be here, but I still have that fear of not having a set of strong shoulders to lean on.

"I'll be here, baby." He presses a chaste kiss to my lips. "See you soon." With that, he's gone, walking out the door, and taking a piece of me with him. He's offering me everything I've ever dreamed of. I'm just worried it's too good to be true.

After Owen left, I was just simply going through the motions. I avoided Linda as much as possible, needing time with my thoughts. The trouble with time is that I'm even more confused than when I clocked in this morning. My heart tells me to take the leap that Owen Riggins is my savior, and my head is telling me that I can only trust myself.

Glancing at the clock, I know he's going to be here in an hour to pick me up. He's going to want an answer, he leaves tomorrow, and I don't know what I'm going to do.

"You done hiding?" Linda asks from behind me.

I sigh and continue to wipe the bar. "I'm not hiding."

"Avoiding me is hiding, Layla," she says in what I could imagine would have been her mom voice had she had children. "What's going on with you?"

"He offered me a job."

"So you've mentioned. What are you thinking?"

"It's in Nashville. He and his brothers own some kind of logistics company. They need office support."

"Have you talked about salary?"

"It's four times what I make here."

"Wow," she breathes, leaning against the bar next to me.

"Yep."

"Tell me where you're at. What are you thinking? Have you made a pros and cons list?" she asks.

"Cons, leaving you and Ronnie. Pros, just about everything else. Including more time with Owen. At least, I think that's a plus." It's a good thing if we work out. If not, I'm starting over again in a new city with no one.

"What do you mean, you think?"

"He wants more, and before you ask, he claims he wants to date me. That I'm the 'magic' he's been missing in his life. Crazy, right?" I ask her. When she doesn't answer, I finally turn to face her. "Linda?"

"Not so crazy." She smiles. "Look, Layla, life is full of hard decisions. You don't need me to tell you that. You've had to make more of them than most at your age. However, you can't let fear hold you back."

"I barely know him. He said I could live with him, but if I didn't want to that his future sister-in-law has an apartment that she hasn't let go yet. It's all too easy," I say, exasperated.

"Layla, sweetheart, not everything about life is hard. There are just as many good moments. Most of the time more than the bad. You were dealt a bad hand in life, and my heart breaks for you that you don't see the good. You deserve the good."

"I don't want to leave you and Ronnie."

"You know where we live. You're welcome in our home anytime."

"The two of you are all that I have," I say, my voice cracking.

"You have me."

My head pops up to see Owen standing before me. He's in worn jeans and a T-shirt, and those blue eyes of his are dark and intense as they stare at me. "Hi," I say, wiping the lone tear that cascades down my cheek.

In a few long strides, he's around the counter and has my face cradled in the palm of his hands. "You have me. You have my crazy family, and we'll come back as much as you want to visit. Ronnie and Linda can come and visit and stay with us, or me, or whatever. I promise you, you will not be alone. I won't ever let you be alone again." The look in his eyes tells me he means every word he's saying.

"Oh my," Linda says breathily, and I can't help but chuckle.

"There she is." Owen smiles down at me. "No more tears, baby. Only smiles for you from here on out."

"There are going to be tears, Owen," I say, taking a step back, putting some space between us.

"I don't like to see you cry."

"That's a part of life. Tears. Pain."

He nods. "You're right. I'll just have to hold you through them."

"If you don't go with him, I will," Linda says, not bothering to lower her voice.

"Linda! What about Ronnie?"

"Phew," she says, smiling and fanning her face with a menu. I burst out in laughter, which is exactly what she was going for.

"My life is in pieces, Owen. I'm a mess, and barely holding it together."

"Let me put you back together. Piece by piece, I won't stop until you feel whole."

I don't tell him that when I'm with him, I feel whole. I feel alive. My breath hitches when I realize that Linda is right. It's my fear, but I didn't let fear stop me before, and now I have Linda and Ronnie to come back to. Never again will I be alone. Reaching for the cordless phone that's lying behind the counter, I dial the number he gave me for Sawyer. I memorized it, because well, I just did.

"Hello."

"Sawyer, hi, this is Layla." Owen's eyes widen.

"Layla! Hi, it's so good to hear from you. What's up? You keeping Owen in line?"

"Is that even possible?" I ask, making her laugh.

"He is a Riggins, but I'll let you in on a secret, they're just a bunch of big softies. Sexy, infuriating softies." She laughs.

My eyes find Owen's. "I'm going to need some pointers."

"You got it. So, what's up?"

"I was wondering if the job was still open, and Owen mentioned you had an apartment for rent?"

"Yes, and yes. Both are yours if you want them."

"I do." The words are past my lips, and I can't take them back. Not that I want to. I want this adventure he's giving me. I'll have a job, and my own place, and maybe if I'm lucky, I'll get more of Owen too. It's risky to take this leap, and I'm scared to death. However, I'm the only one who can change my future. I'm the only one who can reach for the stars as I try and hang the moon.

"Thank God. I wasn't ready to deal with a sad, brooding Owen. I had enough of that with Royce."

"Sounds like a story." I don't comment on the sad and brooding Owen part. I'm sure she's exaggerating.

"Yes, one I'll fill you in on once we meet in person. I'll get the ball rolling on my end. You coming home with Owen?"

"Yes." *I'm going home with Owen.* Those five words elicit fear and happiness and hope for what's yet to come.

"Awesome. I can't wait to meet you. We're on our way to balancing all the testosterone in the family." She laughs.

I can't help but laugh at her dramatics. Surely Owen and his brothers aren't that bad. "Thank you, Sawyer."

"You're welcome. See you soon." I end the call and place the phone back behind the counter.

"Layla?" His voice is thick.

"You ready to put those muscles to use? I have some packing to do."

He engulfs me in a hug, lifting me from my feet. His lips mold with mine, and his reaction alone tells me I made the right decision.

I'm not going to let my fear keep me from fighting for what I want. I don't know exactly what that looks like yet. I do know I want a better home in a safe neighborhood. I'd like a job that pays more so I'm not living less than a paycheck to paycheck, and I'd like to find a man to spend my time with. Maybe even fall in love. I don't know if Owen is that man, but there is a desire in me that can't wait to find out.

CHAPTER
Owen
ELEVEN

HITTING THE CITY limit sign for home, I glance over in the passenger seat, and Layla is still sleeping peacefully. Somehow, we managed to pack her stuff and fit it all into my rental. Even more astonishing is that I was able to convince her to leave her car behind. Ronnie is going to sell it for her and send her the money. I told her I have three vehicles, and that she's welcome to one of them. I assumed she would fight me on it, but I think that she realized her car is still on its last leg, even with the recent repairs.

It's all gone smooth sailing since the moment she called Sawyer. The further we drive from Florida, the easier my breathing became. She's here, in my hometown, and we're doing this. We get to explore this thing between us even further, and Layla, well, she gets to better herself. I want that for her, as much as I want her for me.

Instead of taking her to Sawyer's apartment, I drive to my place. I want her there. I can't explain it, but there's a need for her to be in my space, in my home. I don't take women to my house unless their last name is Riggins, or if it's going to be Riggins. Layla's different, and one day, I can only hope I'm that lucky bastard who gets to change her last name.

Once I've pulled into the driveway, I turn off the engine and unbuckle my seat belt, turning to face her. Her head is tilted toward me, her eyes closed, and just looking at her makes my heart race. I can't believe she's here.

Reaching out, I move her hair that's fallen into her eyes. "Lay," I whisper. She doesn't move, so I lean in and press my lips to her forehead. When I pull back, her eyes are open, watching me. "There she is." I smile.

"Are we there yet?" she asks, sitting up straighter in her seat.

"Yeah. We're home." I don't miss the way my heart seems to stall in my chest at the thought of this being *our* home.

"Come on, and I'll show you around." Climbing out of the rental, I meet her at the passenger door and offer her my hand. She takes it with ease, and I guide us to the front porch. Punching in the code to unlock the door, I push it open and usher us inside.

"Wow." She turns to face me. "You live here? On your own?"

I nod. "I fell in love with it. I added the outdoor kitchen and the pool, but everything else is how it was when I bought it."

"Why do you need such a big house just for you?"

I shrug. "It's close to my parents and my brothers, and I hoped that one day I might have a family, and we'd need all the space."

"You bought this place on the chance that you would need it?" she asks, her eyes wide.

"I have four brothers, and if they ever need a place to stay, I have space. I'm the second oldest, so our younger brothers would come home from college and stay with me instead of our parents."

"What about your older brother? Royce, right?"

I nod. "He was married at the time to the woman who wasn't nice or right for him."

This time it's her turn to nod. "So, you were their place to stay by default."

"Not exactly, we're all really close. We're stair-stepped in age, two years apart between each of us. We were a rowdy bunch growing up," I say fondly, thinking about all the fun me and my brothers had. Still do.

"I don't know how your parents did it. Five boys." She's smiling as she shakes her head.

"There was never a dull moment in the Riggins' house. Hell, we're all grown men living on our own, and there still isn't."

"Tell me more about them," she asks.

"Let's go on a tour of the house, and then we can talk all you want. I want you to feel comfortable here."

"I'm not staying here, though, right? I'm staying at Sawyer's place?"

"That's your choice, Layla. I'd love nothing more than for you to be here with me all the time, but I understand if you're not ready for that."

"And you are? Ready for that, I mean?"

"Yeah, baby." I slide my arm around her waist, pulling her into my chest. "I'm ready for that."

"We barely know each other."

"So you keep reminding me," I tease. "Come on." I lead her out of the foyer into the living room. From there, we tour the entire first level before moving upstairs. "There are four more bedrooms up here."

"Five bedrooms," she croaks, shaking her head. "Your kitchen is the size of my apartment back in Florida. This house…" She turns to face me. "…is incredible, Owen. So beautiful. You should be proud of where you are."

"I am now that you're here." Again, I snake my arm around her waist and pull her into my chest. She fits there.

"These are all extra bedrooms. You're welcome to stay in any of them or stay in my room with me. The choice is yours." Before she can form a reply, I keep going. "You hungry?" I ask.

"No," she says over a yawn.

Without a word, I turn us, and we head back downstairs. I lead us to my bedroom, knowing that the front door is locked, and kick off my shoes. "I'm exhausted," I say, turning on the bedside lamp.

"I told you I would drive," she says over another yawn.

"I know, but I was good. Now, I'm tired." I strip down to my boxer briefs and climb into bed. "You coming?" I slide over to the middle of the bed and hold the covers up for her. "We're just sleeping, Lay. I promise. Now come here. It's late, and I know you're still tired, you can't stop yawning."

I can see the indecision warring in her eyes. "Owen, I don't know if this is a good idea."

"Why not? You've slept next to me before."

"That's why. I can't let myself get used to the safety and comfort of sleeping next to you."

I sit up, letting the blanket pool at my waist. "I want you to get comfortable, and I always want you to feel safe. You are safe with me, Layla."

She's already shaking her head before I'm finished. "I'm not." She taps her hand over her heart. "Right here," she whispers. "I'm not safe right here."

Just like that, another piece of my heart breaks off and finds its way floating toward her. "Come here, baby." I pat the bed next to me. I'm prepared to argue my case, but she surprises me when she kicks off her shoes and asks for a shirt to sleep in. "In that dresser." I point behind her. "Top drawer. The bathroom's through that door." I point, showing her.

"I'll be right back." I watch every move as she retrieves a T-shirt and disappears behind the bathroom door. I decide to send my brothers and my parents a message, letting them know I made it home in our group text.

Me: Just got in.

Royce: Layla?

Me: She's with me.

Mom: Can't wait to meet her.

Dad: Welcome home, son.

Marshall: When you bringing my girl over, bro?

Grant: Owen's in Looovee.

Conrad: Owen and Layla sitting in a tree...

Mom: Leave your brother alone.

Me: Good night.

I power off my phone, knowing that my idiot brothers can keep their teasing going all night long. Normally it would annoy me because, before Layla, there was no one I would bring home to them or consider letting stay in my home. Things have changed. Layla has changed me.

The bathroom door opens, and I can't help but stare as she makes her way toward the bed. "You want me to turn this off?" She points to the lamp.

"Do you need it? To feel safe?" I add.

"No," she says, shaking her head at the same time.

"Turn it off." She reaches for the lamp, and the room goes dark. "Layla." My voice is husky even to my own ears. "Come to bed, baby."

I feel the bed dip as she climbs in beside me. I reach for her in the darkness and pull her to my side, my front aligned with her back. My hand rests on her bare thigh, and my thumb traces her silky-smooth skin. With each pass of my thumb, I feel her body relax into me.

"Owen?" Her voice is soft as it fills the quiet room.

"Yeah?" I ask, my voice rough.

"Goodnight."

"Night," I reply, sliding my hand to her belly and holding her close. It doesn't take long for my body to relax and for sleep to claim me.

I'm standing at the stove frying bacon when I feel her. "Hungry?" I ask.

"How did you know I was standing here?" she asks, her voice moving closer.

"I could feel you."

"Feel me?"

Pulling the bacon out of the pan, I place it on a plate lined with a paper towel, a trick I learned from watching my mom cook for us growing up. Turning off the burner and sliding the skillet to the back, I turn and wrap my arms around her. "Yes, I could feel you. I don't know how, but I knew the moment you walked into the room."

"Is this more of that magic you were talking about?" She smiles up at me.

"This is you, Lay, all you, baby," I say, pressing a kiss to the top of her head.

"How did you know I love bacon?"

"Room service. That's the first thing you went for. Bacon, and toast and jelly." I nod to the island where I have several slices of toast sitting on a plate.

"Be careful, Riggins. You keep spoiling me like this I might never leave," she teases.

Two things cross my mind. First, I love that she's teasing and happy. I love the fact that she's opening up and being herself around me. Second, I plan to spoil the hell out of her, and if that helps my case to get her to stay with me, so be it. Hands on her hips, I lift her up onto the counter. "Strawberry or grape?" I ask.

"What?" She cocks her head to the side, a smile playing on her lips.

"Strawberry or grape jelly?"

"Both." She grins.

"Coffee?"

"Yes, please," she says, swiping a piece of bacon off the plate as I set it on the counter next to her. "So, what are we doing today? I assume we need to drop my things off at the apartment so we can take the rental back?"

"I thought we'd just put your things in the garage here, and then I'll have you follow me in my car to turn the rental in. If we get there before noon, they won't charge me for another day." I'm not worried about the charge. The money isn't the issue. I'm not ready for her to leave, and I'm hoping with time she'll just stay with me and forget about Sawyer's apartment.

"Can't we just drop my stuff off on the way?"

"Yeah, but I don't have a key. It's not much, so it will be fine," I assure her as I hand her a cup of coffee. I busy myself cutting a piece of toast in half slathering one side with strawberry jelly and the other with grape. "My queen," I say, holding the jelly-covered toast to her lips. She giggles and takes a huge bite. I add grape to another piece and step between her thighs where she's still sitting on the counter. Together, we eat breakfast in the most unconventional method, but it's ours. I couldn't think of a better way to start this day or our time together.

CHAPTER

Layla

TWELVE

I'M LIVING IN a fairy tale. I know that at any moment, I'm going to wake up and be in my shitty apartment in Florida. This can't be real—this new life that literally just developed over a matter of weeks, all from meeting a handsome stranger.

"Layla." Owen's deep timbre pulls me out of my thoughts. "Where did you go?" he asks, cocking his head to the side.

"Pinch me," I say, holding out my arm.

"What?" he asks incredulously.

It's not like I told him to kick a puppy. "Pinch me so I'll wake up. I have to be dreaming."

"What's going on in that head of yours?"

"You just told me that you want me to drive that." I point to the shiny car that costs more than I'll probably ever earn in a lifetime.

"Yes, that's my car. I assumed you didn't want to drive my truck or my SUV since you are used to driving a car."

"Why does one man have three vehicles?" Three! Who needs three vehicles?

"A man has to have a truck, and I take the SUV grocery shopping, it holds more, and the car, it's just a luxury. I usually drive it back and forth to work."

"Three, Owen. You have three. All of them probably nicer than anything I'll ever own, and you want me to drive that one," I say, pointing at the car again. "The shiny one that looks super expensive. I can't do it. I'll drive the rental."

"Babe, you're not listed on the rental." He smirks.

"Since when are you a rule follower, Owen Riggins?" I ask, my hands braced on my hips.

He throws his head back and laughs. "Ask my brothers, I *am* the rule follower, trust me. Now, this is just a car. I have insurance, so if you wreck it, I don't care. What I do care about is you being safe. The car can be replaced. Do you think you're going to feel unsafe driving? I can call one of my brothers." He's already reaching into his pocket for his phone before I can reply.

"No. I don't feel unsafe, but I'll be a nervous wreck the entire drive. I've never even sat in a car this nice before."

"Layla…" He slides his phone back into his pocket and reaches for me. I go willingly because, in a short amount of time, I've learned that there is nothing better than being in his arms. "Life is about to change for you. You're going to be making good money, enough to stand on your own. You're going to be able to afford new shoes, and a new car if that's what you want. Get used to this. This is your new normal."

"It's scary," I admit. "I want that, but it feels like it's a fantasy and not my life. I've never had financial security. I don't even know what that looks like."

"I'm right there to guide you. I'm not going anywhere."

"Sure, until you get tired of my freak-outs." I rest my head against his chest. "I'm sorry, this is just all new to me, and I'm having a hard time understanding how I got so lucky."

"Hey." He tilts my chin up with his index finger. "I'm the lucky one. Don't ever forget that." His lips press to my forehead, and I can feel my body relax into him. It's as if I have zero control over the way I react to him, to his touch, or to his kisses.

"Fine," I concede. "Don't say I didn't warn you," I say, holding my hand out for the keys.

"It's going to be fine. After, we can grab some lunch."

"We just had breakfast," I remind him. His eyes heat at the mention of breakfast. We did nothing more than steal a few kisses, yet it was intimate, and I loved every minute of it. If you had told me a year ago I'd enjoy spending time with a man who was bossy and liked to feed me, I would have told you that you'd lost your damn mind. Now, today, it's not so bad. Not when it's Owen.

"I'm a growing boy," he says, rubbing his stomach and grinning.

There is nothing boy-ish about the man. "Uh-huh, let's go," I say, taking the offered keys from his hands, and climbing behind the wheel of his extremely expensive car.

"See that wasn't so bad, was it?" Owen asks as we pull out of the lot of the car rental place.

"No, it wasn't bad, but I white-knuckled it all the way here." That's not an exaggeration. My grip was so tight on the wheel my knuckles literally turned white.

He reaches over and takes my hand in his, bringing it to his lips. He takes his time placing a feather-soft kiss on each knuckle. "Thank you," he says softly, not taking his eyes off of the road, and effectively melting me into a pile of longing.

"Now where to?" I ask him.

"I thought we could stop by Royce and Sawyer's place to get the keys to the apartment."

"Oh, okay," I say, suddenly worried about meeting his family.

"What's that about?"

"I just didn't realize I'd be meeting them today. I'm a mess." I motion at my body that's covered in worn cutoff jean shorts and a tank top. The only new item I'm wearing that's not a hand-me-down or purchased at a second-hand store are the flip-flops on my feet. They're one of the pairs Owen bought me the day we went shopping.

"You're perfect," he assures me.

Biting down on my bottom lip, I try to push back the anxiety that's threatening to take over. I'm meeting his brother and his brother's fiancée. Am I just the new girl at Riggins Enterprises? Am I more? I don't really know, and that causes my anxiety to spike. I know it's crazy; he's told me that this is more for him, but there is this constant worry that the other shoe is going to drop. It's like Owen Riggins fell right out of the sky, and my life with him in it is better than I ever could have imagined. I'm scared I'm going to lose that.

"Lay, baby, what's going on? Tell me what you're thinking?" His soothing voice washes over me.

"Who are you going to tell them that I am? I mean, I don't really know what we are, and I'm not sure if it's just between us or if it's more. I just… I don't know, Owen. I'm not good at these kinds of situations. This is all new to me." He surprises me when he signals and pulls the car over to the side of the road. I watch as he puts the car in Park and turns to face me, or as best as he can with his seat belt still intact.

"What this is between us is just that. It's us. That means it's just you and me. There is no other woman in my life and no other man in yours. However, that doesn't mean that we're hiding what we are to one another."

"What are we? This is all crazy, Owen."

"We're dating. Seeing where things go."

"But I work for you."

"There are no rules against that. Trust me, Royce and Sawyer went through this, and he tried to use that as an excuse to push her away. I'm learning from my big brother's mistakes. I don't give a fuck who you work for, and I'm not letting you go."

"So we tell them that we're dating? Are they going to give you a hard time? We've only known each other a small amount of time."

"No. Royce met Sawyer on a plane, and he knew then that she was it for him, but he fought it. I'm not fighting it. There are no rules or timelines we have to follow. We just have to do what's best for us. What's best for me, is you." He leans in and presses his lips to mine. Just a soft, quick peck, but it does wonders at calming my nerves.

"Okay."

"Just like that?" He grins.

"Yeah, I have no examples to go on here. My life wasn't filled with dates or watching a healthy relationship. I'm learning as I go, and I trust you, Owen."

"Good." He gives me another kiss before turning in his seat and pulling back out on the road.

"Wow. Do all of you own huge houses?" I ask as we pull into Royce's driveway.

He laughs. "Just me, Royce, and Grant. Conrad and Marshall, who are the youngest, still live in apartments. They actually live in the same building. It makes it nice when I have to pick their asses up after a night of drinking and drive them home. I only have to make one stop."

"That's nice of you."

"They're my brothers."

He says it so simply, like there is no other option for him. I wish I knew what that felt like. I've never felt that kind of connection with anyone.

Ronnie and Linda are the closest I've come to having someone to depend on, and even then, I fought it. I didn't want to get used to having them for the fear they might not stick around. That fear is there when it comes to Owen as well, but he doesn't let me hide behind it. We talk about it, and he assures me he's not going anywhere.

For the first time in my life, I'm trusting someone, leaning on them, depending on them to hold me up and catch me when I fall.

I want more than anything for that person to always be Owen. No matter what happens between us, he will always have a piece of me for all the kindness he has shown me. Not just kindness, but he's proved to me that there are good men out there. The kind who is happy to just hold you close as they lie in bed next to you. The kind that asks before taking, not just assume that the world is theirs.

Owen is my unicorn. I never thought I'd ever meet a man like him.

"You ready?" he asks, pulling me out of my thoughts.

"As I'll ever be."

He nods, and we both climb out of his car. His hand finds its way to the small of my back as he leads me up the steps of the porch and to the front door. Owen knocks, and the door swings open. Before me stands a man and a woman, both smiling wide. I recognize them from the video call.

"Glad to have you back, brother." Royce leans in and gives Owen one of those man hugs. You know, it's kind of a mix between a handshake and a slap on the back kind of thing. "You must be Layla," he says, pulling back. He surprises me when he tugs me into a hug.

"Royce," Owen says, his voice sounding very similar to a growl.

"Oh, boy, here we go," Sawyer says, standing next to Royce. "We had enough of that with this guy." She points to her fiancé. "Layla, I'm Sawyer. It's nice to finally meet you."

"It's nice to meet you. Both of you. You have a beautiful home."

"Come on in." Sawyer reaches out and grabs my hand, pulling me inside. I trail along behind her as she leads us to the living room and takes a seat on the couch, offering for me to do the same. It's not until I'm sitting that I notice she's dressed just like me. Cutoff jean shorts and a tank top, and her feet are bare. "How was the drive up from Florida?" she asks.

"Not too bad. Owen drove the entire time. I offered to take a turn, but he refused."

"Get used to that. If he's anything like his older brother, he thinks he has to spoil you. Not that it's a bad thing. It could be worse, but sometimes a girl just wants to drive herself to the damn mall," she says, exasperated, making me laugh.

I nod. "I can definitely see that in Owen."

"All five of them. I swear I don't know how Lena and Stanley did it."

"Their parents?" I ask.

"Sorry, yes, they are the sweetest people you will ever meet. How they raised five hoodlums is beyond me." She winks, and there's a twinkle in her eye telling me she's kidding.

"Thank you for letting me rent your apartment. Are you sure you don't mind?" I ask as the guys join us.

"Not at all. This one—" She points at Royce, who plops down on the couch next to her, throwing his arm over her shoulders. "—has been bugging me to break my lease for months. There are three months to go, and you're welcome to let it go or stay once that time frame is up."

"There is a slight delay," Royce speaks up. "I called the cleaners to come in and have the carpets cleaned, and they're doing that this weekend, so you won't be able to move in until Monday."

"Oh, I can just go to a hotel or something until then."

"The hell. You can stay with me," Owen pipes up. "Just like you did last night. You know I have the space."

Something passes in his eyes that I can't explain. He glances at Royce and quickly pulls his gaze back to me. "Thank you, Owen."

"Why would you even suggest a hotel?" he asks, not caring that we have an audience.

"I didn't want to assume or overstay my welcome." I look down at my hands where I'm wringing them together in my lap.

"Layla." The deep timbre of his voice has me lifting my head to face him. "You are welcome in my home. If it was up to me, you'd be staying with me. You know that. What's this about?"

"I know you said that, but this is so overwhelming and new. I wanted you to have the opportunity to back out if you wanted to." My voice is small, mindful of Royce and Sawyer being witness to our conversation. I can feel the heat of the embarrassment coat my cheeks.

"He's not backing out," Royce chimes in.

"Layla, you're welcome to stay here if you'd rather not stay with Owen," Sawyer offers.

"No. It's not that I don't want to." I blow out a breath. "I grew up... not like this," I confess. "This is a life that I'm not used to. My mother was only that because she gave birth to me. She had a revolving door of men, and the job, the move, I've been on my own for so long that this is hard to grasp."

Owen pulls me into his chest as Royce moves to the edge of his seat, resting his elbows on his knees. His eyes bore into mine. "Welcome home, Layla," he says softly.

I blink hard, fighting back the hot tears that threaten to fall. "I've never really felt like I had a home." I realize as the words leave my mouth that it's true. Sure, I had a shitty apartment back in Florida, but it was never a home. It was a warm, dry place to lay my head at night. There was nothing "homey" about it.

"I'm starving. Layla, you want to help me get the salad ready in the kitchen while the boys grill us some steak?" Sawyer cutting through the tension has me sighing in relief, thankful for the change in topic.

I nod. "I'd love to help." Just like that, they've accepted me for who I am. We spend the rest of the day just hanging out and talking, getting to know one another. I see a lot of similarities between Royce and Owen. Their mannerisms, and the way that they are with Sawyer and me. Owen treats me like Royce treats Sawyer, and I know just by watching them together how in love they are.

I can't help but wonder if Owen and I will get there. If I'm being honest with myself, I'm already falling hard. I'm scared as hell, but I'm not going to fight it. With life comes heartbreak; I know that better than anyone. I also know that sometimes you have to take a risk if you want the reward. That reward is Owen, and he's worth all the risks.

CHAPTER THIRTEEN
Owen

W HEN THE LIGHT of a new day begins to shine through the window, I realize I've lain awake all night. I was able to convince Layla to sleep in my bed again, promising her I just needed her close. I pulled her body into mine, and minutes later, she was sound asleep. Another night with her in my arms was exactly what I needed, but I couldn't seem to turn my mind off. This is where she belongs, here with me. Not just in Tennessee but in my bed. In my arms. I ran through hundreds of different scenarios to keep her here permanently.

"Why are you watching me?" she asks, her voice gravelly from sleep.

"You're beautiful." A light shade of pink coats her cheeks at my compliment. "I've slept alone for thirty years. Never craved the warmth of a woman in my arms until you."

She blinks a few times and tilts her head up to look at me. "You've never slept next to someone?"

"Unless you count my brothers when we were younger and would go camping out at the lake, no."

"How is that possible?"

"Never wanted to until now."

"You don't have to lie to me, Owen. I'm a big girl. I can take it."

I wrap my arms around her and pull her into my chest. I want her as close to me as possible. Always. "I'm telling you the truth. I've never been serious about anyone. I've never had a girlfriend. All of my experiences have been casual and never overnight."

"What? You bring your dates here, and then kick them out of your bed?" She grimaces as she asks the question. No one wants to talk about this shit—especially not me when the woman of my dreams is in my arms.

"They don't come here. We go to their place or a hotel, never here. This is my home."

"A hotel? That's such a waste of money," she says.

"That's all you got from that confession?" I ask with a smile. "I can afford it. Besides, those days are done."

"Done?" I can hear the hope in her voice.

"Why would I need them when I have you?" Her mouth forms the perfect O, showing her surprise. "You're the only one I see, Layla."

"I guess we should move me into Sawyer's place today. I didn't realize that I was breaking a rule," she says, pulling out of my arms. At least she tries to.

"Hey," I say, pulling her back into me. "What are you talking about?"

"No one stays here, and I've done it now two nights in a row, and you didn't even get a happy ending," she says, her frustration showing in her voice.

"Layla, you're not listening to me. I wanted you here. I want you here in my bed next to me. I want to sleep beside you every night and wake up to you every morning. You're the exception."

"I shouldn't have come," she says, once again, trying to pull out of my hold.

"You are exactly where you should be. Where I want you to be. Where is all of this coming from?"

"I moved to a state where I literally know no one, and he tells me that he doesn't have serious relationships. I thought we might have more. I hoped that we would be, but now you tell me this. I need to go." She tries to move away, and I do the only thing I can think of to stop her.

I kiss her.

My hand slides behind her neck, holding her lips to mine as I trace them with my tongue. She opens for me, and my tongue moves against hers. I kiss her until we're both starving for breath. Only then do I pull away.

"I want you to be mine, Layla." She opens her mouth, but I stop her. "Before you say I don't own you, I know that. I don't want to control you, but I want you in my life. I want you to be the one I call after I've had a shitty day and the first one I celebrate with when I've had a good one."

"That's what girlfriends are for, Owen." She sighs.

"Beautiful, Layla." I lean in and kiss her cheek, my lips trailing to her ear. "Will you be my girlfriend?" I whisper—five words I've never said in the same sequence before in my life. My heart is pounding as I wait for her to answer me.

"Owen," she breathes.

"Only you, Layla. I want you here with me. I don't want you to go to Sawyer's apartment. I want you to live here with me. I want you in my bed every night."

"H-How can you say that? Are you doing this for sex? Because I'm warning you, I might be bad at it."

I might be bad at it. Her words repeat over and over in my mind. Does that mean? No, she can't be. Can she?

"Oh, God." She covers her face with her hands, and the action snaps me into motion. She moves to slide off the bed, but I'm able to sit up and pull her into my lap before she gets too far.

"Layla, what do you mean you might be bad at it?"

"Do you not understand the English language?"

"Baby, are you a virgin?" The words feel like grit. I can't believe I just asked her that question. She's fucking gorgeous, with a body that would bring any man to his knees. How is she a virgin?

"My life growing up was rough. I didn't want to end up like my mother, and I knew I needed to get out of that house, out of that town. So it was better for me to abstain. Once I made it to Florida, I was barely keeping a roof over my head and food on the table. No way could I take care of a child too."

"Yet, you fed the homeless men, who looked like a group of thugs that sat outside on the stoop of your building."

She shrugs. "They needed it, and it was like they looked out for me. They scared me at first, but as time went on, they looked out for me. It was nice knowing there was someone around if I needed them."

"That's me. I want to be that someone."

"What is your family going to say? I've never met them, and you what? Just want me to move in with you? Come on, Owen. Think about what you're asking."

"I have thought about it. I know what I want. You've met Royce and Sawyer, and the others will love you just as much as we do. In fact, you get to meet them today at Sunday dinner."

"Love me?" she croaks.

"My sweet, Layla. My heart is yours. Piece by piece, you've stolen it from me, and I never want it back."

"S-Sunday dinner?" she croaks.

I'm overwhelming her and didn't want to do that, but that's just how this conversation happened to turn out. "My parents have Sunday dinner at their place every week. Those who can make it do. Now we're all living in town, it's very rare that any of us miss."

"I can't meet your family today."

"Why not?"

"Because I'm me." She slaps her hand against her chest. "They want better for you than me. I know they will."

"You're wrong. What they want is for me to be happy. They want me to find someone to live my life with and to give them grandchildren." I chuckle. It's as if I can hear my mother now asking when she's going to get grandkids. Royce is the oldest at thirty-two, and now that he's with Sawyer, the pressure is on. I have no doubts when she meets my Layla, she's going to be asking me... us too.

"I don't know."

"Come with me today. Meet them. Let them prove to you that your background has no bearing on who you are to me. You can't help the circumstances of which you were raised. That's not who you are, that's who your mother was. You're not her, Layla." I lean in and kiss the corner of her mouth. "Please, come with me?"

"And the apartment?"

"Think about it. In the meantime, I want you here with me in my home, in my bed. I want it to be our home and our bed."

"This is a lot. I mean, I know you said you wanted to try, but living together? Owen, that's a huge step."

"I know it is, but it's one I want to take with you."

"I'll go to dinner." I start to thank her, but she holds her index finger to my lips. "But don't say I didn't warn you. Once they find out about my family...." Her voice trails off.

"They're going to welcome you into ours. Trust me, Lay. Please."

She nods. "That's what I'm doing. That's why I'm here. I do trust you, Owen."

"That's my girl," I say, kissing her softly. "Now, let's make some breakfast." I pull her to the kitchen and point to the island for her to sit while I make us scrambled eggs and toast. Not exactly gourmet, but I make a mean scrambled egg.

"Oh, before I forget." I reach into the drawer in the kitchen and retrieve the new cell phone I bought her. "This is for you."

"You bought me a cell phone?" she asks in disbelief.

"I added you to my plan. It was nothing."

"Owen—" She starts, and I pin her with a look that tells her I don't want to hear it.

"I like taking care of you, Layla. I'll feel better knowing you have a phone where you can reach me if you need to. I added the number of all of my brothers, my parents, and Sawyer as well. It's yours. Use it to stay in touch with Ronnie and Linda."

Tears well in her eyes. "Thank you, Owen. I'll repay you."

"You being here, that's all I need."

"Wow," Layla breathes as we pull up to my parents' place a few hours later. I try to see my childhood home through her eyes.

"Just a house, babe," I say, trying to ease her fears. Speaking of fears, my hands are sweating, and by the way my heart seems to be beating at a rapid pace in my chest, I'm a little bit nervous myself. I have no reason to be. This is my family, and I know they will love Layla. There isn't anything not to love about her. However, this is a first for me. I've never walked through the front door with a girl on my arm. Not one that I wanted to declare is mine.

This is not only a first for her but a first for me. That's when it hits me. It's not nerves that are making my hands sweat or my heart race. It's excitement. The pieces are all starting to fall together. It's Layla, and the idea of us, here together. Not just here but our future. The one that I want for us more than I want to take my next breath.

Glancing over at her, I flash her a grin—something the me before her wouldn't have done so easily. Now, with Layla by my side, I feel lighter, maybe even a little more laidback, like my younger brothers. Hell, even Royce now that he has Sawyer in his life. "Ready?"

"If I say no, will you take me home?"

"Depends. Where are you referring to as home?" I smirk, knowing I have her.

"Your home."

Reaching over the console, I slide my hand behind her neck. "Our home. And this is my family. I want to share them with you. Will you let me do that, Lay?"

She sucks in a deep breath. "How am I supposed to say no to that?"

"You're not." Leaning over, I kiss the tip of her nose and pull away, climbing out of my truck. I start around the front to her door, and to my surprise, she meets me halfway. I thought I might have to pull her out against her will, but my girl once again proves how strong she is. She's scared and nervous, but she's with me. Right where she will always be.

"Come on." My hand finds hers, and our fingers lock as I lead her up the steps and to the front door. I don't bother knocking as that's not how this family works, and step inside.

"Owen," Layla hisses under her breath. "You can't just walk in like you own the place."

"Of course, he can," a deep male voice greets us. "His momma and I wouldn't have it any other way. You must be Layla," my dad says.

"Y-Yes, sir."

"None of that. Bring it in, darlin.'" Dad holds his arms open wide and steps into her personal space, wrapping his arms around her in a hug. "It's nice to meet you. I was starting to think the two of you weren't coming."

"We're early," I remind him.

"Yep, but you, my son, are usually the first one here."

"Who beat me?" I ask, realizing I didn't bother to look at the vehicles when we pulled up, my mind too occupied on bringing Layla here for the first time.

"Marshall."

"That's my baby brother," I explain to Layla. I've been down the family tree a few times, but there are five of us, and we're a lot to take on all at once.

"I heard that!" Marshall calls from what sounds like the kitchen.

"He hates that." Dad laughs.

"Hates what?" Layla asks.

"When I call him baby brother." My grin is wide and genuine when I think about how my words have annoyed Marshall. "Come on. I'll introduce you." With her hand still wrapped in mine, I follow my father down the hall to the kitchen.

CHAPTER
Layla
FOURTEEN

MY STOMACH IS in knots as I walk next to Owen, following his dad into the kitchen. He must feel the tremble in my hand that he's holding. He gives it a reassuring squeeze, but it does nothing to calm my nerves.

"You're late, brother," a handsome guy who I assume is Marshall says as soon as we enter the kitchen.

"You're never early, what gives?" Owen asks.

"Oh, you know, wanted to be here when my girl got here."

"Your girl?"

"Yep." Marshall stands from the stool he's sitting on and comes to stand next to me. "Thanks for picking her up for me," he says, slinging his arm over my shoulder.

"Marsh," Owen says, his voice low and kind of menacing. The look on Marshall's face tells me he's not a bit afraid of his big brother and that he got the reaction he was hoping for.

"Come on, babe, let me introduce you to my mother," Marshall says with a chuckle.

"Back off, baby brother," Owen says with humor lacing his voice. His hand slides around my waist, and he pulls me into his side and away from Marshall.

"Mom, Owen keeps calling me baby brother," Marshall says in a whiny voice, barely able to contain his laughter.

"Oh, hush, you two. Marshall, leave your brother alone, and Layla too. You're going to scare her off before I get a hug."

"He started it," Owen singsongs, and I can't hide the giggle that escapes.

I rush to cover my mouth with my hand, my eyes wide as I glance around the room. "I'm sorry," I mumble, finally looking up at Owen.

He's grinning, his white teeth shining brightly through his beard, and his eyes are twinkling. I open my mouth to apologize again; it was rude to laugh, but come on, that shit was funny. He beats me to it when he leans down and kisses the corner of my mouth.

"He can razz me all damn day if that's the reaction I get out of you. Love to see you happy, Lay," he whispers, just for me.

"Back up," his mom says, smacking at his chest lightly. "Layla." She smiles, and the dimple in her cheek peeks out. "I'm Lena, the mother to this brood. Welcome." She opens her arms for a hug, and I feel Owen release his hold on me. I step into his mother's embrace and have to swallow hard to fight off the emotions. My own mother never hugged me like this. Not one moment of my past do I ever remember getting this kind of affection from her. "We're glad you're here," Lena says, pulling away.

"Thank you for having me. I hope I'm not imposing," I say, remembering the manners that I learned on my own. Just something else dear old mom didn't offer me.

"Of course not," Lena assures me. "There is more than enough room at the table, and I always make way too much food. Something I got used to raising five teenage boys."

"Mom made sure to have a table big enough for all of us to have a guest," Marshall explains. "We just thought Owen would be the last of us to make that happen." He smirks.

"Fuck off," Owen grumbles good-naturedly while Lena smacks his arm.

"Language in my kitchen, Owen Riggins."

"Sorry, Momma," he says sweetly, bending to press his lips to her cheek.

"See, Momma's boy. You would think he's the baby brother," Marshall jokes.

"You feeling insecure again, Marsh?" another male voice asks, joining us.

"Nope. Just stating facts. Owen has always been Mom's favorite."

"I don't have favorites," Lena assures her sons.

"Owen was the son who rarely caused any trouble. If he did, it was at his brother's influence, older and younger," his dad, Stanley, adds.

"Dad!" The newcomer clutches his chest as if he's been wounded. "Mom, tell her that's not true."

"You boys." Lena just shakes her head and grins.

"Can I help with anything?"

"You sure can. You can sit with me," the newcomer says. He reaches for me, but Owen is faster, wrapping his arms around me from behind and holding me close to his chest.

"Find your own woman," Owen tells him.

"Oh, so it's like that, is it?" the newcomer asks.

"It's like that," Owen confirms.

"Hey, beautiful, I'm Conrad, the sexy brother."

Marshall laughs, spitting water across the room. "You wish you were as sexy as me."

"Sorry, boys, that title's all mine," another newcomer says. He turns to me, where I'm still wrapped in Owen's arms. "Message received, brother." He nods at Owen, then turns his gaze back to me. "Grant, it's nice to meet you." He holds out his hand for me to shake. I offer him my hand, and he pulls it to his lips, kissing my knuckles.

"Fuck, can you all not hit on my girlfriend?" Owen says, exasperated.

"Just showing her she has other Riggins options." Conrad grins cheekily.

"She doesn't need any other options," Owen tells them.

"Give the girl some room." I hear a familiar voice and turn my head to see Sawyer standing in the doorway next to Royce. "Come on, I'll save you." She holds her hand out for me, and I take it, letting her pull me from Owen's embrace. Everyone watching us knows that him letting me go never would have happened if he wasn't willing. The realization causes a warm, soothing sensation to settle in my chest.

"Thanks," I tell Sawyer.

"They're a bunch of softies. You just need to know how to handle them," she tells me.

"Sis," Owen says, his tone nothing but playful.

Sawyer waves him off. "Especially that one. It's the quiet ones you have to worry about," she teases.

"Why don't you boys go find something to do so us girls can get to know each other better?"

"Ah, Mom, you always make us miss the good stuff," Marshall whines.

"What's the matter, baby brother? Feeling left out?" Owen taunts.

Marshall ignores his brother and turns his gaze on me. "See what I mean? I'm the fun brother, not this killjoy. It's not too late to change your mind."

"Come on." Stanley laughs, placing his hand on Marshall's shoulder. "I'm not going to stop him when he comes after you. You better stop while you're ahead."

"Conrad? You got my back, right?"

Conrad's loud, boisterous laugh fills the room. "You do see how he looks at her, right? There is no saving you, and I'm not getting in the middle of that." He points between Owen and me.

"Out. Go on, get. Ladies only in my kitchen."

I chance a look at Owen, and he's smiling wide. In two long strides, he's standing next to me. His lips press to my cheek. "I'll be in the other room if you need me." He says the words just low enough for me to hear, giving my hip a gentle squeeze, and following his dad and brothers out of the room.

"Wow," Sawyer breathes.

"Finally!" Lena throws her hands in the air. "Another one bites the dust." Her smile is wide and genuine.

"I'm confused," I say the words, but I'm not nearly as confused as I want them to think that I am. I just need a minute to process what just happened. His family, they accepted me, accepted us without question. When they know where I came from, that's going to change, and I don't know that my heart will survive not being a part of this amazing group of people.

"What's wrong?" Lena asks.

I can feel the hot tears prick my eyes. "My mother is a drug addict and a drunk. I grew up hungry and poor and locking myself in my room at night, fearful of the men she would have over." I blurt the words before I can think better of it—nothing like just ripping off the Band-Aid and letting the word vomit fall from my mouth. I cover my face with my hands as my embarrassment takes root.

"My sweet girl." I hear Lena say the words as her arms wrap tightly around me. It's not long after that I feel the second set of arms, and I know without opening my eyes that they belong to Sawyer. "I'm sorry for what you've been through," Lena whispers. For a few brief seconds, I allow myself to imagine that these two amazing women were permanent parts of my life.

"I'm sorry," I say, pulling away from them. "You're all being so nice to me, and I didn't want to dump the sordid details of my life on your lap, but it's better to get this over with now."

"Get what over with?" Lena tilts her head to the side, confusion marring her features.

"I'm not good enough for him. I want to be. More than anything, I want to be, but the fact remains that I'm not. I couldn't stand losing all of you after getting attached, and I'm already attached to him. I just—I thought it was best to get it out there."

"Layla, sweetheart." Lena takes slow steps until she's standing in front of me again. "You are not your mother, and you are not your past. You decide your future." She gives me a soft smile. "All that I've ever wanted was for each of my boys to find a good woman to love. A woman who will love and respect them, enjoy life with them. That's all that matters. You do that for my Owen. He's vibrant, and it's all because of you."

"She's right," Sawyer adds before I can think to disagree with them. "Owen has always been quiet and just kind of stands on the sidelines. Earlier, he was ribbing his brothers and smiling. Not that he didn't do those things before, but he was more content to sit back and watch the shenanigans, not take part in them. You've brought him to life." Sawyer smiles softly. "Now, I know a thing or two about loving a Riggins man, not as much as this one." She points at Lena. "But we've got your back."

"He's going to mess up, that's what they do. He's going to drive you crazy at times, but I can promise you he will love you through it all. Every moment that love will burn bright."

"We've not known each other long," I remind them.

Lena shrugs. "Love doesn't know time, Layla. I know what I see, and trust me, I know my boys. Just take it day by day and embrace it. Embrace him. You love him right and that's all I can ask of you. You love him, and you will always have a place in our home."

I can't control the tears as they race down my cheeks. "Th-Thank you. I'm sorry." I smile through my tears. "I'm a mess."

"You're human," Lena says, stepping back toward the stove.

"What are you, ladies…." Owen's voice trails off when he sees me. "What's wrong?"

"Nothing." I shake my head, wiping at my eyes, trying to hide the tears that I know he's already seen.

"Lay," he says, his tone telling me he's not going to give up until he finds out.

"Girl talk," Lena chimes in. "Leave her be. All women deserve a good cry every now and then."

"That." Sawyer points at Lena. "What she said."

"Baby?" Owen bends his knees to bring himself eye to eye with me. "You okay?"

"More than okay." I smile, and it's genuine. I'm not just saying that I'm fine to placate him. Lena and Sawyer eased my fears, and I'm not going to fight this, fight him, or the connection we have. I may end up with a broken heart in the end, but I'd rather know that I tried than to always ask myself what if.

He exhales, stands to his full height, and pulls me into his chest. I feel his lips press against my temple, and I know this is exactly where I'm supposed to be.

"We're starving out here," one of his brothers, I think Conrad, says, joining us in the kitchen. He spots Owen and me and grins. "Layla, if I would have known you needed me, I would have been here." He moves toward us, but Owen is faster, pushing me behind him.

"Get your own woman." Owen laughs.

Conrad chuckles. "Ma, what can I carry?"

"Grab that basket of rolls and stop pestering your brother," Lena says, not bothering to look up from where she's pouring gravy into a dish.

"Yeah, Conrad. Stop pestering me," Owen taunts.

"Owen Riggins, you hush. You three go ahead and make your plates." She turns to face us and sets the gravy on the island.

"I knew I was your favorite." Owen laughs.

"Don't tell your brothers." Lena winks, causing Sawyer and me to throw our heads back in laughter.

Hours later, Owen and I are lying in his bed. The room is dark, and the only sounds are our deep, even breaths as we start to fall asleep. "Owen?" I whisper.

"Yeah?"

"I want to stay. Here, I mean. I want to stay here with you."

"You sure?"

"Just me and you, right? We're exclusive?" I ask, feeling nervous.

"You're damn right we are," he assures me, pulling me a little closer. Something I would never have thought possible a few seconds ago. "I want you here, Layla. In my arms, in my bed, in my heart."

"I don't know why you came into my life, Owen Riggins, but I will forever be grateful that fate brought us together."

"It's the magic, baby."

"Maybe, but I think it's all you."

"There goes another piece," he says, kissing my shoulder.

"What?" I turn to look at him, even though it's dark. When he doesn't answer, I roll over and blindly reach out, placing my hand against his cheek, running my fingers over his beard. "What did you mean?"

"Another piece of my heart belongs to you."

I don't know what to say to that. This man robs me of my words. Unable to speak, I bury my face in his neck and breathe him in. A flash of what our future together has the potential to be streaks through my mind. I want him, and all the pieces he's willing to give me.

CHAPTER *Owen* FIFTEEN

MY EYES POP open when I feel a soft hand wrap around my hard cock. *Layla.* Her eyes are watching as she strokes me gently, and she doesn't realize that I'm awake. Biting down on my bottom lip, I try to remain still, but when her grip tightens, I can't hold back. She's snuggled up to my chest, so I pull her close. "What are you doing, baby?"

"I wanted to touch it."

Fuck. I swallow hard, letting her do her thing. I've imagined her hands on me for weeks, and my imagination didn't do justice to the sensations she's causing inside of me right now. "Tighter," I murmur. Moving my hand to lay over top of hers, I guide her strokes, and it doesn't take long for her to gain a rhythm of her own that causes my eyes to roll back in my head. "Lay-la," I croak out. "Babe, you need to stop."

"I don't want to stop."

"Things are about to get real messy, beautiful," I murmur,

running my fingers through her hair, trying not to think about how incredible it feels to have her hands on me — trying not to lose control.

She continues to stroke me from root to tip when her head lifts, and her eyes meet mine. "Life is messy, Owen. If anyone knows that, it's me. There are good messes and bad messes. I think this is going to be a good mess." The corner of her mouth tilts up in a grin, and I have to kiss her.

Sliding my hand behind her neck, I fuse my lips to hers. I want to fucking devour her, but with each stroke of her hand on my cock, she leaves me breathless. "You don't have to do this," I pant. I don't want her to stop. Fuck me, I never want her to stop touching me, but I want her to do it for her. Not for me.

"I want to do this. I've never felt comfortable enough to explore. Men, well, they make me nervous, but not you. You make me feel at ease, and I want to experience this with you. I want so many things I've been too afraid to reach for."

"Come here," I murmur, pulling her lips back to mine. I kiss her like she's the air that I breathe. I kiss her until I feel my spine start to tingle. Pulling away, I rest my forehead against hers.

"I want to watch you let go," she says softly.

As if her words have a direct line to my cock, I bite down on my bottom lip as I spill over into her hand, and onto my belly. I hear her suck in a breath and force my eyes open to watch her witness my embarrassment as if I'm a teenager all over again. Instead, what I see steals the breath from my lungs and causes my cock to remain hard as steel. "Layla." I all but growl her name. She ignores me as she swipes her index finger over the head of my cock and brings the now wet digit into her mouth.

I watch as her nose scrunches up. "Not as bad as I thought, but not exactly yummy," she says quietly, almost as if she's talking to herself.

Her words have laughter bubbling up inside me. "Come here, you." I pull her into me, and she squeals.

"Now, we're both messy."

"You started it," I say, kissing her softly.

"Thank you, Owen."

"Um, babe, after that, I'm the one that should be thanking you."

She rolls those baby blues and a smile tilts her lips. "I mean it. I feel alive. Like I'm really living for the first time in my life, and I have you to thank for that."

I sober my features. "I was living, and I have a great support system, but I didn't really feel like my life was my own, not until I found you. I work for the family business, and I love it, but it was just something I kind of fell into. Don't get me wrong, I would never change that, but you, you're just for me, you know?"

"I'm all yours, Owen Riggins."

"All mine?" I raise my eyebrows. "Then I should get to do with you as I please," I say, running my hands down her back to cup her ass.

"Oh no, you don't, mister. We have to work today. My first day. I can't be late." She climbs out of bed and makes her way to the bathroom.

"Hey, Lay," I call out for her. She sticks her head out the bathroom door. "What if we made other plans?"

"Other plans?"

"Yeah, you know, the 'stay in bed all day' kind of plans."

"Nice try." She grins.

"Can't blame a man for trying." I climb out of bed and gather clothes for after I've showered in the bathroom down the hall. I want nothing more than to join her and repay her in spades for what she just gave me, but I know I need to take things slow with her. In fact, I want to. I don't want to scare her away. If I have my way, she'll be changing her last name, so we have all the time we need.

I'm sitting at my desk trying to think of a reason to go see Sawyer and, by default, Layla. I can't concentrate for shit knowing she's here. It's not that she's distracting me. No, she's been busy with Sawyer all morning in training. A few times I'll hear their voices or laughter filter down the hall, and I have to force myself to sit here and not go to her. I want to see her smile, catch a glimpse of the way her eyes sparkle and her entire face lights up. I want all of her smiles.

"You look busy." I hear Royce say from behind me.

Spinning around in my chair from where I've been staring out my office window, I nod. "Can't seem to get my head in the game today."

"It gets easier," he assures me. "Took me some time when Sawyer started working here."

I don't bother to ask him how he knew what was wrong. I had a front-row seat to him and Sawyer and the push and pull between the two of them. "Yeah, well, you fought it. I'm not fighting her, brother."

"No." He chuckles. "I'm glad you learned from my mess-up. But I still know what it's like to know that your woman is in the building, and all you want to do is get your hands on her, be next to her, but there's work that needs to be done."

"That about sums it up," I admit. I've been gone for a few weeks, and the amount of paperwork on my desk is daunting, but I can't focus.

All I see is her.

Layla.

"Stop!" I hear Sawyer's laughter ring out. Royce immediately turns and leaves my office, and I know he's going to her. I understand the pull better now than ever. I know he loves her, but it never really clicked for me until I met Layla. If he can go see them, then so can I. It's the excuse I've been waiting for all damn day.

I'm hot on his heels as we round the corner and find Marshall and Conrad leaning against the desk, their hands waving wildly with smiles on their faces.

"I shit you not," Conrad says, holding his hands up in front of him.

"H-He s-screamed like a girl," Marshall barely gets the words out through his laughter.

"What did we miss?" Royce asks, standing with his arms crossed over his chest.

"What are you two? The Men in Black?" Marsh asks.

I look over at Royce and then at myself. I'm standing the exact same way, and we're both in black suits today.

"No, I'm your boss," Royce fires back.

"CEO big brother, not my boss." Marshall wags his finger at Royce.

My eyes find Layla. "What's so funny, baby?" I'm aware of the stares of my brothers, but I ignore them, keeping my eyes on my girl.

Layla's eyes soften at the endearment. "Oh, you know, Conrad and Marshall were just telling us about a skiing expedition out on your family's lake." She grins.

"It's been years since I thought about that," Grant says, joining us.

"Do you all not have work to do?" Royce asks, trying to pretend to be annoyed, but there is zero annoyance in his tone.

"In a minute." Conrad waves him off. "You remember the one, right, O?" he asks me.

"I remember." I nod, barely able to keep from cracking a smile. It's been years, and I can laugh about it now. Back then, I wasn't impressed.

"So it's true?" Layla asks.

Another nod. "Unfortunately," I tell her.

"Why am I just now hearing this one?" Sawyer asks our group.

"We have so many stories," Grant tells her. "We have to save the really juicy ones to embarrass the others when the time is right. You know, like in front of your new girlfriend." He gives me a pointed look. He's baiting me to bite back that she's not mine, but those words will never pass through my lips. Not when it comes to Layla.

"I was young, probably nine or so, but I still remember O's white ass shining in the sun, with his shorts around his ankles," Marshall recalls.

"I'll give you credit, brother," Grant chimes in. "You never let go of the rope."

"Owen's always been the best skier between all of us," Royce says, throwing me a bone.

"I've never even been on a boat," Layla tells them.

"What? We need to fix that. Stat," Conrad tells her.

Her eyes find mine. "Maybe we can go sometime?"

"Baby, my parents have a lake. We can go whenever you want."

"This weekend?" she asks with hope in her voice.

Again, I feel the stare of my brothers. The lake is sacred, and I know they're waiting to hear my answer. "Yes. The water will be cold this time of year since it's early May, but we can take the boat out on the water. You'll need to wait a few more weeks before we can get you on some skis. You're used to Florida weather."

"You're right. It took me some time coming from Indiana but it was a nice change of pace for sure. We can wait if that's better."

"Nah," Royce chimes in. "We've all been itching to get the boat out on the water. You two want some company?" He looks over at me.

"Yeah, I think a day on the water is just what we need."

"We should call Jase and Sam and see if they want to join us."

"What about the baby?" Marshall asks.

"Are you kidding me? Between Jase's mom and his sister, Logan, they will have no trouble finding a sitter."

"It's all set," Grant says, slapping his hands against the counter. "Noon?" he asks.

"Done," Marshall and Conrad say at the same time. "We got the drinks."

"I'll work on the food," Sawyer tells the group.

"I can help. Just let me know what we need," Layla offers.

It's a simple statement, but it has my heart flipping over in my chest. She so easily fits into the fold of my family and me. I can imagine us years to come, our kids playing with their cousins just as my brothers and I used to out on the lake. It's clear to me—every piece of the future I want for us.

"Get back to work," Royce says. He steps around the desk and plants a kiss on Sawyer's lips. "Love you," he whispers, but we all hear him. Not that he cares. He would shout it from the rooftops if he had the chance.

He steps back, and I take his place, leaning in to kiss the corner of Layla's mouth. It's on the tip of my tongue to repeat Royce's words to tell her that I love her.

Wait.

I'm in love with her.

It's crazy to think that she just came into my life, but I know without a doubt that this feeling, the fluttering in my chest, the way she's always on my mind, I know that it's love. Crazy or not, it is what it is.

I want so badly to whisper those words to her. I've never been envious of my big brother, but here and now, I wish I had the freedom with my emotions as he does. I don't want to scare Layla away. I know she needs time, and I'm determined to give it to her. She'll get to where I am. I'll make sure of it. "I'm glad you're here," I say instead.

Those baby blues sparkle when she looks up at me. "Get to work, Riggins," she teases.

Unable to resist, I place another kiss on her lips and pull away. "Yes, ma'am."

"Hey, I only got one." Royce winks as he leans in and kisses Sawyer again. "There. That's better." He pulls away and turns, stalking toward his office. I do the same, even though the pull to stay near her is strong. So strong, in fact, that I get not a single thing accomplished the remainder of the day.

By the time five o'clock rolls around, my computer is shut down, and I'm standing next to her desk, waiting to take her home with me—our home. So much has changed in my life in such a short span of time, but they're all for the better. Instead of going home alone to work, I'm going home to hold her. To kiss her soft lips. There is nothing in this world I'd rather do.

CHAPTER SIXTEEN
Layla

"**T**HAT MAN..." SAWYER plops down in the chair next to me. "I swear he's got a corncob shoved up his ass today," she huffs.

"Trouble in paradise?" I ask, raising my eyebrows. Sawyer and I have gotten close over the last month. We work side by side here at Riggins Enterprises, and we spend a lot of time out of the office together too.

"He's just being broody Royce today."

I can't help but laugh at her. I learned quickly that Sawyer claims there are many layers to Royce. At first, I thought she was exaggerating, but as time passes by, I can see it. He wears many different hats, and running the company is a lot of stress on him. More so than his brothers, next to Owen, of course. He has the financials. My man is hella smart. "What did he do this time?"

"I simply suggested he was burnt out. He's been working endless hours the last three months trying to get the new location in Michigan up and running. He bit my head off and said there was no time for breaks. I know he's stressed, and he's going to apologize once how he spoke to me settles into his mind, but damn, it's been a while since I've dealt with broody Royce. He's been my sweet, loving fiancé for so long I almost forgot this layer of his personality existed."

"We should go out to dinner tonight, maybe grab a drink," I suggest. "Maybe the two of you just need a break."

"We do spend a lot of time with them, don't we? How are things with you and Owen?"

"Good." Sawyer grins, and I know I can't hide the dreamy tone of voice. It's just something that happens when I think or talk about Owen. I can't control it.

"Ah, the honeymoon phase. Royce and I had that as well, once he pulled his broody head out of his ass," she says, smirking.

"Dinner?"

"Yes."

"Call Sam, see if she can get out for a couple of hours. We'll make it a girls' night." Six months ago, that suggestion would have never come out of my mouth. I've grown as a person since moving to Tennessee. I know it's Owen's influence on my life. I have more money in my bank account than ever before, a safe place to lay my head at night, and a man I've fallen madly in love with, even if he doesn't know it.

"Good idea. Too bad Hadley and Derek are visiting his grandparents." Sawyer reaches for her phone to call Sam, who, from Sawyer's reaction, quickly agrees.

"Where?" Sawyer asks me, pulling the phone away from her ear.

"Anywhere." I shrug. "You pick, or Sam can pick. I'm easy."

"Not my place." I hear Sawyer say. "Royce is being broody." She listens for a beat. "Yeah, your place is out. We know Jase will hover." She laughs. "Let me ask her." She pulls the phone away again. "Hey, Sam suggested one of our places since she's still nursing Aria. Jase is home, so he'll hover, and my place is out. What about yours?"

"I-I don't know. I'd have to ask Owen."

Sawyer tilts her head to the side and opens her mouth to speak but is interrupted by the sound of Owen's voice. "Ask me what?" he asks, as we both turn our heads to look at him.

"Um, well, we wanted to get together and just hang out."

"Girls' night," Sawyer adds. "Your brother is being an ass, and Jase will hover. Aria will be there because Sam is still nursing. We asked Layla if we could do it at her place," she fills him in.

"Lay?" Owen speaks, and I turn my head to look at him. "It's your home, baby. You don't have to ask me for permission to invite someone over. You don't have to ask my permission to change the paint on the walls or buy a blanket for the couch. It's our home, baby." His voice is low, and his deep blue eyes bore into mine, willing me to accept the words he's saying.

"Perfect." Sawyer grins. "Sam, be at Layla and Owen's at six. I know you can't drink, so I'll bring the supplies for virgin daiquiris. Oh, and we're going to need your guacamole," she tells her. They talk for a little longer, but I tune them out as Owen takes one step, then another until he's standing right in front of me.

"Hey." I smile up at him.

He shakes his head and reaches for my hand. "Come with me." I don't hesitate to follow him down the hallway and into his office. Once we're inside, he shuts the door, and the sound of the lock clicking into place echoes throughout the room. With my hand still in his, Owen leads us behind his desk, where he moves everything to the side with the push of his hands, before resting those same hands on my hips and lifting me up onto his desk.

I let out a squeak of surprise that has him grinning. "What's it going to take, Layla?"

"What do you mean?"

"To trust that this is real? What's it going to take for you to feel comfortable in our home?"

"I do." I say the words, but we both know that my insecurities are rearing their ugly head.

"Baby, it's me you're talking to. Tell me what's going on?"

"Why won't you have sex with me?" I blurt out. Now that the words are out there, I can't take them back, and to be honest, I don't want to. It's something that's been bothering me. He lets me touch him, and he will kiss me until we're both breathless. He's touched me over my clothes, but he never takes it any further. "Is there something wrong with me? How am I supposed to relax and accept us if you haven't?"

I watch as his face goes white, and his eyes turn an even darker shade of blue. "Is that what you think? Layla, no," he's quick to add, not letting me answer his question. He grabs his hand and places it over his hard cock. "This, baby, this is what you do to me. It's taken every ounce of willpower I can muster to take things slow with you. I know you've never…." His voice trails off.

"You let me touch you."

He hangs his head, almost as if he's ashamed. "I know."

"Owen, look at me. Please." He lifts his head, and I place my hands on either side of his face. "I want you, Owen Riggins. You are the only man to ever make me feel desired. You are the only man who I've ever trusted enough to have access to me… like that."

"Like what?"

"Sex, Riggins. I want it to be you. Only you. How can I trust that we're both in this when you're holding back? I've given you all of me. At least I want to. I moved away from the life I built to be with you. The family that I chose, I left to be with you. I took a chance on the feeling I get here." I remove a hand from his face and place it over his heart. "Anytime I think of you, I have to catch my breath. My heart gallops in my chest, and my body… my body tingles at the thought of being with you. I want there to be an us, Owen, but I need to know that you're in this too. You say all the right things, and you treat me like I'm made of glass, but I'm not. I've lived through so much, fought to be where I am, and I'm not going to shatter now. Especially not with you by my side."

"There is nothing I want more in this life than to be with you. In every way," he adds. "I didn't want to rush you. I'm here for the marathon, baby, not the sprint. We have time. I want you to feel comfortable and safe."

"I sleep in your arms every night, Owen. It doesn't get much safer than that."

His forehead rests against mine, and I can see the rapid rise and fall of his chest. "Fuck it," he murmurs. He stands to his full height, and with his hands on my hips, he lifts me from his desk, setting me back on my feet. "We're leaving."

"What? We can't leave. It's not even lunchtime yet."

"Layla," he warns. "We're leaving, baby." With one hand holding tight to mine, he doesn't touch anything in his office, except for opening his desk drawer and grabbing his keys. He guides me out in the hall and reaches around to lock his office door before closing it. When we reach the reception desk, which is my desk, Sawyer is still there filling in for me. "We're leaving," Owen tells her. His voice is commanding, and if I didn't already know better, I'd think he was pissed.

"Everything okay?" Sawyer's eyes flash to me, and I nod. Reaching into the bottom drawer of my desk, I grab my purse and phone, all while Owen's hand is tightly clasped around mine.

"Fine. Layla will be expecting you and Sam at six. Not a minute sooner." He looks down at me, and the heat in his gaze sets my body on fire.

"Oh, oh." Sawyer grins. "Got it. Not a minute sooner. Layla, I've got you covered today."

"Owen, you have a meeting this afternoon," I remind him.

"Cancel it," he says, not looking at Sawyer, but she replies anyway.

"Got it, O." Sawyer sounds thrilled to be canceling his meeting.

"Thanks, sis," he says, finally tearing his eyes from mine. He drops my hand only to throw his arm over my shoulder. "No calls, not until six," he says, guiding us to the door.

"Where are they going?" I hear Royce ask from behind us.

"They're making it an early day. Oh, and it's girls' night tonight." The elevator doors slide closed before I can hear his reaction.

Owen doesn't stop moving until we reach his car. Silently, he opens the door for me and waits until I'm buckled in to close it.

My eyes trail him as he walks around and slides behind the wheel. Leaning over the console, he slides his hand behind my neck and presses his lips to mine. All too quickly, the windows are fogging up, and we're both gasping for breath.

"I'll show you, baby. I just need to get you home first." With that, he buckles his seat belt and pulls out of the parking garage. His hand finds mine, our fingers tangled, and resting between us for the entire drive.

When he pulls into the garage, the silence continues as he climbs out of the car. I don't wait for him to open my door, opting to meet him at the front door. With his hand on the small of my back, he guides me into the house.

We don't stop until we reach his bedroom, *our* bedroom. The sound of the door closing behind us is loud. Then again, my nerves are on edge. I want this. I want him, but I still have those insecurities that I don't know what I'm doing, that I won't be good enough, and everything we have will end. Poof. Just like that.

"Stop thinking, baby," his husky voice greets me. He steps up behind me, aligning his front to my back. "It's just me, just us. You tell me if I make you uncomfortable, and I'll stop. It's as simple as that."

"I won't want you to stop. I want you," I tell him, my voice breathy and filled with need. I turn in his arms so that we're face-to-face.

"I'll go slow. You tell me if it's too much. There is nothing you could ask of me that would make me not want to be with you. Tell me you understand that, Layla."

I nod, unable to speak from the lump of emotions forming in my throat.

This. Is. Happening.

Finally.

"I need your words, Layla."

"I understand."

"You're my heart, Layla Massey. I'm so in love with you. I can't see past how you make my heart race."

"D-Did you say you love me?"

"Caught that, did ya?" He gives me a boyish grin. He slides a hand behind my neck and bends his knees so that we're eye to eye. "I love you. Piece by piece, you've stolen my heart, and I gotta tell ya, baby. I don't want it back. It's yours. I'm yours. Forever." Then he kisses me. Not just any kiss. No, this kiss is slow and deep as if he needs to prove to me with his lips molded to mine that the words he speaks are true.

My body trembles as I let this all sink in.

Owen Riggins loves me.

That's when it hits me that I didn't say it back. "Owen," I say, pulling away. His lips trail down my neck.

"Less talking. More kissing," he says, nipping at my ear.

"Owen," I try again. He continues to run his lips over every part of my exposed skin, and I can't think with his lips on me. "Stop, just for a minute." Just like that he's gone. His body is no longer aligned with mine, and his lips are no longer caressing my skin. "Hey." Reaching up, I place my palm against his cheek as I move my body in close to his. I miss his warmth. "I liked what you were doing, but I needed your attention. Your full attention."

He nods, blowing out a breath. "You have it."

"You sure?" I ask, my voice playful.

"You've always had it, Layla." His hands slide around my waist, pulling me even closer, and I didn't think that was possible. "Now, talk. I'm listening. It's not my fault your sweet skin distracted me."

I roll my eyes, making him laugh. "You sure? You're listening? This is important."

"I'm all ears, Lay. What's going on?" He sobers, and I know I've got him.

"Owen Riggins." I stand on my tiptoes, bringing my mouth a breath away from his. "I love you."

He sucks air into his lungs and fuses his lips to mine. This time I won't be stopping him.

CHAPTER
Owen
SEVENTEEN

WORDS ARE POWERFUL. Hers bring me to my knees. I will never forget this moment. Never. Hearing her tell me that she loves me is like a jolt of electricity running through my veins. I can't kiss her long enough, can't get her close enough. This woman in my arms is my entire world.

Her hands make their way to my dress pants. I have to force myself to pull my lips from hers and take a step back. Her chest is heaving, and her eyes are glassy from need—all for me. "Strip, Layla," I say. My voice is deep and barely controlled. I need her naked, and as much as I'd love to take my time with her, the need inside me burns too hot. I know I need to be gentle, but time is not on our side. Not this time. I need to feel her heat wrapped around me.

"Like this?" she asks her hands, starting at the top button of her blouse.

I swallow hard and nod. "Like that."

"What about you?" I can see it in her eyes. She's nervous, and that's not going to work for me. Faster than ever before, I rid myself of my clothes and grip my cock as I watch her undress for me.

"Better?" I ask. She nods, biting her lip. "Layla?"

"Yeah?"

"Faster, baby." She fumbles with the buttons of her shirt. When she's finally to the last one, she lets it fall from her shoulders and onto the floor. Her eyes never leave mine as she reaches behind her and unclasps her bra. She hesitates, holding the material to her chest.

"You're beautiful, Layla. It's just me, baby. The man who loves you. You can trust me. Show me, baby." Slowly, she drops her hands, taking her bra with her. Her full pert breasts are finally on full display for me. "Fuck," I croak, at a loss for words for the gorgeous woman standing in front of me. She stands with her arms at her sides, her eyes locked on mine. I can see the tension in her shoulders. I step toward her and drop to my knees. My hands find the zipper of her skirt and give it a gentle tug. "Step," I say once the material is pooling at her ankles.

Settling her hands on my shoulders, she lifts one leg then the other. "Almost there, baby." My hands roam over her calves, and the smooth skin of her thighs. Reaching her white thong, I slide a finger under each side of the waistband, and slip the tiny piece of fabric over her hips, and down her thighs. She steps out one leg at a time.

"Owen." Her voice trembles.

"I'm right here, Layla. I'm not going anywhere. Tell me what you need."

"You," she whispers, her voice so low I almost didn't hear her. "I need you."

Unable to resist, I lean in and place a kiss on her belly before climbing to my feet. It takes Herculean effort to keep my eyes on hers and not let them trail over her delectable naked body. I know she needs my attention, and that's what she's going to get. We have a lifetime for me to memorize every inch of her.

"Can I touch you?"

She exhales loudly. "Finally."

I don't even try to hold back my chuckle. "Oh, she's got jokes," I say, lifting her with my hands on her hips and toss her on the bed. Before she's done bouncing, I'm crawling over the top of her. My lips find hers, cutting off our laughter. I kiss her until her body fully relaxes under me. Knowing I need to protect her, I pull away and reach for the box of condoms I bought when we got back from Florida from the nightstand. Tearing open the box, I toss a foil packet on the bed next to us, before dropping the box on the floor.

"You good?" I ask, needing to know this is still what she wants.

"I'm good." Her hands roam down my chest.

"Not this time, beautiful. You've had your fun for weeks. It's my turn, and I need to make sure you're ready for me."

"I'm ready," she assures me.

"Yeah?" I settle onto the bed next to her, resting my weight on my elbow so I can look down at her. "Let me see," I say huskily.

There is a slight tremble in my hands as I cup her breasts, rolling her pert nipple between my thumb and index finger. Layla arches her back off the bed, telling me without words that she likes what I'm doing. I shimmy down the bed a little, and capture a nipple in my mouth, while still playing with the other. Fuck me, but her skin is soft and sweet—not that I expected anything less from my Layla. Her hands roam over my back, and her nails begin to dig in.

My lips trail from one breast to the other, while my hand glides over her belly until I find the lips of her pussy. With my index finger, I test her wetness, before sinking one digit inside her.

"O-wen," she breathes my name.

"Too much?" I lift my head to gauge her reaction.

"No." She shakes her head. "It's not enough."

My lips find their way to hers, and I kiss her lazily. I need her relaxed and dripping with need so I don't hurt her. I lose track of time as we kiss, adding another finger and lazily pumping in and out of her.

"Please," she begs against my lips. "More, Owen. I need more. You're driving me insane."

"More of this," I say, adding a third finger.

"Unh, th-that's nice, but I need you."

"This is me."

"No, this." She slides her hand between our bodies that are slick with sweat and grips my cock.

"You want my cock, baby?"

"Now."

My girl is demanding. She's ready. I move to hover over her, fisting my cock, stroking from root to tip as I stare down at the love of my life. "I love you, Layla. This is going to be uncomfortable, so you tell me if you need me to stop."

"I won't shatter, Owen." She reaches for the condom and tears it open, handing it to me. She watches intently. I'm sure so she can do it on her own the next time.

She's right. My girl is strong, a fighter. She's fought to be where she is, to make a better life for herself, and I'm humbled she chose me to live her life with. Leaning down, I brace my hands on either side of her head. "Guide me in, Layla. We're going to take this nice and slow."

Her soft hand grips my cock as she aligns me at her entrance. I'm torn. I want to watch her eyes as we feel each other for the first time, but I also want to distract her from the pain. I need to watch her to make sure she's okay. I bend my head to kiss her lips but pull back as I push into her one slow, torturous inch at a time.

"Oh." Her mouth forms the perfect O as I push in a little further.

"You good, babe?"

"F-Full. So full."

"More?"

"Yes." Her nails dig into my back as I give her more. "I want all of you, Owen," she says breathlessly.

"I don't want to hurt you."

"You would never hurt me." The look in her eyes tells me she believes those words deep in her soul. She's right. I would never do anything to hurt her.

"Give me your lips," I say, dropping a little lower to kiss her. My tongue slides past her lips as I push all the way in. She raises her hips, taking everything I have to offer. I still once I'm fully sheathed inside her—partly because I want to memorize this moment, and partly because I'm close to falling over the edge. It's been years, high school since that happened to me. Yet, here we are.

"Wh-What's wrong? Why did you stop?" Layla asks, pulling her lips from mine.

"I need a minute, baby."

"What did I do?" she asks, her voice small.

I can't help but laugh. "You're breathing, Layla. That's all it takes for me to want you. I'm close, baby. I just need a minute to get it under control."

"You can do that?"

"Sometimes, but if you keep lifting your hips like that, I'm not going to be able to."

"You mean like this?" she asks, lifting her hips, and I slide a little deeper, something I didn't think was possible.

"Fuck me," I murmur.

"I thought that's what we were trying to do?" she sasses.

"We might be fucking, Layla, but there will always be love in our bed. Tell me that you know that."

"Yeah," she agrees softly. "I love you too, but can we get back to the... you know..." she asks, her voice trailing off.

"Say it, Lay. What do you want to do?"

"Move. I want you to move."

"Like this?" I roll my hips and pull out, pushing back inside her.

"Oh." Her eyes roll back in her head. "That works," she pants.

I freeze, and her eyes pop open. "I need you to say it, Lay. Tell me you want me to fuck you."

She licks her lips, and I see not only need but determination in her eyes. "I want you to fuck me, Owen."

"This is going to be fast." I pull out and push back in, finding a steady rhythm. "You good?"

"So good," she pants.

Moving my weight to my forearm that's resting beside her head, I slide my hand between us and begin to circle her clit with my thumb. "I need you to come for me, baby." My voice is a caress in her ear.

"Th-There, don't stop. There," she says again. Her eyes fall closed, and her head tilts back further into the pillow. I feel her walls begin to squeeze my cock like a vise.

"I love you, Layla. Come for me," I whisper as she detonates around me. I follow her over the edge of ecstasy in the most intense orgasm I've ever had in my entire life. Everything is better with her, kissing, work, Sunday dinners, sex, all of it.

Life is better with Layla.

Mindful of my weight, I move to lie next to her, holding her in my arms. We're both struggling to pull air into our lungs as we bask in the glow of our lovemaking. Our bodies are drenched with sweat, but I couldn't care less. I need to hold her.

"Owen?"

"Yeah, baby?"

"When can we do that again?" she asks.

My laughter fills the room. I've never been able to laugh and love during sex. It was always a means to an end. That changed today. "You're going to be sore," I tell her.

"I'm okay." She turns in my arms to look at me. "Promise."

"You have a girls' night to get ready for, remember?"

"That's tonight."

"We need to shower, and then I'm taking you to the store to get whatever you want for tonight, and I'm going to help you do whatever it is that we need to do to get ready. Then I'm going to disappear for a few hours. I'll probably go see one of my brothers or maybe see if they want to meet up for a beer."

"You don't have to leave."

"I know that, but it's girls' night. This is your home, Layla. I want you to be able to do whatever it is you women do on girls' night without worrying about me lingering."

"I don't really know. I've never had one."

"Come on, we're going to shower, and then you're going to call Sawyer, and then we're going to the store. In that order." I kiss her nose and climb out of bed, holding my hand out for her.

"What about that?" She nods to my still semi-hard cock and the condom.

"I'll take care of it."

"Is it uncomfortable?"

"It's fine. Come on." I lead her to the bathroom.

"We don't have to use them. Condoms, I mean. I'm on the pill, have been for the last couple of years. It helps with some female issues."

"That's your choice, babe."

She bites down on her lip. "I want to know what it feels like. Just you, nothing between us."

"Fuck, are you trying to kill me?" I ask her, reaching and turning on the shower. I turn back to find her watching me curiously. Reaching down, I rid myself of the condom, and stroke my cock that's ready to go again. "This, Layla. I can't have you again so soon, and now look."

"I can help with that." She reaches for me, and even though I know that I should stop her, I don't.

"Shower," I croak. She steps under the spray, with me following along behind her. She then proceeds to help me with my hard cock. What she doesn't realize is now that I've had her, now that I know what it feels like to lose myself inside her, I'm going to walk around like this all the damn time.

CHAPTER
Layla
EIGHTEEN

"**T**HIS IS SO good," Sam says, holding her hand over her mouth. She's just taken a bite of my German chocolate cake I made when Owen and I got back from the store earlier this afternoon.

"Thanks. It's actually a recipe I got from the hotel restaurant where I used to work."

"Will you get in trouble for making it?" Sawyer asks, taking a bite. She moans and closes her eyes. "I don't care if you do. I have bail money. I'll make sure the boys spring you from the pen. This is delicious," she says, making us laugh.

"No. The managers and I were close. It's an old family recipe of theirs. So technically, it's not even the hotel's."

"Can you make wedding cakes?" Sawyer asks, taking another huge bite.

"Um, I don't think so." I laugh.

"How are the wedding plans coming along?" Sam asks.

"They're not. Not really. The only thing I know for certain is that I want it to be at the lake."

"It's beautiful there. Summer? Fall?" I ask, taking a bite of my own piece of cake.

"I kind of want it to be winter. I know that sounds crazy, but it was cold out when he proposed, and it might be sentimental of me, but that's what I want."

"Not at all. Get some outdoor heaters, and they have tents that you can rent with sides and all that. I'm sure you can make it happen."

"What does Royce think?" Sam asks.

"I haven't really told him yet."

"Ah, that explains the broodiness." Sam chuckles.

"Maybe. He wants to get married now. He doesn't want to wait, so telling him he has to wait until late November or early December is going to send him into orbit."

"Pfft, you're kidding, right? That man would give you the moon if he could. Just tell him what you're thinking."

"Yeah, what if he assumes you not wanting to commit to a date means you're having second thoughts?" I ask her.

"I never thought about it like that," Sawyer confesses.

Aria begins to fuss, and Sawyer jumps into action, setting her plate with her half-eaten piece of cake on the table and grabs the baby from her Pack 'N Play. "Hello, sweet girl," she coos to the baby.

"Besides," Sam looks at me and winks, "you need to get on that wedding planning so you can get you one of those. Aria needs some cousins to play with."

"She has cousins, and pseudo cousins." Sawyer laughs.

"Yeah, but she needs more. Besides…" Sam chuckles.

"Is this pick on Sawyer night?" she asks. "They're mean to Aunt Sawyer, aren't they, baby girl?" she asks Aria.

"Fine." Sam rolls her eyes dramatically. "Layla, how are things with Owen?"

"Great." I smile at her.

"Oh, I know that smile." She grins.

"Does this have anything to do with the fact that you left the office before noon today?"

"Owen left early? And it wasn't for work?" Sam asks in disbelief.

"Yep. He also instructed me that everything could wait until tomorrow. He didn't want to be interrupted."

"Traitor," I say, trying to sound offended, but my smile shines through my voice. I can't help it. Today was incredible. Better than I ever could have imagined it could be.

"I've seen a change in him, and we have you to thank for that."

"Wait, is this déjà vu?" Sam asks. "Didn't I tell you the same thing when it came to you and Royce?"

"Similar," Sawyer agrees. "It's true, though. We all see it. You're good for him."

"He's good for me." I don't tell them that life for me before Owen was dull and void. I know they know my story. There is no use in bringing up the bad when there is so much good to talk about and celebrate. "All right, baby hog. Hand her over," I say, setting my now empty plate on the table and holding my hands out for the baby. These women, they accept me, and make me feel like we've all been friends forever. I can't believe I almost didn't come to Nashville. That would have been the biggest mistake of my life.

"Aw, do I have to?" Sawyer says, her eyes shining with mischief.

"Yes, now hand her over." I reach for Aria, and she comes to me with ease. "Hello, beautiful," I coo at her. She's such a gorgeous baby. She has her daddy's blue eyes and her mommy's dark brown hair.

"I'm telling you, Sawyer, you need one." Sam points at Aria. "You both do."

"Someday," I admit. "Everything is still so new for us."

"Love is love, Layla. The only timeline you're on is set by you," Sawyer tells me.

"Royce told you that, didn't he?" I ask her.

"Possibly." She shrugs.

"Owen said something very similar to me."

"Let's not talk about timelines. Jase and I broke records." Sam laughs.

The sound of the front door opening catches our attention. "Well, they held out longer than I thought they would," Sam jokes.

"There's my girl." Jase leans down and kisses Aria on the head, where I'm holding her in my lap, before heading toward the chair that Sam is sitting in. Without a word, he takes her hand, pulls her from the chair and takes her seat, pulling her down onto his lap.

"You ladies have a good time?" Royce asks, sitting on the loveseat next to Sawyer, kissing her temple.

"Girls' Night, Riggins," she answers.

"Hey, it wasn't just me this time. These two jokers couldn't stand to be away either."

I feel the couch dip, and I turn to look at Owen. Aria reaches out and latches onto his beard, and he chuckles. Carefully, he removes her hand from his beard and takes her from my arms. I watch in fascination as he leans in and blows raspberries on her chubby cheeks, making her giggle.

"We need one of those." I hear Royce say, his voice low. I don't hear Sawyer's reply, but I don't need to. It looks like baby Aria took the broody right out of her uncle Royce.

"You both need one," Jase chimes in. "It's the best, man. I'm telling you."

Owen looks at Jase, then turns his gaze toward me. "We do have some bedrooms to fill." My heart trips over in my chest, and an emotion that I've come to associate with Owen clogs my throat.

Happiness.

I wasn't sure I would ever find it, but this man sitting next to me... he is my happiness. And those bedrooms he says we need to fill. I can see it. Our kids running and playing in the backyard. Maybe a big swing set. I know that we're nowhere near ready for that, but I want to be. Someday I want that vision to be our truth.

"Damnit, Sawyer," Royce pouts. "We either need to start trying without a date or set a wedding date," he tells her.

"I want to get married at the lake," Sawyer blurts.

"I know that. I told you I don't care where it is as long as the end result is that you're a Riggins."

Sawyer looks at Sam, then over at me. We both give her nods of encouragement. "I want it to be winter, around Thanksgiving, but before Christmas, just like our proposal."

"Done."

"Wait? What?" she asks, surprised.

"I told you I want it to be a day you've always dreamed of, one we will always remember and can tell our kids about one day. You want to recreate that night, and I'm going to make it happen."

"I thought you would fight me on it. It's a few months away."

"Four to be exact, and I'm not waiting a minute longer. I'm ready for you to be my wife," he says, leaning in and kissing her. "And you two—" He points to Owen and me. "We get to have the first Riggins grandchild. I am the oldest, after all." He smirks.

"Is that a challenge, big brother?" Owen asks.

"Oh, Lord, just wait until the other three hear about this. They're all going to be trying to knock up the town just to rise to the challenge."

"Nah, Con and Marsh are still sowing their wild oats, and Grant, he's too level-headed for that."

"I would have said the same for you." Sam laughs.

"I didn't accept the challenge. Not my fault, this guy is a Neanderthal and wants to knock up his fiancée."

"Hey!" Sawyer laughs.

"You did say that you have bedrooms to fill," Jase chimes in.

"Heard that did you?" Owen smirks.

Aria begins to fuss, and Jase is lifting Sam off his lap, and rushing to Owen to take her. "Hey, baby girl. You missed your daddy, huh?" he asks as she coos up at him, no longer fussing.

"You've got her spoiled," Sawyer comments.

"Of course I do. I spoil both of my girls," Jase replies.

"We should probably be getting her home," Sam says, looking at Jase and Aria with so much love in her eyes.

"Us too. Thanks for having us. Our place next time."

"Next time?" Royce asks.

"Yep. This is going to be our new thing. Girls' night." She looks at me and then at Sam, and we both nod.

"As long as Layla makes this cake."

"Cake?" Jase asks. "I want cake."

"Layla, you've been holding out on us," Royce says, pretending to pout.

"I'll go cut a few slices for each of you to take home. We can't eat it all anyway." I go to the kitchen and dig in the cabinets until I find two containers and add two pieces of cake to each.

"You saving me some of that?" Owen asks.

"Yes. There are two pieces left," I say, placing the lids on the containers. Together, we walk back to the living room, so I can pass out the to-go containers. After a round of hugs, and a kiss on the cheek for baby Aria, we're alone again.

"Don't look at me like that, Layla. It's too soon."

"I feel fine."

"Sleep, beautiful. We need to sleep. It's been a long day."

"Fine." I roll my eyes, and he smacks me on the ass.

"I'm going to have me a piece of cake first and lock up."

"Okay. I need to fold the load of laundry from earlier."

"I'll help." He starts to follow me.

"No. I've got it. Go enjoy your cake." I stand on my toes to kiss the corner of his mouth and head toward the laundry room.

Fifteen minutes later, we're snuggled up in bed. We've easily fallen into a routine, one I hope lasts us a lifetime.

"I'm so glad you came," I tell Sam, giving her a hug.

"Logan has Aria for a few hours. After last night, I decided we needed a break. It was hard to get Jase to agree, but I have my ways."

"Oh, I bet you do." We share a laugh. "Just think, you get to be witness to my epic fail on the skis."

"First time?" she asks.

"Yep."

"Hot damn!" Jase claps his hands and rubs them together. "This is going to be fun."

"What did we miss?" Royce asks, joining us with his hand tightly clasped around Sawyer's.

"Layla's a first-timer." Jase grins.

"Don't worry, beautiful. I'll be there to catch you," Marshall says, stepping up next to me and slinging an arm around my shoulders.

"I thought I told you to get your own?" Owen's deep voice comes from behind us.

"I did. O, meet Layla. Lay, meet my brother Owen," Marshall quips.

"Fuck off." Owen shakes his head, a smile playing on his lips. He pulls me from Marshall's arms and into his.

"O, what have I told you about having your hands on my girl?" Conrad says, joining our circle, crossing his arms over his chest.

"Are you trying to be me?" Owen asks over a splutter of laughter.

"What? I don't do a good Owen?" He makes a face I've never seen Owen make, and we all throw our heads back in laughter.

"Idiots, the lot of you. Everyone knows Layla's my girl," Grant says as he walks past us with a cooler in his hands.

"What the fuck? Did they do this to you?" Owen asks Royce.

"They tried."

"Sawyer knows when she's ready for the sexy Riggins brother to call me," Conrad says, pretending to hold his phone to his ear. Royce reaches out and smacks him on the back of the head.

"Pfft, he whines too damn much. We know you can take it, O." Marshall grins.

"Besides, we all know Layla's your girl," Conrad says soothingly. "She turned us all down," he says, then turns and runs, his laughter trailing behind him.

"You better run, fucker!" Owen calls after him, making no effort to chase him.

"You'll get your chance for payback," Royce tells Owen. "Just wait. Someone is going to come along for each of them and knock them on their ass. I'm taking notes, brother, as should you."

I love the dynamic between Owen and his brothers. I love that they can laugh and joke, but I know if any one of them needed something, the others would be there, no questions asked. I've never known this kind of family dynamic, and I'm thrilled I can be a witness to it. That I get to be a part of it, even for a little while.

"Did we come here to spend the day on the water or whine about your brothers?" Sawyer pulls her hand out of Royce's and links her arms through Sam's and holds the other out for me. I step out of Owen's hold and we head off toward the boat that's hooked up to Grant's truck.

The rest of the day is filled with much of the same. The brothers, and Jase giving each other a hard time, and loving every minute of it. Sam, Sawyer, and I laid out in the sun, swimming, and getting caught up. We helped Sawyer brainstorm ideas for the wedding while watching our guys in the water. I got up on the skis and lasted an entire minute before falling into the water, which is a win in my book. It was one of the best days I can ever remember having.

"I'm exhausted," I say as I place our wet clothes into the washing machine. "I'm ready for a shower and bed."

"You did great today, babe," Owen says, carrying our bag into the kitchen.

"I wouldn't call a minute great, but I did it, and that's more than I thought possible. I was sure I'd never make it to stand up on those things."

"You'll get the hang of it."

I nod. "I'm determined to be able to ski next to you and your family and not look like a fool."

"You didn't look like a fool."

"Oh, I did." I laugh. "But I'm good with it. I had a great time. I can't believe this is how you grew up."

He steps next to me and wraps me in his arms. "My brothers and I raised a lot of hell out on that lake."

"Raised?" I ask. "To hear Sam and Sawyer tell it, that's an every summer occurrence."

"Maybe." He smiles. "Ready for that shower?"

"Depends. Are you going to help me?"

"Am I breathing? You can bet your sweet ass if you're in our shower naked, I'm going to be standing next to you."

"Race ya!" I say as I take off running toward the bedroom. His long legs catch up to me, and in no time, we're both stripped naked, and standing under the hot spray. Owen roams his hands over every inch of my body and then makes sweet love to me before we fall into an exhausted sleep.

The perfect ending to an already perfect day.

CHAPTER
NINETEEN

"**I** THINK THAT wraps it up," Royce says as we come to the end of our weekly meeting. He scans over his list. "One final item. We need to decide who is going to the gala for the children's hospital this year."

My three younger brothers groan, and normally I would be joining them, but not this time. An image of Layla all dressed up as we sway across the dance floor plays like a movie reel in my mind. "Lay and I can go," I tell Royce.

"Yeah?"

I shrug. "I think she'd enjoy it. It's something new for her. Besides, I don't think it will be that bad with a woman I actually like on my arm." That causes all four of my brothers to not only laugh but nod in agreement. We all hated finding dates for these things. The media always made them out to be more than what they were, and if you asked a clinger, it would sometimes take months to shake her until she got the message that it really was just a date.

"Taking one for the team, I like it," Conrad comments.

"This year," I tell him. "Mom and Dad went last year, and Royce the year before that, so you three better start duking it out or drawing for straws or some shit," I tell them.

"My prediction is one of them is going to fall ass over heels for a woman, and like you, will have no problem showing her off," Royce says smugly.

I try like hell to hide my laughter at the expressions on my brothers' faces. Well, the younger two. Grant just looks... indifferent. Hmm, very interesting. I'm going to have to keep an eye on him. Maybe see if Layla has noticed anything since she's working closely with all of us.

"Now, get to work." Royce grins at each of us, and I can't help but send a silent thank-you to my future sister-in-law. Sawyer has been so good for him. She brought my brother back to life, and we owe her the world for that.

Leaving the conference room, I head to the front of the office to see Layla. I need to break the news to her about the gala that I signed us up for. Then I'm going to call my mom and see if she will take her shopping. One, I don't want her to pay for anything, and my mother will make sure that happens. Two, I don't know what she needs for this thing, but my mom will. It's a win-win for Layla and for me.

As I approach her desk, I hear her soft voice as she answers the phone. "Riggins Enterprises, this is Layla." There's a pause. "One moment please." She looks at me and smiles before buzzing Conrad and letting him know that the call he's been waiting on is on line three. "Hey, handsome. How was your meeting?"

I love that she's opening up more and being free with her feelings and affection. "Good. Although, you and I have a date in two weeks."

"A date?"

"Yep. Every year one of us from the company goes to represent at the Annual Children's Hospital Gala. We get dressed up, eat some really expensive food, dance a couple of dances, write a big check from the company, and then we can head home."

"Is it really that boring?" she teases.

"It won't be with you there." I lean down and kiss the corner of her mouth. "You're going to need a new dress."

"What kind of dress?" she asks, eyeing me suspiciously.

"A fancy one. Don't worry. Mom will go shopping with you. She's going to love every minute of it too. You don't know how many times we heard growing up her saying she loves her boys but wished the good Lord would have blessed her with a girl to do girly things with. That's why she's always insisted on a dining table larger than life. She was sure each of us would find the perfect counterpart and bring them home to her. Then she would have five daughters and five sons," I explain.

"You really think she won't mind? I could ask Sam or Sawyer."

"Trust me, she's going to be hurt if you don't ask her." I pull my phone out of my pocket and dial Mom's number, hitting the speakerphone button so that Layla can hear our conversation.

"Hello, my second oldest," she answers, her voice as chipper as ever.

"Hey, Ma. I got a question."

"Sure, what's up?"

"Layla and I are the chosen ones for the Children's Hospital Gala this year. I was wondering if—" I start, but she cuts me off.

"We have to go shopping. Tell Layla to call me when she's free. There is this cute little dress shop downtown where I usually find most of my dresses."

I look at Layla and grin. "She heard you. You're on speaker."

"Layla, honey, what does your schedule look like? I'm ready when you are," Mom tells her.

"When is the gala?" she asks.

"Two weeks."

"I guess we should start sooner rather than later. It might take some time to find something," Layla suggests.

"I'm paying," I tell her. "You're going to this event because of me, and I refuse to go without you." Again, I leave out the fact that I volunteered us for the job.

"Owen," she starts, but I hold up my hand to stop her.

"Nope. It's on me. Mom, make sure you get her anything and everything she needs. I'll give you my card."

"Oh, my son, don't you worry. I have no problem spending your money." Mom laughs.

That's the thing. Mom knows what we make and that this shopping adventure the two of them are about to go on is nothing but pennies in my bank account. That's still hard for Layla to grasp. She'll get there. One day what's mine will be hers. Hell, it is now, just not in the eyes of the law. That will all change when her last name is Riggins.

"Layla, how about we go this evening when you get off work? We can grab dinner just the two of us?" Mom offers.

Layla looks to me, eyes wide and full of panic. I step closer and take her hand in mine while still holding my phone with the other. I nod and watch as she swallows hard. "Thank you, Lena. I would really appreciate that."

"Sweetheart, you're doing me a favor. I'm getting out of the house with a woman!" Mom says excitedly. "It's been ages since I've gone shopping. I'll meet you there at the office at five."

"Thank you," Layla says as the line goes dead.

"She's excited. Thank you for humoring her."

"Me? She's giving up her time to help me."

"Layla, she wants to do this. You heard her. She offered before I could even mention it to her. You're not alone anymore, baby. You have my big, crazy-ass family and me behind you. We're here for you, and it's not conditional. We're not going anywhere." I lean down and press my lips to hers. Just a soft peck, but the spark I feel anytime I touch her is still there from the heat in my hand that's holding hers, to the electricity that passes through our kiss.

I hope it's always like this. I hope we never lose the fire that seems to burn between us.

The house is empty without her. I'm used to her riding home from work with me, us fixing and eating dinner together, and tonight, I'm all alone. I hate it. Layla has brought so much into my life. I didn't realize how lonely I was until this moment.

I miss her.

Pulling my phone out of my pocket, I scroll through social media. An ad pops up for a jeweler, and I click on it. Over the next hour, while I wait for her to come home, I look through pages and pages of engagement rings, but none of them are what I want. Hell, I don't really even know what I want, but none of them scream Layla to me. Closing out of the screen, I pull up Royce's number and hit Call.

"What's up?" he asks.

"I was hoping to call in a favor," I say, clearing my throat.

"Anything," Royce replies.

"I need a ring." I don't need to say more. I don't have to explain what kind of ring, or that I know it's soon, but I love her. I don't have to tell him that I've never felt this way before and that I know with a feeling deep in my soul that she's the one for me. Now and forever.

"Tell me when and where."

"She's out with Mom now, shopping for the gala. She should be home soon, but she knows my schedule. I was kind of hoping we might be able to get Sawyer in on it. Maybe tell her to invite Layla shopping or to a movie, or whatever it is that they do?"

"Babe," Royce says. "Can you get Layla out of the house this weekend?"

"Sure, what's going on?"

"Owen and I have a mission," he tells her.

"Is he going to propose?" Sawyer's excited question filters through the line.

"O, you're on speaker," Royce says, and I can hear the background noises better, including Sawyer.

"Is he?" she asks.

"Hey, sis. Yeah, I'm going to propose."

"*Eeek!*" she shrieks. "Tell me what you need."

"I was hoping you could get her out of the house this weekend. Saturday. Royce and I can go shopping."

"You have to take her to a different part of town," Royce tells her.

"I know that," she replies, and I can imagine her rolling her eyes at him. I love that she doesn't put up with his shit.

"Done. I'll talk to her about it tomorrow at the office."

"Thanks, sis."

"Are you kidding me? You helped Royce pick out my ring, and now I get to be involved. I'm so excited for both of you."

"Thank you." There is a warmth in my chest with the knowledge that Layla is going to be my wife. Be by my side forever. That is if she says yes.

"She's going to say yes," Sawyer adds.

"What? You're a mind reader now?" I ask her.

"No, but I speak Riggins. I know the five of you almost as well as I know myself. Layla loves you. You have nothing to worry about."

The garage door opens. "She's home."

"We've got you, Owen," Royce replies.

"What he said," Sawyer agrees.

"Thanks. I'll see you both tomorrow," I say, ending the call and sliding my phone back into my pocket. I don't even bother to try and look busy, or like I didn't miss her. I'm on my feet, standing, and heading toward the garage when she walks in. Her face is lit with a smile, and I know, without a doubt, my mom took care of her for me. "I missed you," I say when she reaches me, wrapping my arms around her.

"I missed you too, but I had a good time with your mom. She's so sweet, and exactly what I imagine a mother should be."

There is a ping of sadness that hits me when I think about her childhood and everything she had to endure, and everything that she missed out on. "We have a lot to make up for," I tell her.

"No, that's not why I said that."

"I know, but I want to give you the world. When we have kids, you're going to be an amazing mother."

"When?"

"We talked about filling all these bedrooms, remember?"

"Yeah." A slight blush coats her cheeks. "I remember."

"So, did you find a dress?" I have to make myself pull away from her and ask the question. All I want to do is drag her to our room and start working on those kids we were just talking about.

"I did. But your mom took it with her."

"Why?"

"She thinks it's going to be fun to have a big reveal, and me get ready at their place. She said that you should have to come and knock on the door for me," she says over a giggle. I love hearing her happy. "We were talking about how fast we fell, and she said that's how it happens sometimes, but because we missed the 'dating' portion for the most part, and because I never went to my high school prom, this is the perfect opportunity for me to experience getting all fancied up. Her words not mine. And have a young man just as fancy knock on the door to pick me up."

I love my mother. The excitement in her eyes, tells me she's on board for this, and I'm thrilled to be able to give this to her. "Done. Although, it's not going to keep me from asking questions. Like what color is it? Or, does it show off these legs?" I ask, letting my eyes rake over her.

"Nope. Owen Riggins, you're just going to have to wait."

"This isn't our wedding day." The words slip before I can think better of it. She cocks her head to the side, studying me, and my palms begin to sweat, worried that my slip of the tongue gave me away.

"No, it's not."

"It will be though. One day soon, I'll make you my wife." What the hell? Might as well plant the seed and let it take root. That way, when I do get down on one knee, she's not completely taken by surprise.

"I want that, Owen. More than anything."

My posture relaxes as I pull her into my chest. "Me too, baby. Me too."

CHAPTER *Layla* TWENTY

I HAVEN'T SEEN Owen since I left the house earlier this morning. Lena arranged for my hair and makeup to be done at her salon. It's been years since I've gone to something other than one of those hair-cut-only places that have specials for ten dollars. The end result of today's visit has me not recognizing myself.

"Gorgeous," Stanley says when we enter the house. "My boy's not going to know what hit him." He smiles warmly.

"Which one?" Lena laughs. "You know, if the youngers are here when this goes down, they're going to give him a hard time." Lena shakes her head, talking about her sons' antics.

"Yep," Stanley agrees. "Owen's going to have to put his foot down."

Lena points at me. "Not thinking that's going to be an issue, dear."

"Maybe I should just go back home. I mean to Owen's and get ready." I feel my face heat. I still feel self-conscious over the fact that I just met him, moved across the country with him, and moved in with him in a matter of weeks.

"That's not happening. We have a plan, and you're going to stick to it, missy." Lena points her finger at me. "Besides, I want to see my son's expression when he sees you all fancied up."

"You'll learn to read between the lines, Layla girl, that means she wants to take a thousand pictures just like she did when the boys were in high school."

"That's my right," Lena fires back. "Now, how about a late lunch before we put you into that dress?"

"I'm not sure that's a good idea. It's tight."

"And you're a tiny thing. Trust me. You'll be nervous enough tonight around all those stiffs. Eating now is important. We don't need you passing out on us."

"Don't think my boy could handle that." Stanley chuckles.

I follow them into the kitchen where I help Lena make us some chicken salad sandwiches with chips. "Thank you both for everything," I say as we sit down to eat. "The boys are lucky to have had the two of you growing up."

"You have us now too. I don't know the extent of what your childhood was like, but I do know that you are a part of this family. We're always here if you need us," Lena says sweetly.

"Remember that, darlin'," Stanley adds. "No matter what, we're here for you. That's what family does."

Not all families, but I keep that to myself. They already know that this is new to me. "I'm nervous," I admit. "About tonight. I've never been anywhere fancy. What if I use the wrong fork or say something wrong? I don't want my lack of experience with these kinds of things to look bad on you or your company."

"It's the boys' company now." Stanley chuckles. "Besides, there is nothing you could say or do to damage anything."

"Just be you, Layla. Let Owen guide you, and you'll be fine. There will be some stuffy people who will tip their nose up at you. But remember, if we were there, they would be doing the same thing. It's not you. It's them. They think the zeros in their bank account give them the right to be rude. They live in a fantasy world. They are no better than the rest of us but pretend to be," Lena explains.

I nod, letting their advice sink in. "I'm excited too," I tell them. "This is new for me and something I always wanted to do, just never could." I stop myself before going on to tell them our money woes and that I worked to keep food on the table, and drugs in my mother. Going to prom like a normal teenager wasn't even on my radar.

Staring at my reflection in the full-length mirror, I feel and look like a princess. My dress is dark navy blue. The fabric crosses over one shoulder, leaving the other exposed. The length flows to the floor, with a slit up the side of my leg. I'm wearing strappy silver heels with a thick heel because I'm new at this. Lena assured me a thick heel would make it easier, and she was right. I'm a little wobbly but able to stand and walk without the fear of breaking my neck.

A soft knock at the door pulls me from the mirror. "Come in," I call out.

Lena sneaks her head inside the door. "Oh, Layla," she breathes. "You're breathtaking. Owen isn't going to know what to do with himself." She smiles widely. "I have something for you." She steps further into the room and closes the door.

"Lena, thank you for everything. For shopping and today. I've never had these kinds of moments, and I've really enjoyed my time with you."

She nods as her eyes shimmer with tears. "I've enjoyed it too." She hands me a small black box.

Slowly, I take the box from her hands and open the lid. I gasp when I see a pair of diamond stud earrings. "Lena, they're beautiful."

"Thank you. I thought they would complete your outfit."

"I can't wear these. What if I lose them?"

"Sweetheart, you won't, and if you do, that's okay. They're

material things. As long as my family is safe and healthy, losing an earring isn't going to affect us."

"I've never worn anything so beautiful or expensive."

"Well, there's a first time for everything. Try them on. Owen will be here soon."

My hands shake as I place them in each ear, then pivot to look in the mirror. "Are you sure about this?" I ask, turning to look at her from over my shoulder.

"Positive. You're beautiful, Layla." She nods, her own eyes shimmering with unshed tears. The doorbell rings and her smile grows. "That's him. Stanley told him he had to knock." She giggles. "Now, I'm going to go down and call for you. That way, you can make a grand entrance."

"Is this really necessary?" I ask.

"You bet it is. My boys have always had it too easy when it came to women. Please don't take that the wrong way, but those Riggins genes are strong. I knew that when one came along that made each of them work for it, I was going to enjoy it. Please don't take that from me." She bats her eyelashes.

"Oh, fine," I concede with a laugh.

"That's my girl. Now, you have a good time this evening. Just be you, Layla."

"Thank you." I lean in and give her a hug. "I promise I'll return your earrings. I'll take good care of them."

"Just take good care of you and my son, and we're all set." Deep voices carry up the steps. "He's not going to let us play this game long. Not knowing you're up here. I'll call for you." With another quick hug, she's rushing out the door and back down the stairs.

Glancing around the room, Owen's childhood room, I try to picture him growing up here. Trophies are still sitting on top of his dresser and there's a football jersey framed and hanging on the wall. I would have loved to have known him then.

"Layla! Your date's here," Lena calls up the steps.

"Really, Ma?" I hear Owen chuckle.

"Here goes nothing," I whisper into the quiet room. With one foot in front of the other, step after step, I make my way downstairs. I hear Owen's intake of breath as our eyes lock. I get lost in an ocean of dark blue as his heated gaze stays on me. Once I reach the bottom step, he holds out his hand, helping me clear it.

"Hey, baby." He leans down and kisses my cheek.

"No funny business with my girl," Stanley says. He tries to sound stern but fails miserably as Lena smacks his arm.

"I need a couple of pictures."

"By a couple, she means a couple hundred." Stanley laughs.

"You're—I don't have the words, Layla. Breathtaking, gorgeous, beautiful, magnificent, Hell, all of it. You're everything," Owen says, sliding his arm around my waist and pulling me to his side.

"I'm going to need you all to look at me for a few of these," Lena announces.

I turn to face her and realize she's been snapping pictures. I can't wait to see them. "Don't worry, sweetheart, I'll make you copies," she assures me, reading my mind.

Owen and I pose for countless pictures, and she even has Stanley join us and then has him take a few of her with us as well.

"Mom, we really need to get going."

"Have a great time." She hugs me then Owen. We wave goodbye, and with my arm hooked inside of his, we walk outside, and I gasp.

"W-What is that?"

"A limo."

"Where's your car?"

"I knew I wouldn't be able to keep my hands off you tonight, and it's a special occasion. I took the off chance that you hadn't ever ridden in one before."

"We're going to look silly, pulling up in this thing."

"No, we won't," he assures me. "The majority of those there tonight have their own drivers who will be driving them in their own personal limos. Trust me."

I nod. "This is like a fairy tale," I say, more to myself than him, but he hears me.

"Just call me Prince Charming," he says, kissing my temple.

The driver opens the door for us, and I dip my head, sliding across the soft leather seat. "This is so cool," I say, looking at Owen. "I'm sorry, I know that's lame, but—" I start. He places his index finger over my lips.

"It's cool," he agrees. "You know what else is cool? You are. You're also sexy as fuck."

"Sexy, huh?" I tease to lighten the mood. I like the way his eyes are taking me in.

"So sexy," he says, sliding his hand under the slit in the side of my dress.

"Owen Riggins!" I scold. "I'm nervous enough. I don't need to be walking up in there smelling like sex."

"Just a taste, come on, Layla. You're killing me here."

"Tonight. When we get home."

"Oh, I forgot to tell you. We're not going home tonight. The gala is held at a swanky hotel downtown. I got us a room, just like we would have if it were prom night."

My mouth falls open. "You had a hotel room on prom night?"

He shrugs. "Everyone did."

"And your parents let you?"

"Hold on now, don't go talking crazy." He chuckles, the deep sound warming me. "They thought we were staying at a friend's, and in turn, that friend's parents thought they were staying with us."

"You never got caught?"

"Nope."

"I bet they knew."

"No way. Dad would have called us out on it. Hell, Mom would have too."

Before I can reply, the limo pulls up in front of the hotel. "Let's go have some fun." Owen grins.

"You trimmed your beard," I say, noticing just now.

"Had to clean up for my girl."

"I love you the way you are."

"I love you too." He leans in for a kiss, and I don't bother to warm him about my lipstick. He can smear it. Hell, it can be gone for all I care. I'm not passing up on a kiss from my man over lipstick.

Once we're outside the limo, Owen offers me his arm, and I slide my hand into the crook of his elbow. He smiles down at me, and I stand tall, keeping my head held high. I don't want to embarrass him, so I'm just going to have to fake it until I make it. I make a mental note to once again thank Lena for the thicker heels.

Owen gives the gentleman at the door his name, and we're granted access into the ballroom. My eyes scan the room. It's stunning, and unlike anything I've ever witnessed. I wasn't kidding when I said I felt like I was in a fairy tale. This ballroom is reminiscent of something you would see on a movie screen, not a local hotel that I'm in, as an invited guest at that.

"You good?" Owen asks, leaning in close, his lips next to my ear.

"Yes. Thank you for bringing me. This is incredible."

"No, baby. That title's all you." He kisses the corner of my mouth as a man calls out his name.

I mentally remind myself to smile politely, to stand tall and not to fidget. I want people to see us together and think that we belong together because piece by piece, our hearts are twisted, and for me, there's no going back.

CHAPTER  TWENTY ONE

EVERY MAN IN this ballroom has had his eyes on my girl. I get it. She's fucking gorgeous, but I can only take so much. I need to get her out of here, and under me, or over me. I'm not picky as long as I'm inside her.

"Mr. Riggins, a picture?" The photographer holds up her camera, and I nod, pulling Layla close. Her hand rests on my chest as she leans into me. The flash goes off, and we're on the move before the words "Thank you" are out of the photographer's mouth.

"What's the rush?"

"I need you out of this dress," I say, not bothering to lower my voice. I don't care if all of the fuckers who have been staring at her all night hear me.

She's mine.

They need to recognize that and focus on their own dates.

"Owen," Layla gasps, but I don't stop moving toward the door that will lead us to the bank of elevators that will take us up to our room. Our room where I can strip her out of that dress that's been taunting me since I arrived at my parents' place. I place my hand over hers that's resting in the crook of my arm as we wait for the elevator. Luckily for us, when it arrives, we're the only one waiting. As soon as the door slides shut, I'm all over her.

Her back hits the wall, and my lips mold with hers. I kiss her like I've been dying to do all night. I pull her leg up to wrap around mine, as she buries her hands in my hair. "O-Owen," she pants, turning her head to the side. That's fine. My lips trail over her exposed shoulder. I've been dying to taste her here all fucking night long.

The door chimes and slides open, and I have to force myself to pull my lips from her soft skin. With her hand clasped tightly in mine, we make our way off the elevator and down the hall to our room. It takes me three tries to get the keycard in the door. Not because I'm nervous; it's because I want her with an intensity that makes my hands shake as they ache to touch her.

Finally, the light turns green, and I push open the door, allowing Layla to walk in before me. Dropping the key card to the floor, I pull her into my arms and kiss her hard. Her taste, a mixture of champagne and Layla, explodes on my tongue. I can't get enough of her. Can't seem to get her close enough.

"I need you out of this dress," I say, bunching it up around her waist.

"Don't rip it," she says, reading my mood expertly.

Stepping away from her, I place my hands on the back of my head. My chest is heaving as I struggle to pull air into my lungs. "I need you naked, baby. I know you love the dress. I can buy you a new one." I reach for her.

She jumps back out of my grasp. "No. I love this dress. You're just going to have to wait."

I grip my cock that's straining against the zipper of this monkey suit I'm wearing. "I'm dripping with need for you, Layla. I can't wait." My words are strained as I try to reach for her, but she's a tiny thing and fast as she again evades me.

My eyes are glued to her as she turns her back to me. "Can you unzip me?"

I step close, my hands falling to her back as I slowly pull the zipper down. She steps away before I can rip the offending piece of fabric from her body. "I want you," I tell her.

"I want you too, but I love this dress." I watch as she carefully slides the fabric over her shoulder and shimmies her hips, letting it slide to the floor. When she bends over to pick it up, her tits look as though they are about to fall out of the strapless bra she's wearing, and her ass in that thong... I want to bite it.

"What would your mom say if she knew you tore my dress and why?"

"I don't give a fuck, and can we not talk about my mom right now?"

Soft laughter fills the room as she turns to face me. "I need you naked, Owen," she says, her hands on her hips.

"Gladly." I begin to rip off my clothes—jacket, tie, shirt, with my buttons flying across the room. Next, I fumble with my belt as I unclasp it. I make sure to latch on to the waistband of my boxer briefs and remove them with my pants. Letting it all fall to the floor. "You're next," I tell her, gripping my cock. I watch in fascination as she walks to the other side of the room, pulling a chair from the small dining table in the corner. She carries it with her, setting it in front of me.

"This is for you."

"What am I supposed to do with that?" I ask, staring at the chair.

"Sit."

"Babe, we can talk later. I need you." I look down at my hard cock gripped in the palm of my hand.

"Sit, please," she says, batting those baby blues at me. I can't say no to her, so I sit in the chair. With slow, gradual steps, she comes toward me, stepping between my legs. My hands grip her hips, any excuse to touch her. "I like this," she says softly, running her hands over my newly trimmed beard. "I like the way it feels against my bare skin."

Fuck. Is she trying to kill me? "Layla," I croak.

With a hand on either side of my face, she bends so that our mouths are barely a breath apart. "I love you, Owen Riggins." Her lips press to mine, and I try to deepen the kiss, but my girl has other plans as she pulls out of my hold, taking a step back.

She stands just out of reach, and I want to go to her, toss her on the bed and have my wicked way with her, but something tells me that she needs this. That she needs to feel in control, and we both know Layla holds all the control, along with every single piece of me. The breath whooshes from my lungs when she reaches behind her and unclasps her strapless bra, letting the tiny scrap of material fall to the floor.

I keep my mouth shut and my hands fisted at my sides as she slides an index finger on either side of the waistband of her thong, and shimmies her hips yet again, letting it fall to her feet.

"Did you know that I can't think when your hands or your mouth are on me? It's like you turn my brain to mush. You always get to take the lead, and I thought it would be fun to mix it up a little, but I can't have you touching me. I'll lose focus."

My throat is dry as I reply, "You want to seduce me, baby?"

"Something like that." She smirks.

Unfurling my hands, I raise my arms and open them wide. "I'm yours for the taking, Layla. Do with me what you wish."

"There are so many things," she says, tapping her index finger against her chin.

"Do your worst, baby."

"Oh no, that I won't do. I'm thinking tonight is going to be filled with nothing but the best." She licks her lips, causing my cock to twitch.

"Fuck," I murmur, making her chuckle.

"That's the plan, handsome," she assures me. "Hands behind your head."

I've never been one to take orders from a woman, but this woman I'll do anything she asks, so I place my hands behind my head, interlocking my fingers. I sit silently and wait for further instruction, but it never comes. Instead, my beautiful Layla drops to her knees, settling between my thighs. She doesn't utter a single syllable as she grips my cock, strokes me from root to tip, licks her lips, and takes me into her mouth.

"Son of a…." My voice trails off as my eyes roll to the back of my head from the mere pleasure of having her lips around my cock. Over and over again, her head bobs between my legs. As the pressure begins to build, I need to be inside her. That's where I long to be. That's where I belong. "Layla, baby. I need to touch you. I need to feel you."

Slowly, she lets my cock slide out of her mouth before peering up at me, her blue eyes blazing with desire. She wipes her mouth with the back of her hand and stands. "I was enjoying that." She pretends to pout. She might have been enjoying it, but I can tell from the gleam in her eye, she has something else planned for us, planned for me. What I didn't expect was for her to straddle my lap.

"You can touch me," she says huskily as she removes my hands from behind my head and places them on her hips.

"Tell me what you want, baby. This is your show." I love her newfound confidence that grows every day. I want her to have this. Hell, it's not a hardship to let the love of my life seduce me. I win no matter who's calling the shots. At the end of the night, we both get to find our pleasure in each other, falling asleep in each other's arms. That's all that matters.

"This." Reaching between us, she lifts until I'm aligned at her entrance, and slowly settles back onto my lap, burying me inside her.

Wrapping my arms around her back, I crush her to me in a hug so fierce I'm not sure either of us is getting any oxygen into our lungs. I love this woman with every piece of my soul. Every minute with her only makes me fall further in love with her. There is a spark every time we touch, and I hope we never lose it. I never want to stop feeling the way I do right now in this moment. With her settled on my lap, our arms around each other and my cock buried deep inside her.

Loosening my grip, my hands roam over her back, relishing in the feel of her soft skin against the palm of my hands. My fingertips trail over her spine, and I settle my hands on her ass. My lips find hers in a slow, sensual kiss, that if I wasn't already sitting would have had my knees buckling. Not breaking our kiss, I lift her slowly off my cock, leaving just the tip, before lowering her back onto my lap. I repeat this process over and over, all while devouring her lips. We settle into a steady rhythm as the tension builds.

"Owen," Layla pants as she buries her hands in my hair.

"I got you, baby."

"How is it better every time?" she asks.

Honestly, I don't know, but then it hits me. "It's the magic, baby." When I stand from the chair, she wraps her legs around my waist, and I move us to the wall. One at a time, I slide my arms under her legs, pressing her back against the wall, rock my hips and let loose, fucking her hard and fast. I feel her nails dig into my shoulders, but it only fuels my desire for her. To have her lose control on my cock, the way she makes me feel as though I'm losing control anytime I'm around her, and every time I'm inside her.

Her walls clamp around me at the same time a deep guttural moan falls from her lips. "Owen!" She calls out for me, and I snap, spilling over inside her. My legs feel like jelly, but I manage to walk to the bed, sitting down with her still wrapped around me, and my cock still buried deep inside her.

"I don't know where that came from, but when can we do it again?" she asks through staggered breaths, making me laugh.

"I'm all yours, baby. You tell me when and where... I'll take care of the rest." I kiss her bare shoulder. "Come on. We need to shower and then get some sleep." She climbs off my lap, and I'm already regretting my decision for a shower. Losing that connection of our bodies, the warmth of her draped around me, is a feeling I will forever crave.

We manage to shower, taking our time to let our hands roam over each other's naked bodies. By the time we climb into bed, we're both exhausted and sated. Layla snuggles close, her naked body aligned with mine, and my last thought before drifting off to sleep is I get to do this every night of our forever.

CHAPTER

TWENTY TWO

I CAN'T STOP smiling. I couldn't control it even if I wanted to. I've never been this happy. I've never felt as though I belong as I do with Owen. Not just with him but with his family and my job. It's like all of the shit I had to live through growing up, was my fight for my happily ever after — the one I've found here in Nashville.

"Hey, sis." Conrad stops at my desk just as the phone rings.

Holding up a finger, I shrug and answer the phone. "Riggins Enterprises, this is Layla," I say as chipper as ever. "Hello?" I wait for someone to speak. "Riggins Enterprises, how can I help you?" I ask again. I can hear someone breathing on the other end, but they're not saying anything. Feeling a chill race down my spine, I place the phone back on the cradle. I'm overreacting. I can imagine Owen and his brothers doing the same thing as kids.

"No one there?" Conrad asks.

"No. Well, maybe. I could hear someone breathing, but they didn't say anything."

His brow furrows. "That's odd."

I nod. "Yeah, I've gotten one of those same calls every day this week."

"Really? Have you told the others?"

"No. I'm sure it's just some young kid playing games." I wave off his concern. The phone rings again, and I smile with a roll of my eyes. "Riggins Enterprises, this is Layla," I say into the line. I listen as the caller asks to speak to Conrad. "May I tell him who's calling?" I ask politely. I listen as the caller relays their name. "One moment." Parking the call, I look up at Conrad. "Joseph Bauer is returning your call," I tell him.

"That's what I was here to tell you." He chuckles. "Give me a few to get back to my office and put him through." Conrad smacks the desk lightly with the palm of his hands and heads toward his office.

Placing one earbud back into my ear, I get back to work on typing the letter that Royce dictated when the phone rings again. I swear, I'm not getting anything accomplished today. "Riggins Enterprises, this is Layla."

"Baby." Owen's deep voice greets me.

"Yes, sir?" I reply, and he groans in my ear. The sound turns me on more than it should, and at work no less.

"Can you come and see me?"

"Sure. Let me just have Sawyer watch the phones."

"Called her first. She's on her way to you."

"Okay, is something wrong?"

"Yes, something is wrong. We've been here for hours, and I've yet to lay eyes on you."

"It's two in the afternoon. We've both been busy, you know working, that thing that gives us our paycheck."

"Bring your smart ass to my office." He laughs and ends the call.

I look up to find Sawyer smirking. "Take your time." She winks.

"Oh, that will not be happening," I tell her, reading between the lines.

She shrugs. "Don't knock it until you try it."

"Sawyer!" I laugh.

"You've seen my man, right?" She grins.

"What about me?" Royce asks, stepping up behind her. He places a kiss on her cheek. It's like they have roaming devices on us. It never fails Royce and Owen always knows where we are. If I didn't love him as much as I do, I might find it creepy. However, coming from the life I lived, it's nice to know I have people who care.

"Office sex." Royce wags his eyebrows at Sawyer when she speaks. "Not us, Lay and O," she tells him.

"We get next," Royce quips.

"That," I say, giving them a pointed look, "is not happening."

"What did he do for you to cut him off?" Royce asks, and I can't help but laugh because he truly believes Owen must have done something to upset me.

"Nothing. We're at the office."

"Don't knock it until you try it," Royce says.

"See!" Sawyer points at me. "Go, don't keep your man waiting."

Their laughter, combined with mine, follows me down the hall to Owen's office. "You rang?" I ask, stepping into his office.

"Shut the door."

"I think it's better if we keep it open," I say, taking a step further into the room.

"Babe, if you think that door being open is going to stop me from tasting you, you're wrong."

"Not here," I hiss as he stands from his chair and meets me halfway.

"These lips, baby." He grins as he traces my bottom lip with his thumb. "What did you think I meant, Layla? Huh? You thinking about me tasting your pussy? I could, you know. I could set you on the edge of my desk, hold your legs open, and soothe the ache with my tongue."

"W-We didn't lock the door."

"Told you." He smirks, placing a kiss on my lips. "I've missed you today."

I push away from him and take a step back. "That—" I point to him. "We can't be doing that here." I shift my stance, rubbing my thighs together to quell the ache that is, in fact, strong as ever, at least until we get home from the office.

"It's going to happen, baby. It's like a rite of passage to fuck my girl on my desk."

"Whoa." I hear from behind us. I groan, covering my face with my hands. "Looks like I got here just in time," Marshall jokes. I groan again, and the room fills with laughter from the brothers.

"Trouble. The lot of you Riggins boys are trouble." I walk to Owen and pull on his tie until he bends to my height. "I'm going back to work. Love you." I kiss the corner of his mouth.

His eyes are soft. "Love you too, Lay." I turn to face the door, and he smacks my ass.

"Glad to see you happy, brother." I hear Marshall say as I walk back to my desk and just like that my smile is back.

Owen keeps checking his phone, and it's driving me crazy. "Are you waiting on a call?" I ask him.

"What?"

I point to his phone.

"Oh, no. Royce asked me to help him with something for Dad today. Something on the garage. He's supposed to text me and tell me what time to meet him."

"Good. I'm glad you won't be home alone while I'm out shopping."

"I left my card on the dresser. Did you get it?"

"No, and I'm not going to. I have money, Owen. You never let me pay for anything, and my salary at Riggins is more than generous. I can afford to go shopping."'

"I want to spoil you."

"You do. Do you need anything while I'm out today?"

"Not that I can think of. You should take my card in case you see anything you want for the house."

"I have money," I say yet again, wrapping my arms around his waist in a hug. A horn blares outside, which tells me Sawyer is here. "I'll be back later. Have fun with Royce and your dad." After a kiss that could be considered anything but quick, which is interrupted by Sawyer's honking, I'm out the door for another day of shopping.

A couple of weeks ago, Sawyer asked me to go with her, and of course, I said yes. We had a great time and even met Sam and baby Aria for lunch. I assume we're doing the same today. Either way, I'm sure it will be a fun time. Girls' days are new for me. I could never afford it before, and really Linda was my only female companion, and one or both of us was usually working.

"So, are we looking for anything particular?" I ask, putting on my seat belt as she pulls out of the driveway.

"What? Do we need an excuse to go shopping?" She chuckles.

"Not at all, just wasn't sure if we had an agenda."

"Nothing certain. I'd like to stop at the wedding store across town and look at dresses. Not trying anything on today, but I want to see what's out there. Maybe they have a book or something that I can look through."

"Eep! Yes, I am so excited for you and Royce. A winter wedding at the lake is going to be so romantic."

"What about you? Are there wedding bells in your future?" she asks.

"We haven't talked about it specifically. He says things like when we fill up the bedrooms with kids and changing my name and stuff, but that's about it."

"So, Owen drops to one knee, what's your answer?"

"Hell, yes," I say, and we both laugh.

"That's what I thought."

"It's crazy. It's so soon, but I've never felt like this. I love that man with all that I am."

"You're good for him. He's more open and spends less time working and by himself. They say when you find the right person, you just know. I knew with Royce. Sure, I didn't know if he was there, but I was certain of my love for him. Look at us now."

"Getting married."

"Getting married," she echoes. "And my man isn't near as broody now that we've set a wedding date." She chuckles.

The rest of the drive we talk about ideas for the wedding. It's going to be freezing cold that time of year, and Sawyer wants the service to be short and sweet, considering it's outside. "Let's go to the dress shop first," I suggest. "All this talk about dresses and wraps has me itching to see what you pick."

"I'm just looking," she reminds me.

"You say that but what if you find *the* dress? We have to buy it."

"Most brides look for months before they find their dream dress for their weddings."

"Maybe, but I'm feeling lucky." She throws her head back in laughter as she parks her SUV outside the dress shop. "Let's do this," I say, reaching for the door handle.

"Layla," Sawyer breathes my name. Reaching out, she grabs my arm and stops me. "There are so many."

She's right. This bridal shop is huge, and there are rows and rows of dresses. "I'm thinking we're going to need some help."

"What can I help you find today?" an older lady asks as she approaches us.

Sawyer just stands there in awe of our surroundings. "Hi, I'm Layla, and this is Sawyer, the bride. She's having a winter wedding, so we would need something long-sleeved, and thicker, I'm guessing."

"Of course, it's nice to meet both of you. My name is Mary. Sawyer, congratulations."

"Thank you," Sawyer says, finding her voice.

"Now, are we having an indoor or outdoor wedding?"

"Outdoor. Just for a quick ceremony. Then I'm hoping we can rent tents and heaters for the reception."

"Perfect. Right this way." She leads us to the back of the building where we see a sign indicating Winter/Outdoor.

"Wow, you're really organized," Sawyer says.

"We have to be," Mary replies. "With a building this size and over five thousand dresses to choose from, we need all the organization we can get. Now, tell me what you're thinking."

We spend the next ten minutes or so telling Mary all of the elements that Sawyer and I discussed on the way here. Mary leads us to a private dressing room and excuses herself to bring us a few options.

"I should FaceTime Hadley. She's going to be pissed that she missed this."

"Hey, it's not your fault she's on vacation."

"Right? We'll have to remind her of that." She pulls her phone out of her pocket and initiates a video call with her best friend. "Hey, Had." She turns the phone so that I can wave. "This is Layla, Owen's girlfriend."

"Nice to meet you. What are the two of you getting into?" Hadley asks.

"Well, I'm at a bridal store, dress shopping."

"No way! Layla, how did you get her to do that?" Hadley asks.

"It was her idea. I'm just moral support," I manage to answer, still reeling by being referred to as Owen's girlfriend. I love the sound of it.

Hadley's laughter fills the air. "Sawyer, give Layla your phone. I'm settling in for this."

"I know you're on vacation. I just wanted you to know."

"We're lying on the beach. Derek is sleeping next to me." She pans the phone so we can see a tanned Derek sleeping on a towel under the umbrella next to her. "I was too engrossed in this book to fall asleep," she says, closing her Kindle and tossing it into her bag. "This… the two of you have my full attention."

"Here you are," Mary says as she enters the room, pushing a rolling cart with several dresses hanging. "Sawyer, have a look and let me know what you're thinking."

Grabbing her phone, I point it so Hadley can see what's going on. Sawyer walks up to the cart and begins to sift through the dresses. When her eyes light up, Hadley squeals, and I know she's found the one. You don't get that look for just any dress.

"Try it on," Hadley and I say at the same time.

Sawyer looks over at me, and I nod. I watch as she carefully takes the dress from the cart and disappears behind the changing curtain.

"Layla?" I turn the phone so I'm now facing the screen. "You can't let her back out. She's going to look gorgeous, and she's going to try and talk herself out of it. Don't let her. I'm not there to kick her in the ass."

"I'm all over it." I chuckle.

"She's going to say it's too much, but we both know Royce will have other ideas about that."

"For sure. If she balks, I'll call him."

"Perfect," Hadley says just as Sawyer calls out that she's ready.

I turn the phone back around, and when she appears, Hadley and I both gasp and tell her that she looks beautiful. She does. The dress has a fitting bodice that flares at the hips, long-sleeved, and a white faux fur shawl wrapped around her shoulders. It's perfect, and she looks like a winter angel.

Sawyer looks up, and her teeth are digging into her bottom lip. "Say it, Sawyer," Hadley prompts.

"I love it," she says so low we can barely hear her.

"Buy it," Hadley says immediately. "It's perfect, and you look gorgeous."

"A winter angel," I say, voicing my earlier thoughts.

"I don't know," she says. I pull my phone out of my pocket. "Don't make me call Royce," I threaten.

"It's so much money."

"You're only doing this wedding gig once. Might as well go all out," I tell her.

"Right, like you wouldn't think the same way if you were standing in my shoes."

"We're not talking about me," I fire back, making her laugh.

I can see the indecision warring in her mind. I tap the screen of my phone and call Royce. Making sure to leave it on speaker so that Sawyer can hear, he asks, "Layla?"

"Hey, Royce, sorry to bother you. I know you and Owen are helping your dad today. I just wanted to tell you that your girl found the perfect wedding dress."

"Did she buy it?" There's excitement in his voice.

"No. She's—" I start, and he talks over me.

"Sawyer, baby, you're getting the dress. Layla, send me the details of the store, and I'll call and take care of it."

"Royce—" Sawyer calls out, but he talks over her too.

"Nope. You want it. It's the dress you want to be wearing when you become a Riggins. It's yours. I'll take care of it. Layla, thank you."

"Anytime," I say, sticking my tongue out at Sawyer. "You boys behave," I tell him, ending the call.

"I can't believe you did that."

"Layla, if I was there, I'd be high-fiving you," Hadley says.

"Looks like you got yourself a dress." I grin at Sawyer. The smile that tilts her lips tells me she's thrilled, and I couldn't be happier for her. I say goodbye to Hadley with the promise to have Sawyer call her once we're back on the road. As I look around the room, I can't help but imagine myself being the one looking for a dress.

Layla Riggins has a nice ring to it.

CHAPTER
Owen
TWENTY THREE

WALKING INTO MY parents' house on Sunday, we're the last to arrive. If the vehicles in the driveway weren't indication enough, the sounds when I open the door would have been. With Layla's hand held tight in mine, we follow the laughter of my brothers to the kitchen.

"There they are. The celebrity couple," Grant boasts.

"What the fu—" I glance at Mom as she gives me the side-eye. "—heck are you going on about?" I ask.

"Layla, you're apparently breaking hearts all over Nashville," Marshall speaks up.

"Explain," I say, my voice quiet and low.

"This." Conrad passes me what appears to be this week's paper.

"What's that?" Layla asks.

"You two made the paper," Grant explains.

"Is that a bad thing?" Layla asks.

"No, sweetheart," Dad assures her. "In fact, it's good for business."

Grabbing the paper from the table, I open it, and sure enough, there we are on the front page.

Hearts Are Breaking All Over Nashville

It appears Royce Riggins isn't the only Riggins bachelor who's off the market. Pictured above is his younger brother by two years, Owen, and his date. Sources tell us that Owen didn't let the beauty out of his sight the entire night, and when they left, it was to a room upstairs. I know, I know, the Riggins brothers of Nashville's Riggins Enterprises are dropping fast, but don't worry, ladies. There are three more brothers, and our sources tell us that they are indeed single and ready to mingle.

The article goes on to talk about the gala and the support it receives every year from Riggins Enterprises and is accompanied by the picture taken of Layla and me as we were leaving the gala. Her hand is on my chest, and my arm is around her waist, holding her close to me. The picture is intimate in the way we're standing, but what takes it to another level is the way I'm looking down at her. I'm not surprised. I couldn't take my eyes off her all night long. I do know for a fact the photographer also got a shot of me looking at the camera. I guess the paper thought romance would sell. I wonder if I can get a copy of that picture? I make a mental note to call the paper and find out.

"Well?" Grant asks.

"They're not wrong. Well, I don't know about the hearts breaking across Nashville part, but I am indeed off the market, and you jokers are as single as they come."

"The final three stand-strong brothers," Conrad says, puffing out his chest.

"Just wait," Dad tells him. "You can't stop the magic."

"Here we go," Marshall whines. "More of the magic. I get it, you and Mom had a connection. That's not going to happen for all of us."

Dad gives him a pointed look. "Ask your brothers."

"Royce?"

"Like pulling rabbits out of a hat." Royce grins. "The old man knows what he's talking about."

"Owen?" Marshall asks me. "Come on. You've always been the sensible one."

"Abracadabra, little brother."

The room erupts in laughter.

"All right, it's time to eat." Mom expertly herds us into the large dining room.

Layla takes her seat next to me as we all fill our plates. Conversation flows easily, as it always does. I take a minute to look around the table. Royce will be married in a few months, and hopefully, Layla and I will be not far behind him and Sawyer.

My three younger brothers claim they want nothing to do with commitment, but I can see the envy in their eyes when they watch Royce or me with our ladies. When Royce fell for Sawyer, it was different. He was coming off a bad divorce, and his heart was shattered from deceit. When he met Sawyer, it had nothing to do with him not wanting to settle down, but his fear of trusting. She smashed those fears and brought my brother back to life.

The younger three, I can't wait to watch them fall.

The magic, whether it's a Riggins thing, or a love thing, is fierce when you find the right woman to share your life with. Mine is sitting next to me, and her ring, the one I picked up from the jeweler yesterday while she was shopping with Sawyer, is hidden in my safe in my home office. Now I just need to find the right time to ask her for her forever.

"Have a good day, Lay." I kiss her quickly before making my way down the hall to my office. I never thought I would enjoy working with my significant other. To me, it always seemed like it was too suffocating, but now Layla is in my life, I know I was wrong. Again, it all goes back to finding the right woman to change your view on life and relationships.

Firing up my laptop, I get lost in spreadsheets and numbers. My job has always come easy to me, and I'm proud to know my role here at Riggins is important. It's pretty cool to think about how all five of us found our niche within the business. It was all our doing. Mom and Dad never pressured us to work for the company. They gave us the freedom to follow our own path; it just so happens all five of our paths lead back to family, and Riggins Enterprises.

My eyes are blurry from staring at the screen all morning. Glancing at the clock, I see it's lunchtime just as my stomach growls.

"Knock, knock," Layla says, stepping into my office.

"How did you know my tired eyes needed to see you?" I ask her.

"I didn't, but I did know that you were lost in your work and would be getting hungry." She holds up a bag from the deli across the street. "Wanna have lunch with me?"

"I heard wanna have me for lunch," I say, sliding my chair back from my desk and patting my lap.

"You're incorrigible, Owen Riggins." She laughs, taking the seat across from my desk. I watch as she unpacks two club wraps, two bags of chips, and two bottles of water. "How's your day going?" she asks, passing me my food.

"Good. Just working on the budget. We're still deciding on whether adding that new location in Wisconsin is a good idea, so I'm crunching numbers and listing the pros and cons from the finance side. How about yours?"

"Good. I got a text from Linda today. It was a picture of her and Ronnie on the beach. They actually both took time off from the restaurant together."

"Good for them. Did you invite them up?"

"No. I know you had said that I could. I wanted to check with you again before I extended the invitation."'

"Layla, it's our—" I start, but she cuts me off.

"Our home. I know. It's just… still hard for me to grasp the idea at times. I'm glad you don't know where I came from. I mean, you know, but you didn't see it. Saying that times were rough… that's an understatement. Any money we did manage to get, paid the rent and went to drugs. There was hardly ever food in the house, and more times than not, I was locked away hiding in my room."

We've talked about her life before Florida, but it still gets my blood boiling anytime I think about her having to suffer through that. Being scared to fall asleep in her own home, going to bed hungry. If I ever have the chance to meet her dead-beat mother, I'm not going to be able to control my anger or my hatred toward her.

"I can see you stewing, Owen. Trust me when I tell you she's not worth it. I got out, and it could have been much worse than it was. There are many who were in my exact same situation and had to deal with sexual and physical assault. For all of her wrongs, my mother never hit me. She just didn't care."

"I'm not a fan," I say, trying to keep the anger out of my voice.

"I'm not either." She takes a bite of her wrap and places it back on the wrapper. I do the same, needing to give myself some time to cool off. I'm not mad at her, but I'm sure as fuck mad for her. "When I was at the deli, I heard there's a new bakery opening up just around the corner. It should be nice for grabbing pastries for meetings."

"Is there any way to not tell Grant that? He has a sweet tooth. We'll never keep him in the office." I laugh.

"Sorry, don't think I'll be able to hide a bakery." She shakes her head.

"Trust me, that boy can eat the hell out of some donuts."

"How does he stay so fit?"

I shrug. "We all work out or run, not religiously, but we do. I guess it's just good genes. Look at Dad. He's in his sixties and still looks slim and trim."

"They say that if you want to know what your partner will look like in thirty years, you need to look at their parents."

"You crushing on my dad, babe?" I tease. Her cheeks turn a light shade of pink.

"No. But I will admit he looks great and doesn't look his age at all."

"Well, I know for a fact you are not going to be like your mother."

"She was pretty. She used to be. When I left Indiana, she was hardened by all of the drug use and drinking. She looked closer to seventy than her thirty-six years of age."

"She's young."

"Yeah, she got pregnant with me right out of high school. I never met my grandparents, and she claims to not know who my father was. I guess at least she kept me."

"Lay, you're breaking my heart here," I tell her honestly.

"Sorry, I don't mean to be a downer. I guess it's just seeing how amazing your family is. After spending the day with them yesterday, it's in the forefront of my mind on what I missed out on, and what I had to live through to be where I am today."

"You are exactly where you are supposed to be." This time when I push away from my desk and pat my lap, she comes to me, sitting sideways and wrapping her arms around my neck.

"This is going to sound crazy, but I can breathe easier when you're close to me."

"Not crazy," she says, running her fingers through my hair. "I feel the same way. Like when we're close, or when you're touching me, nothing else can. Everything is right in my world."

"Come on, guys," Conrad says from the doorway. "This is a professional establishment," he says, walking in and taking the seat Layla was just sitting in.

"What happens in my office, stays in my office," I fire back at him. "What's up?" I ask, tightening my hold around Layla's waist when she tries to move.

"I smelled lunch," he says, eyeing the table.

"Didn't you have a lunch meeting?" Layla asks him.

"Yeah, but it was at some stuffy restaurant where the portion size is smaller than half of the palm of your hand, and five times the cost."

"Want me to order you something? I can run across the street to the deli and grab you a sandwich or a wrap," she offers.

"Thanks, Lay, but I'll run over there and get something."

"Are you sure? I don't mind."

"I'm sure. Besides, I don't want this guy in my ass because you're buying me lunch." He winks.

"He's just a big teddy bear," she says, resting her palm against my cheek. Her thumb traces over my beard that I happen to know that she loves when my face is buried between her thighs. "I need to get back to work." She leans in for a kiss, before standing and gathering my trash, and wrapping up the rest of hers and placing it in the bag.

"You didn't finish eating."

"Did you see the size of that thing?" she asks.

"Wow, I didn't think you shared, O" comes from the doorway.

"Oh my gosh! I'll be at my desk." Layla laughs and scurries from the room.

"Gotta admit, bro, that blush of hers is damn cute," Marshall says, leaning against my desk.

"Yeah," I agree. Then again, everything about Layla is cute and sexy in my eyes.

Another look at the clock tells me we have just four, short more hours until I can get her home and in our bed where I can lose myself inside her. It's without a doubt, my favorite place to be.

CHAPTER
TWENTY FOUR

"**W**OW, LOOK AT you," I say to Sawyer as she approaches my desk. "Did Royce see this outfit?"

"No," she says with a laugh. "He had to be here earlier than me. I got to sleep in."

"He's going to flip," I tell her.

"Meh, he'll be fine."

"I loved it when you bought it, but I love it even more now. It looks great on you," I tell her honestly.

"Thanks."

"What the fuck are you wearing?" Royce's deep voice echoes throughout the lobby area.

"Uh-oh, broody Royce," I whisper, making Sawyer laugh.

"Sawyer," Royce says, now standing next to her.

"Hey, babe." She smiles up at him.

His eyes soften, which tells me that although he may be

brooding over her outfit, the love he has for her outshines it all. "What is this?" he asks. His hand disappears where I can't see it, and her body moves closer to his.

"It's a new skirt. I bought it a couple of weeks ago when Layla and I went shopping."

"Where's the rest of it?" he asks.

The elevator dings and I turn to watch Conrad walk off. "Damn," he says, fisting his hand and placing it in front of his mouth.

"Keep walking, Con," Royce bites.

"Looking good, sis." Conrad chuckles as he walks past us to head toward his office.

"You have to go home and change," Royce tells her.

"What? I'm not going home to change."

"Yes, you are. Sawyer, I can't work knowing my brothers and every other man, hell, probably some women are ogling you."

"They are not." Sawyer shakes her head. "Conrad is just trying to get you worked up."

"Well, he succeeded."

"What did I miss?" Owen asks. "Conrad just walked past my office, laughing like a hyena."

Sawyer loses control as a giggle escapes her lips. She quickly places her hand over her mouth when Royce glares at her. "You're trying to kill me. That's the only explanation."

"What did you do, sis?" Owen asks her.

"He doesn't like my skirt," Sawyer explains.

"Fuck, babe. It's not that I *don't* like it. I fucking love it, and your ass and your legs look fucking edible. That's what I don't like. That other men get to see you like this."

"Yeah, but I'm coming home with you." She holds her hand up and wiggles her fingers, making her engagement ring sparkle in the light.

"Fuck," Royce mutters. He rests his forehead against hers, and I force myself to look away, giving them their moment.

"I should be back here in time to take you home," Owen says from beside me.

"If not, it's fine. Sawyer already said that she would give me a ride home."

"I hope this meeting doesn't take all damn day."

"Either way, I'll see you when you get home."

"I love that I get to come home to you." He leans down and presses his lips to mine.

"Yeah, well, I love you," I tell him.

"You ready?" Royce asks Owen.

"Yeah. Let's get this day over with."

"Exactly. We've met with this guy more times than I can count. He needs to either shit or get off the pot," Royce grumbles.

"What is it for?" I ask. I'm still learning the ins and outs of the business.

"He's the competition. His company is headed for bankruptcy. We've offered to buy him out, but he's dragging his feet. The further he goes into the hole, the less our number for purchase is," Owen explains.

"Today's it," Royce adds. "I'm done dealing with him. We were trying to be nice and give him a buyout. His only other option is to find someone else to do what we've been offering for months, or file bankruptcy."

"Yikes."

"Yep." Owen leans down and kisses me again. "Have a good day, baby."

"You too." Sawyer and I watch them as they walk away.

"Damn, we are lucky," Sawyer says, turning to face me.

"That we are. He took that well."

She waves her hand in the air. "He's a big softie. They all are."

"I'm starting to see that." The truth is, they all try to be hard, but spend five minutes with any of the Riggins brothers, and you'll see that they are indeed soft-hearted and loving men.

"I better get to work. Lunch today?" she asks as the phone rings.

"Yes," I say, waving to her. "Riggins Enterprises, this is Layla," I answer. I hear nothing but hard breathing, louder this time than the previous calls. "Hello? Riggins Enterprises, this is Layla," I say again. Nothing but more breathing greets me. I don't have time to deal with these kids today. I have two reports for Grant to get done today, so I hang up. Putting the call out of my mind, I get to work. The office is quiet today with both Royce and Owen gone. Then again, maybe it's just because I know Owen's not just down the hall in his office. It's really distracting at times knowing he's so close, while I'm craving to be near him, but knowing it's inappropriate at the office.

With the phones now quiet and two of the five brothers out of the office, I'm able to get lost in the reports I'm doing for Grant. I don't even realize what time it is until I see Sawyer's shadow fall over my desk.

"Ready for lunch?"

"Is it that time already?"

"Yep. The deli across the street is calling our name."

Reaching into my desk drawer, I grab my purse and phone and switch the phones to the out-to-lunch message. "Did I tell you that a new bakery is coming in down the street?" I ask her as we enter the elevator.

"Oh, God, my hips don't need to hear that." She laughs.

"Stop, you're gorgeous. It will be convenient when needing breakfast for those early morning meetings. Hopefully, we can work with them, and they'll deliver. Making our lives easier."

"Good call. When are they opening?"

"I'm not sure. I heard them talking about it the other day when I stopped in at the deli to grab Owen and me some lunch."

"We'll have to keep an eye on it. That's the perfect excuse for us to check it out and introduce ourselves," she says as we exit the building.

Lunch is good as always; this little deli is on point with their food. The company's even better. With each day, Sawyer and I get closer, and I value that friendship. I know she has a best friend in Hadley, but she's quickly becoming mine.

I'm so engrossed in what I'm doing that I'm startled when the phone rings. It's been really quiet this afternoon, and I've been able to mark things off my to-do list. "Riggins Enterprises, this is Layla," I answer. Nothing greets me but breathing again. I'm sure it's just kids, but it's starting to not only piss me off but get a little creepy. "Riggins Enterprises, this is Layla," I say again. Nothing but breathing, so I hang up.

"How was your day?" Owen's voice pulls me out of my thoughts.

"Hey. You're back sooner than I thought you would be."

"It's done. He's playing games, and we're over it. He's going to have to find someone else to bail him out."

"That's sad for them, but at least you and Royce tried."

"That we did. You in a place to head out early?"

Looking down at the clock, it's thirty minutes until quitting time. "I don't know. My boss might get upset."

"Your boss says get your shit, we're leaving," he says, leaning over the desk for a kiss.

I stand from my chair and meet him halfway. "I guess it's time to go then," I say when I pull away from the kiss. "Let me call Sawyer and tell her."

"Go on," Royce says, coming out of his office. "We're leaving for the day too," he says, running his hands through his hair. "Turn off the phones, and let's get out of here."

"You heard the man," Owen says.

Not needing to be told twice, I shut down my computer, turn the phones over to night mode, and grab my purse from my desk drawer, swiping my phone from the desk, following Owen to the elevator.

Before the elevator doors close, Owen has his arms around me, and I'm leaning into him. "What do you say we pick up dinner on the way home?"

"I don't mind cooking."

"I know, but I just want to hold you." He kisses the top of my head. "I'm exhausted, and all I want to do is spend the rest of the evening with you in my arms."

"How can I say no to that?"

"I was hoping you would say that. What sounds good?" We step off the elevator.

"Honestly, wings." I grin up at him.

"Even better, they deliver. You can call and order when we get in the car, and it should be there not long after we get home."

"Wings and my man. Sounds like a good night to me."

"I love you." He chuckles. My reply is to blow him a kiss as he opens the car door for me. Before we are even out of the garage, I have my phone to my ear ordering dinner.

"I'm going to grab a shower," Owen says when we get home. "Here's my wallet to pay for dinner." He reaches into his pocket and hands me his wallet.

"I can—" I start, and he gives me a look that tells me not to argue.

"I'm buying dinner." His shoulders are slumped, and he's been quiet since we got home.

"You okay?"

"Yeah." He sighs. "I'm just over today. I hate that we wasted so much time on this company, only to not have a deal in the end."

"Go shower, wash the day away, and I'll be here waiting for you." That earns me a kiss, but not just any kiss. One that curls my toes as he heads to the shower. Not two minutes later, our food arrives. I leave it packed for now. I have other plans. When I enter our bedroom, I can hear the shower running. My man's had a bad day, and it's up to me to make it better. Stripping out of my clothes, I step into the bathroom. Owen has his arms braced on the shower wall, letting the water rain down on him. I slide in behind him, wrapping my arms around his waist. He places his hand over mine as I press a kiss to his back.

He turns and lifts me into his arms, pressing my back against the wall. "Having you here means everything to me. *You* mean everything to me," he says, kissing my bare shoulder. "I love you, Layla."

"I love you too." His lips find mine, and I open for him, giving him all of me. When he slides into me, I sigh, relishing the feel of our connection. Slowly, he makes love to me in the shower. It's as if he's memorizing every touch, every sensation. It's intimate, and as my orgasm crashes over me, I can't help but think that my heart also feels as though it's bursting—not from pleasure, but from love for this man.

"Stay here. Don't even bother getting dressed," Owen says, leaving the room with nothing but a towel wrapped around his waist.

Grabbing the hairdryer, I dry my hair enough that it's not dripping wet and pull it up on top of my head in a messy bun. I'm turning off the bathroom light when he comes back into the room carrying dinner and a couple of bottles of beer.

"Dinner in bed?"

"Now you're speaking my language." I smile at him. He looks less stressed after our lovemaking, and I'm glad I could offer him that. He's done so much for me. I want to be the one he can turn to, the one who can turn a shit day into one that's not so bad.

We devour dinner and snuggle up to watch a movie. I think we make it maybe fifteen minutes before we're making out like teenagers, and Owen hovers over me, making love to me for the second time tonight.

It's only Thursday, and this work week has been long. I'm ready for this weekend. Owen and I are going car shopping. He insists I can drive one of his, but I want my own. I've saved all of my money from working here since Owen barely lets me pay for anything. This is something that I want to do on my own. To say that I'm excited is an understatement.

The office is quiet again today. Royce and Owen begrudgingly agreed to another meeting for the company they were trying to buy. The owner called begging. Apparently, he was playing hardball. When Royce told him they were done, the reality of his situation hit him, and he begged them to reconsider. This time they took Grant with them. Something about power in numbers.

My desk phone rings. "Riggins Enterprises, this is Layla." Once again, nothing but heavy breathing, and I've had enough. "Look, I don't know why you keep choosing this number to harass, but this is a business. We don't have time for the games."

"You never were much fun," a raspy voice that I would recognize in a crowded room replies.

"W-Who is this?" I ask, hoping I'm wrong.

"What? You don't even recognize the sound of your mother's voice?"

"M-Mom. H-How did you find me?"

She laughs. It's a haunting sound. "Oh, come on. Did you really think that you just left town and I didn't know where you were? Oh, no, my darling daughter. I've been watching you for years. In fact, you've been making me money, but we can get into that later."

"What do you mean? How have I been making you money?" I can hear the panic in my voice. I would have been happy if I had lived the rest of my life never hearing her voice ever again.

"Now, now, I can't be giving away all of my secrets." She laughs. "At least not until you give me what I want."

"What are you talking about? If you've been following me like you claim to be, you would know that I don't have anything. Nothing. I don't even have a car."

"You're right, you don't, but that man of yours does."

My heart drops to my toes. "No."

"No? I didn't even tell you what I wanted yet."

"It doesn't matter. I won't let you touch him or his family. They're good people. They don't need evil like you in their lives."

"Silly girl, they already have me in their life. They have you. You are a part of me, little girl. Don't forget that."

I shiver at her calling me "little girl." It's what she always called me. I don't know why she bothered to name me Layla. She never used my name. Never.

"Now, like I was saying, I know you don't have a pot to piss in, but you've done well for yourself. Finding a man with money. I taught you well."

"It's not like that. I love him."

"Oh, I'm sure you do. That's why you're going to do what I tell you. I want a million dollars. Cash. You have one week to get it to me, or else."

"No." I push the words past my lips. "I won't use him like that."

"You don't have a choice. I'll be delivering you a package. In fact, it will be there within the hour. I think you'll see things my way once you get it. Don't call me. I'll call you." With that, she ends the call.

My hands shake as I place the receiver back on the base. I can't believe she found me, and what is this nonsense that I've been making her money? I have no idea what she could be sending me, but I feel like I'm going to be sick. I hate her. I know that hate is a strong word, and I shouldn't hold the feeling in my heart, but... I. Hate. Her.

My only saving grace is that Owen is out of the office today. I focus on taking deep, even breaths, willing my heart to slow its rhythm. My concentration is shit, and there is no point in trying to get anymore work done today. The whooshing sound of the elevator doors opening has me standing and watching as a young guy, who can't be older than eighteen if that, approaches my desk.

"I have a delivery for Layla Massey."

"I'm Layla," I tell him.

He hands me the package. "This is for you."

"Thank you. Um, can you tell me who sent you?"

"No, ma'am. I work for a courier service. I just get the packages and the name and address for delivery. Have a great day." He waves. I stand and watch until the elevator doors close, shutting him in before my eyes go to the letter-size envelope sitting on the corner of my desk.

With shaking hands, I retrieve the envelope and slowly tear it open, pulling out the contents. It takes me a minute to decipher what I'm looking at. Once I figure it out, my stomach rolls. With the envelope and its contents clasped tightly in my hands, I rush for the restroom and lose the contents of my stomach.

CHAPTER

Owen
TWENTY FIVE

AFTER OUR MEETING yesterday, Royce, Grant, and I called Conrad and Marshall, inviting them for drinks. Finally, after months of negotiations, we were able to close the deal to buy the small trucking outfit just east of Nashville. The company wasn't a huge competitor, but they were a competitor. A drink was in order, and it's been months since the five of us got together for a beer. I forgot how much fun hanging out with my brothers was. We don't do it nearly enough, and I told them so. They all looked to be surprised by my admission, but we agreed to make sure we get together more often.

It was late when I got home, and Layla was already sound asleep. It was nice knowing she was at home waiting for me. I slid in bed next to her, pulled her into my arms, and slept like a baby. All was right in my world, until the light of day, and there isn't a doubt in my mind that something is going on with her. She's been quiet all morning and barely touched her breakfast. It's not just that the smile that's usually shining at me every day is gone.

"You okay?" I ask once we're in the car and on our way to the office.

"Yeah, I'm fine." She smiles, but it doesn't reach her eyes.

"You seem off."

"I have a headache."

"Why didn't you say something? What can I do?" I glance over at her before turning my eyes back to the road.

Another smile, this one genuine but still pained. "Nothing. I just have to wait it out."

"Do you get them a lot?" It's been a few months since she moved to Nashville with me, and this is the first time I've heard of her having a headache.

"I used to get them all the time. It's been years, but when I do, it takes days to kick it."

"I'm going to call and get you into the doctor," I tell her.

"No, Owen, I'm fine. I just took some over-the-counter medicine. I'll be fine."

"If you're not better by tonight, we're going to the doctor," I tell her.

"Owen." She reaches over, placing her hand on my thigh. Her touch goes a long way to soothe my fears about her being sick. I couldn't survive anything happening to her. "It's a headache. I'll be fine."

I don't argue with her, that's the last thing she needs, but I'm sticking by my demand that if she's not better, we go see a doctor. "We're out of the office again today," I remind her. "Marshall will be there if you need anything."

"I'm a big girl. I can take care of myself."

"I know that, but you have a family who loves you, that includes my brothers."

"I know," she says, her voice cracking.

"We should go home," I say, not sure leaving the office and not being close to her today is the right choice. "You're upset."

"It's still a lot to take in, knowing I have so many people in my corner. Sometimes it gets the best of me. This is one of those times."

I pull into my spot in the parking garage and turn off the engine. Removing my seat belt, I turn to face her. My hand cradles her cheek. "You are the most important person in my life. I will always be in your corner. There is nothing in this world that can keep me from being by your side." Her eyes well with tears, and my anxiety piques. I hate to see her cry. "I love you, Layla. You know that, right?"

She nods. "I love you too." She smiles and wipes at her tears. "We should go in. I have a lot to get done today, and you're all supposed to be leaving in twenty minutes."

"I can stay," I offer, but she waves me off.

"I'm fine, Owen. Thank you for worrying about me and taking care of me. I don't know what I would do without you."

"Good thing we're never going to find out." I kiss her one more time on the corner of her mouth and pull the keys from the ignition, exiting the car.

I leave Layla at her desk with the promise to stop by before we leave to check on her again. She rolled those beautiful blue eyes of hers but didn't argue. She knows it wouldn't do a bit of good. Instead of going to my office, I stop by Marshall's. He's the only one of us in the office today. I would have gone to Sawyer, but girl code and all that. I'm afraid she might not tell me if Layla needs me. I know I can count on my brother.

"What's up?" Marshall asks, sitting up straighter in his chair.

"I need a favor."

"Anything." For all of the goofiness that comes from my brothers, the younger two especially, I know that I can always count on them. "Layla's not feeling well. Can you check in on her for me today?"

"Got it." He nods.

"Call me if she needs me. She won't ask," I say, running my hand over my beard.

"I'll check on her," he assures me.

"Can you also make sure she eats lunch? She didn't eat much for breakfast." It's on the tip of my tongue to tell him to forget it, and that I'm staying.

"Owen, I promise you I'll look after her. I'll make sure she eats, and if she needs you, even if she won't admit it, I'll call you."

My shoulders relax at his assurance. "Thanks, Marsh."

"Anytime, brother. She's family."

His easy acceptance of the woman I love has me feeling a little choked up myself. I know that my emotions are feeding off hers, but my brothers, they're my best friends, and Marshall, although six years younger than me, he's got my back.

"Thank you." My words are sincere.

"Go on, do what you've got to do. I've got her."

With that knowledge, I nod and leave his office. I stop by mine to grab a file I'm going to need for today and then make my way back to the front office to see Layla. She's sitting at her desk, looking at something on her computer. "Babe, why don't you at least take it easy today? That computer can't be good on your headache."

"I will. I was just checking my emails to see if there is anything that needed my immediate attention."

"Promise you'll take it easy?"

"Yes."

"Ready?" Royce asks, coming out of his office.

I look at Layla, and she gives me another one of those smiles that doesn't reach her eyes. "Do what you need to do. I'll have my phone on my desk all day. You can check in with me."

"What's going on?" Royce asks, and I can hear the concern in his voice.

"Nothing is wrong," Layla assures him. "I have a headache, a migraine, and Owen wants to cancel the day. I'll be fine."

"You sure? We can move this if we need to."

"Yes, I'm sure. It's Friday. I'll have all weekend to rest up. Besides, I took some headache medicine, and I'm already starting to feel better."

"Layla," I try again, but she gives me a look that tells me I'm pushing my luck.

"Owen, I'm fine. I promise you, I'm fine. If I need you, I'll call you. Marshall and Sawyer are both here with me today. It's not like I'm going to be alone. Go do your job so I can do mine."

"Get Sawyer or Marshall to drive you home if you feel like you're done for the day," Royce tells her. "Don't worry about missing work."

"I appreciate that. Thank you. I'm fine." She stands from her chair and walks to where I'm standing next to her desk. Her arms wrap around me, and she hugs me tight. "I love you, Owen Riggins."

I hold her close to my chest and breathe her in. "I love you too. Take it easy today, babe."

"Got it." She pulls away and salutes me, making me chuckle.

"She good?" Royce asks once we're on the elevator.

"I'm not sure. Something feels off to me. She's not acting like herself."

"She's not feeling good."

"I know, but it feels like more than that."

"Maybe she found the ring?"

"No. It's in the safe. Hell, I don't even know if she knows that the safe is there. I rarely use it. It has my passport and things like that. She doesn't have one, so I didn't have to store hers for her."

"I'm sure she's fine. Marshall and Sawyer will take care of her today. Like she said, she will have the weekend to rest if it's still there. If I know you, you'll make sure she does."

"Damn right," I agree.

"Hopefully, we can get these contracts signed today and get this deal done. I'm tired of dealing with these people."

"You're not the only one. We've put a lot of resources and time into this deal. I'm ready for it to be finished and off our plate."

"Right on."

The rest of the drive we talk about the deal, and what's next for

Riggins. We've opened several new hubs all over the United States, and we want to keep growing. Riggins Enterprises is our family's legacy. I know that all five of us wish to one day pass it onto our kids like our father did with us. Well, I know Royce and I, and I'm sure the others will too, once they settle down and really start to think about their future beyond what's going on that weekend.

As soon as we pull into the lot, I send Layla a text.

Me: We just got here. How are you feeling?

Layla: Better. Do your thing, Riggins. I promise I'm fine.

Me: I love you.

Layla: I love you too.

I slide my phone into the pocket of my suit jacket and climb out of the SUV. Time to put on my CFO hat and get this done.

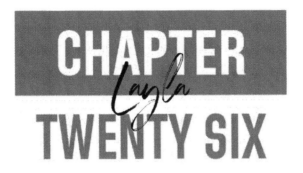

CHAPTER
Layla
TWENTY SIX

MY STOMACH ROLLS with a mix of guilt and nausea. The images that are locked in my bottom desk drawer make me want to be sick, and of course, there's the truth that I'm keeping from Owen. I don't know how to handle this. I'm not giving into my mother's demands, but those pictures.... I place my hand on my stomach, hoping that will ward off the nausea. I don't know how she got those pictures. Pictures of me in my apartment in Florida, and at our home in Indiana. Pictures of me in the shower, of me in my room. Naked pictures. My own mother was spying on me, and she said I was making her money.

Is she selling them?

I have to swallow back the bile that creeps up in my throat.

I can't bring all of this on Owen. His family. They're good people, and they don't need the bad publicity that this is sure to bring their family or Riggins Enterprises. The thought of hurting them tears me up inside. Even more so, the thought of walking away from Owen because of my vile mother has me an emotional mess. I can't do it. I won't give her money, and I don't want to walk away from Owen or his family, or this job. I just need some time to figure out how to beat her at her own game. I need some time to try and stop her.

Maybe I could go to the police?

No, that's not an option. The entire situation would be plastered all over the six o'clock news.

"Think, Layla, think," I mumble under my breath.

"You doing all right?" Marshall asks, startling me.

"You scared me," I say, placing my hand over my chest.

"Sorry," he says sheepishly. "How you feeling?"

I sigh. "That brother of yours told you to check up on me, didn't he?"

"He's worried about you."

"I know he is. I'm fine, Marshall. I promise. I just have a headache that doesn't seem to want to go away today." Probably because my mother is trying to blackmail me, but I keep that to myself.

"Can I get you anything?"

I smile at him. "No, but thank you."

"All right, I'll be in my office if you need me."

"Thank you, Marshall." He nods and turns to head back to his office. I can't concentrate, and part of it is the headache that my mother has caused. It's just a waiting game now. Every single time the phone rings, I jump, and fear grabs a hold of me, thinking it will be her.

I manage to spend the morning getting caught up on emails and rescheduling a few meetings. It's not much, but at least it's something. When the phone rings a few minutes before noon, I feel it in the pit of my stomach. It's her.

"Riggins Enterprises, this is Layla."

"You got my package?" my mother's raspy voice greets me.

"Yes. Where did you get those?"

She laughs. The sound is pure evil, causing the hair on my arms to stand on end. "Little girl, I told you. You've been making me money."

"What does that mean?"

"When you turned eighteen, I lost the money that the state was giving me for putting up with you, so I had to improvise."

"What money?"

She cackles. "Welfare, little girl. I got paid to keep you."

"Then why didn't we have food or clothes?" I ask, my voice shaking.

"You had a roof over your head, you ungrateful bitch. I needed the rest of that money."

"For drugs? For booze? I'm your daughter," I say, my voice growing stronger as my anger takes route.

"You had no idea that we recorded you. We get a pretty penny for your showers on the internet."

"W-What?" I choke out over the lump in my throat. "What do you mean?"

"I mean those are pictures of the videos we stream of you. Don't worry, doll. We don't show your face. At least not yet. If you don't get me my money, I'll have your face plastered all over the internet. What do you think your little billionaire and his family will think about you then?"

"I hate you." The words fly out of my mouth. "Why are you doing this to me? You're my mother."

"You were income, little girl—nothing more, nothing less. And now you're going to be my big payday. I want a million dollars cash by the end of the day on Sunday, or we tell the world who you are."

"I can't get that kind of money."

"Figure it out."

"N-No. I won't do it. I won't take from him, or any of them to feed your habit."

"You will do as I say."

"I'm an adult. You can no longer control me. Go fuck yourself,"

I say, slamming the phone down on the base. I'm breathing heavy, and my heart is pounding so hard I'm afraid it might beat right out of my chest.

Closing my eyes, I take a deep breath in and slowly exhale. I repeat this over and over until I feel as though I have control. That's when the reality of my situation sets in. She's going to expose me for something I'm not. I need to decide what to do.

I don't know how I'm going to face Owen and his family. On the other side, I can't leave them either.

I'm going to fight back. That's my only choice. Leaving Owen isn't something I'm willing to do. Not without giving him the chance to decide for himself. I should be selfless and leave, but I love him too much.

I need to get my thoughts in order. Then I'll go to the police. I'll tell them everything, surely, they can help me. It's going to get out one way or the other. I refuse to take money from Owen or his family, not for her. Not like this. I just hope Owen and his family understands, and they're still here with me when this is all said and done. I'm going to embarrass them, and it's going to look bad on Riggins Enterprises. I know the chances are slim, but it's a chance I have to take. They're more family to me than my own mother, and if they ask me to leave, I'll go quietly.

I've never been happier than my time here in Nashville. I'm not giving that up unless I have to. I need to figure out how to tell them. Maybe after I go to the police, then I'll know more of how this is going to be handled, and maybe if I plead with the police, they can keep it out of the media. I'm a minor in some of those images and videos. My stomach rolls yet again, thinking about the perverts who've been watching me online. Even if there are not videos, she has the pictures.

I refuse to remain a victim of my circumstances of my mother. It's time to fight back. At least I'll know I stood up for what was right. I just hope I don't destroy my heart and happiness in the process.

Picking up my phone, I call Marshall. I could walk back to his office, but I don't want to see him or Sawyer. I just need to get out of here. "Layla," he greets me. His voice is harder than usual.

"Hi, Marshall. I'm not feeling well. I'm going to go on home. Can you tell Owen for me if he comes back to the office?"

"You okay?"

"Yeah, just think I need to lie down."

"You need me to drive you?"

"No, that's okay." Shit, I forgot I don't have a car here.

"Take Owen's car. He rode with Royce. We'll make sure he gets home."

"Are you sure?"

"Yes. You know he would rather you do that than Uber."

"Thanks, Marshall."

"You sure you're okay?" he asks.

"I'm sure. I'll see you on Monday, if not before then."

"Text me and let me know you make it home okay."

"Will do. Bye." I end the call.

Grabbing my purse, I make sure I have the spare set of car keys for each of Owen's cars that he insisted I have. Luckily, I find them in the bottom of my purse. Next, I unlock my bottom drawer and retrieve the envelope that has the pictures. The evidence that I'll be presenting to the police later this afternoon.

I just need a minute to myself. To process what's going on, and how I might lose the love of my life and his family over this.

CHAPTER
TWENTY SEVEN

I TOLD MYSELF that I wasn't going to hover over Layla today. Owen and Royce are protective of their women. If she says she's fine, she's fine. However, I told him I would take care of her, and I meant it. Glancing at the clock, I see it's lunchtime. Saving the document I'm working on, I head to Layla's desk to see if she feels like eating anything.

I stop when I hear her voice. "I hate you." I've never heard Layla talk like that, and the venom in her voice tells me she means those three words with everything inside her.

"I can't get that kind of money," she says.

Who in the fuck is she talking to? She's obviously on the phone since I don't hear another voice.

"N-No. I won't do it. I won't take from him, or any of them to feed your habit."

Him? Is she talking about Owen? I move a little closer to try and get a look at her desk. Sure enough, she's on the phone. Her hand is pressed to her forehead, and she's visibly upset.

"I'm an adult. You can no longer control me. Go fuck yourself." She slams down the phone, and I'm ready to go to her to see what the hell is going on, but give her a minute to compose herself. When she picks up the phone again, and I hear my desk phone ringing in the distance, as quickly and quietly as I can, I rush back to my office.

I get to the phone in time to have her tell me she's not feeling well after all, and that she's going home. I remind her that she rode with Owen, and insist that she take his car, that I'll make sure he gets home to her. I know O gave her keys. He was bitching the other day that she wanted to buy a car when he has one that she can drive. I get her wanting her independence, and so does he. He just wants to take care of her.

"Text me and let me know you make it home okay."

"Will do. Bye."

Ending the call, I stand at my office door and listen for the elevator. Her heels click against the floor, the door whoosh open, and then silence. My feet carry me back to my desk, and I call Sawyer. "Hey, Sawyer. Layla had to go home today. She's not feeling well."

"Really? I'm such a bad friend. I've been buried in work all morning trying to get caught up before next week I didn't even realize."

"Headache," I tell her.

"Oh, well, I'll save what I'm working on and move to her desk."

"Thanks. I'm actually heading out for the day. Something came up."

"I see how it is. Everyone leaves me all alone."

"There's security downstairs," I remind her. "No one is getting to this floor unless they are approved."

"Oh, I know. I was just kidding. I'll see you Sunday for dinner?" she asks.

"I'll be there," I assure her before ending the call. Turning off my computer, I grab my phone and keys and head out. Once I'm in my car, I head to Royce's house. I call him on the way.

"Hey, what's up?" he asks.

"You still with Owen?"

"Yeah, we actually just finished up our meeting."

"Good. I'll meet the three of you at your place."

"What's going on?"

"I'll tell you when you get there. Just make sure you bring Owen, and Grant too. I'm calling Conrad."

"Is it Mom and Dad?" There is worry in his tone.

"No. But we need to rally, brother."

"Noted. We're on our way."

The line goes dead, so I call Conrad. "Hey, Con," I say when he answers.

"What's up?"

"You still working with Dad today?"

"No, we just finished up. The old man can still work like he's in his twenties." Conrad laughs.

"No doubt. Hey, can you meet up with us over at Royce's place?"

"Sure, what's up?" His voice changes. He knows me well enough to know if I'm not joking around, it's serious.

"Just meet us there. I'll explain when I get there. I think it would be easier to do it once."

"I was just with Mom and Dad, who is it?" he asks.

"Layla."

"Fuck. Does O know?"

"No, and I'm not exactly sure what we're dealing with, but we need to rally."

"I'm on my way," Conrad assures me before the line goes dead.

I want to be there when they get there, so I push the pedal a little further to the floor. I don't know what's going on, but I know without a doubt that we're going to get to the bottom of it.

You don't mess with a Riggins and get away with it.

CHAPTER

Owen

TWENTY EIGHT

"**W**HO WAS THAT?" I ask Royce."

Marshall. He wants us all to meet him at my place." He doesn't take his eyes off the road.

"Did he say why?"

"Nope."

He's not telling me something. Realizing I'm not getting anywhere, I pull my phone out of my pocket and dial Marshall. "What's up?" he greets me.

"What's going on?"

"Just need to talk to you all." He evades my question.

"How was Layla?"

"She left about fifteen minutes ago. She took your car. She said she just wanted to go home and rest," Marshall explains.

"Fuck, I knew I should have just skipped today."

"She said she would text me when she gets home."

"Did she?"

"No," he admits. "But she looked exhausted. I'm sure she just went home and went to bed."

"Yeah, you're probably right. All right, we're almost at Royce's, you there?"

"Just pulled in."

"See ya soon." I end the call and debate on calling Layla. If what Marshall said is right, she's sleeping, and I don't want to disturb her. I know she's not feeling well. I decide to send her a text. If she's up, she'll reply.

Me: Did you make it home okay? How are you feeling?"

By the time we pull into Royce's driveway, she hasn't replied. I tell myself it's because she's asleep, but I can't help but worry about her. As soon as we find out what Marshall needs to talk to us about, one of these fuckers is taking me home to her.

Royce parks his truck beside Marshall's, who is parked in front of Conrad. Grant, Royce, and I climb out of the truck, and I'm the first to ask. "What's going on?"

"Let's go inside," Marshall suggests.

"You okay, brother?" Grant asks him.

"Yeah." His reply is not all that convincing, so we follow him inside, waiting to see what bomb he's going to drop on us.

"Let's hear it," Royce says once we're all settled in his living room.

Marshall looks at me. His gaze is intense. "O, I overheard Layla on the phone today at the office."

"Okay?" I ask calmly, even though the idea of whatever this is involving Layla has me on high alert.

"She was talking to her mom," Marshall says, keeping his eyes locked on mine.

"Fuck," I hiss.

"I only heard Layla's side of the call, but she told her she couldn't get that kind of money."

"Son of a bitch," Royce seethes. "What is it with people using us for money?"

"That's not Layla," I say, getting in his face.

"Whoa, I didn't say it was. However, her bitch of a mother seems to have no issue with it," Royce replies.

"I don't have details. Layla was pretty upset, so I didn't call her out on it. I wanted all of you to know first so we can get a game plan together."

"I need to go home," I say, running my fingers through my hair.

"I agree," Marshall says. "She's upset, and I'm sure she needs you. But we all want to be there for her. The two of you aren't dealing with this crazy psycho on your own."

"What he said," Conrad chimes in. "What do you need?"

"Fuck, I don't know. Layla. I just need to see her."

"Have you met her mom?" Grant asks.

"Fuck no. Layla left home the day she turned eighteen and never looked back." I go on to tell them what I know of her life before Florida. I hate that I'm betraying her trust by telling them, but these are my brothers. They're standing here with me, willing to go to battle if that's what it takes. They love her too.

"I think we need to go talk to her. Get her to tell us what's going on, and we can form a plan from there."

"We should call the police," Conrad suggests.

"Probably," Marshall agrees. "But, I think we need to talk to her first. We don't want to steamroll over her."

"I'll do what I have to do to keep her safe," I tell them.

"We got you, brother." Royce's hand grips my shoulder. His phone rings and his eyes light up when he looks at the screen. "Hey, babe." He listens. "Yeah, I'm with my brothers at our place. Layla had a call from her mom, and we're going over to talk to her. Can you go to Mom and Dad's? We don't really know what we're dealing with, and I'd rather you not be here alone."

His words send fire through my blood. I have to get to Layla. I motion with my hand that we need to leave, and he nods, the others falling in behind us as we head back outside. Grant and I ride with Royce, while Marshall jumps in with Conrad. Royce hangs up with Sawyer and immediately calls our parents, letting them know what's going on. I tune him out as I reach for my phone in my pocket.

I try to call Layla, but she doesn't answer. Fear and panic like I've never known washes over me.

Something is wrong.

I hit End and redial her number. Over and over again I call her and keep getting nothing but her voice mail. Grant, sensing my panic from the back seat, reaches up and places his hand on my shoulder. He doesn't say anything, but then again, he doesn't have to. I know my brothers have my back always. I just hope that whatever we're about to walk into, all five of us, and Layla make it out unscathed.

Pulling into our driveway, there is an older model SUV sitting in front of the garage. Royce doesn't even have the truck in Park, and I'm opening my door and jumping out, rushing toward the front door. Trying the handle, it's locked. I fumble with my keys in my pocket, and my hands shake so badly I can't get the key into the handle.

"Let me," Grant says from behind me.

If I'm overreacting, they're never going to let me live this down, but my gut tells me I'm not overreacting. I don't recognize that SUV, and Layla doesn't feel well. She wouldn't invite anyone over. My guess is I'm about to meet my future mother-in-law. Good, I get to tell her to take her demands and fuck off, and to leave my girl alone.

Grant gets the door unlocked and pushes inside ahead of me. I hear a scream, not just any scream but one of pain, and push past him. What I see is something I will never forget as long as I live.

"Get the fuck away from her!" I seethe.

CHAPTER
TWENTY NINE

Layla

THE ENTIRE DRIVE home I'm running through scenarios. Every time I think about my mother filming me, I have to swallow back the bile that rises in my throat. Will Owen still want me knowing that perverts across the world have seen me? All of me? I send up a silent prayer that he will.

My heart tells me he's a good man and he will know that this isn't my fault. He was my first, so he knows I don't sleep around, and we live together. He knows me; at least, I hope he does.

Pulling into the driveway, I hit the button for the garage door opener. The door rises, and I pull his car inside. Grabbing my purse, I climb out, and that's when I hear her.

"Little girl, I've been waiting for you." My mother's raspy voice sounds from behind me.

Slowly, I turn to face her. "What are you doing here?"

"You and I need to have a little chat."

"There is nothing more to say. I won't give in to your demands.

You can tell whoever the hell you want to tell that it's me in those pictures or videos or whatever. I won't extort money from Owen or his family. They're good people."

She laughs. It's manic. The sound sends chills racing down my spine. "You see, that's where you're wrong. I've lost out on a lot of money since you up and left that shithole you called home."

I cross my arms over my chest. "That's rich coming from you. I grew up in filth and shambles."

"You always were an ungrateful little bitch." She raises her arm in the air, making a come-here motion, and I watch as a man, who looks just as rough as she does, climbs out from the driver's side of the SUV. "This is Don. Don, this is—" She starts, but his words stop her.

"Oh, I know this sweet piece," he says, grabbing at his crotch.

"Leave. Both of you. I don't want you here."

"Like you have a say in the matter. Don," my mother says, and the filthy guy comes at me. I try to run, but he reaches me in time to pull my hair and drags me back into his chest. His breath smells like death, making me gag.

"I've got plans for you. All that teasing. It's time to pay up, little girl." His lips press against my cheek, and his tongue slips out, licking the side of my face. I gag, which only makes him laugh. "I've been waiting a long time for you," he whispers in his smoker's voice as he drags me into the house. I hear the garage door start to close, and I pray Owen gets home soon before it's too late.

Don drags me into the house and tosses me on the couch. I scramble to get away from him. Not willing to go down without a fight. I'm so focused on crossing the room I don't see his hand coming until it smacks me across the face.

"Bitch," he seethes. "You want it rough, I can make that happen." This time it's his fist that connects with my jaw, and the hit has me seeing stars and crying out in pain.

"Oh, did that hurt? Just wait." He tosses me back on the couch. I kick out my legs to keep him from advancing on me, but he's fast, moving out of the way. He kicks back, right at my knee, and the pain is excruciating. "Fuck you!" he screams with spittle flying out his mouth.

I'm sobbing, but that doesn't keep me from fighting him when he comes at me with a knife. "Don't move," he sneers, holding the knife toward me. My chest heaves, but I stop my movements, not sure what he's going to do. My body trembles with fear as he takes the knife and slices down the middle of the blouse I wore to work today. It was one I bought on one of my many shopping trips with Sawyer. It was also one of my favorites. "There she is," he breathes the words. "Just like I remember."

"Don! You want a beer?" my pathetic excuse for a mother calls out. "Looks like he's got the good stuff."

"Yeah!" Don calls back.

A few seconds later, my mother appears with two beer bottles. She doesn't even spare me a glance as she hands Don his beer. "I'll go get the camera," she tells him, turning to walk back out of the room.

"This time, you're going to know you're being recorded. And the world will know it's you. I'm not going to hide your face this time. No, that would be a shame. Then they won't be able to see what I've done. They won't be able to see what happens when you fight me." His grin is filled with malice.

"Please let me go. I don't have much, but I'll give you what I have," I plead with him.

"You might not, but that man of yours does. Have you changed your mind? I gotta admit, that would change plans for tonight."

"No." I swallow hard. "I won't take money from him to give to you."

"That dick must be good," my mother says, joining us again.

"She's about to see what good dick is like." Don grabs his crotch yet again. The eye that's not swollen shut closes so I can try to block out what's happening.

I send up a silent prayer. *Please God, if things get worse, don't let Owen be the one to find me.*

"Stand up." Don yanks on my arm. I pull, not wanting to stand. Partly because I'm afraid of what he's going to do next, and partly because the pain in my knee is still throbbing. "Fucking stand up!" he screams. His hand once again connects with my cheek, and it feels as though he pulls my arm out of its socket when he tugs me from the couch.

I stumble as he hauls me along behind him, only to feel another set of arms capture me from behind. "Hold still," my mother scolds me.

"Just need a minute," Don says. The next thing I know his hands are on my waist and he's got my skirt around my ankles. "Fuck, the real thing is so much better," he says. "Get a chair," he tells my mother, as he slides his arms around me and pulls me close. He nips at my earlobe. "You fucked up, little girl. You should have given us what we wanted." With that, he pushes me, and I fall into a hard chair. I'm guessing one from the dining room.

With his hands on my shoulders, he holds me to the chair while my mother ties my arms behind my back. "I'll get the camera set up," he tells her.

"Mom, please don't do this."

"You refuse to get me the money that I want, then I'll take it. Your little moving stunt cost me a lot and I have people that I owe. I told you I would get it out of you one way or the other." She tightens the rope so tight I can already feel the circulation being cut off on my wrists.

"It's showtime," Don says, standing before me. My eye is so swollen I can't see out of it. With my one good eye, I see him advancing on me with the knife held out in front of him. That's when I feel the rope tighten around my legs. "I've missed these," Don says, taking the knife and cutting my bra in the middle. I feel the cups being torn from my breasts.

"Let's get this over with before he gets home," my mother says.

With a nasty grubby hand, Don cups my breast. All I can do is close my eyes as the tears once again begin to fall. I don't know what I've done in life to deserve this, I just pray that I make it through it.

"Open." I hear his gruff voice. I force my one eye open to find him standing over my lap with his dick in his hands. "Open," he growls. My eyes slide close, which is why I don't see the punch to my temple coming.

I sees stars, but I fight. Clamping my jaw shut as tight as I can, I breathe through the pain. I'll bite him if he gets any closer. I swallow back the vomit that threatens to spew from my mouth.

"Fucking make her open," Don tells my mother.

I feel her hands on my cheeks, the pain from her squeezing is like fire, but I fight her on it. I'm woozy from the hit, and all I want to do is succumb to the darkness that's calling me, but I don't. I fight to keep my mouth shut.

"Get the fuck away from her!" an all too familiar voice rings out.

Owen.

So many voices and pounding feet. I hear flesh hitting flesh, and a female scream. I'm pretty sure it wasn't me. Then I hear his voice in my ear. "I'm here, baby. I've got you. We're going to get you out of here."

"Owen." I'm able to croak out his name through my tears.

"I'm here, Layla. I've got you." His voice cracks. "Call a fucking ambulance!" I hear him shout. "Stay with me, baby."

"I-I love you. I-I told them no." I need to explain it to him, but the pain is so unbearable and the darkness is calling. My pain is also blanketed with relief because Owen is here. He's here and it's over. They can't hurt me anymore. He won't let them.

"I love you too. Just stay with me, Layla. Help is on the way."

I open my mouth to tell him I love him. To tell him that the sound of his voice is the best thing I've ever heard. I want to tell him that I'm sorry, that I never meant to bring evil into his life. I try to reply, to tell him everything, but darkness claims me.

CHAPTER  THIRTY

I T'S BEEN TWO long days sitting in this chair next to her hospital bed. I refuse to leave her side. Alice, that's Layla's mom, she and her partner, Don, were taken into custody. Alice sang like a canary claiming Don threatened her. The police didn't buy it, but the police did manage to learn what was going on. Alice and Don had been filming Layla. She was just a preteen when it started. They followed her to Florida and continued to film her in her apartment. When she moved here with me, they lost track of her. That is until the picture from the Gala made the news. That's how they found her. I led them to her, and that's something I will never forgive myself for.

The only saving grace is they never showed her face. Their video of the time at our house, which they'd plan to later upload, was evidence enough. However, the idiots had the camera rolling when they were in the car. They discussed what they had been doing, and how the plan was to extort a million dollars from my family and me and still sell the video. Their stupidity sealed their fate.

It's a good thing.

The two of them behind bars is the only thing keeping me from killing them both. Well, and the fact I refuse to leave her side. I want to be here when she wakes up.

"How's she doing?"

I look up to find Royce standing next to me. I didn't even hear him come in. "No change, really. She's woken up a few times, only to fall right back to sleep. They're telling me it's normal. The hits to her face were severe, as is her concussion. Sleep is what her body needs to heal." At least that's what the doctors and nurses tell me every time I ask about her waking up.

"Here." He hands me the small black box I asked him to stop by my place and pick up.

"Thanks, man."

"Anytime."

"Knock, knock," Sawyer whispers, pushing open the door. She glances at Layla, and her face drops. She doesn't stop until she's standing right in front of me. She bends and wraps her arms around me in a hug, and I have to battle with the emotion that clogs my throat. "We're here for you. Both of you," she whispers.

"Thanks, sis. I'm good. I just need her to wake up."

"She will," Sawyer says, stepping into Royce's arms. "She needs time to heal."

"Can she come back from this?" I ask them.

"She's strong," Sawyer tells me. "So damn strong. She's going to need you, but yeah, she can come back from this."

"I can't take her back to that house. I can't make her live there."

"You can stay with us."

"Thanks." I nod. "Mom and Dad offered too."

"Whatever you need," Royce states. His hand on my shoulder tightens, giving me his support. "We're going to head out. Mom and Dad are on their way, and Con, Grant, and Marsh are in the waiting room."

"Thanks for this." I hold up the ring box. Royce nods.

Sawyer gives me another hug before turning and leaning in to kiss Layla on the cheek. "He needs you," she whispers. "Get better soon."

Fuck me. Hot tears prick my eyes, but I push them back. Not seconds after they leave, my other three brothers come walking into the room. "We're here, brother," Grant says solemnly. He gives me a hug, and the other two do the same. Every day I've sat here with my girl, my family has been here multiple times to visit and offer their support.

She's here in this bed because she was protecting my family and me. We all know that, and the fact is, they loved her before all of this, now she's one of us regardless of whether or not we're together. However, we're going to be together. That little black box in my pocket ensures that.

I'm not giving up until this woman agrees to marry me and has my last name.

"You need anything?" Marshall asks.

He's taking it the hardest. He blames himself for letting her leave the office. He had no way of knowing what was going to happen. He isn't to blame, and I've been telling him that. If anything, I owe him for his quick thinking and getting me to the house as fast as he did. He called in the Riggins cavalry. I don't think he's going to let the guilt go anytime soon. Maybe when Layla wakes up, she can convince him.

"No. You've done enough. You brought me to her."

"Not soon enough, brother," he says sadly.

"This isn't on you, Marsh," I tell him. He nods, but I can see in his eyes he's blaming himself, no matter what I say about it.

"We're going to get out of here. Mom is pacing out there to get in here and see the two of you." Grant grins.

"They were here earlier today."

"You know, Mom. She's a worrywart when one of her kids is hurting. This time it's two of them," Conrad says.

He has no idea how much his words mean to me. That my family sees and accepts how incredible the woman is who's stolen every last piece of my heart.

"Thanks for stopping by," I tell my brothers.

"Oh, here." Marshall hands me a bag that I didn't see until now. "Just a couple of bottles of sweet tea, some Combos, beef jerky. I thought you could use some snacks."

"Thanks, Marsh."

He nods.

After a round of goodbyes, my brothers leave, and my parents push open the door. "I didn't think they would ever leave," my mom says, going to the opposite side of the bed. I watch as she gently picks up Layla's hand, mindful of her IV and holds it in hers. "How's our girl doing?" Mom asks.

"G-Good," I say, clearing my throat. "At least that's what they tell me. I just want her to wake up and stay awake. I want to hear her voice and see those baby blues," I say, looking at Layla. Her eye is still swollen shut, and her face appears to have every color under the rainbow from the bruising. The doctors assure me it's all normal and a part of the healing process. I hate it. Every time I look at her, I want to go down to the jail and strangle her mother and Don for doing this to her.

"She's healing, Owen. It's going to take some time, but she's going to be okay. None of her injuries are life-threatening. The concussion gave them pause, but she's showing great improvement." My mother recites what the doctors told me word for word. That tells me that she's been harassing the medical staff, which has my mouth tilting in a grin.

"You know how she is," Dad says. "When it's one of her babies, she takes charge, and I'm not the only man who can't say no to her." He chuckles.

"Hush," she says, her smile wide. "I wanted to make sure we weren't missing anything." She places Layla's hand back on the bed and digs into her purse. She pulls out some kind of wipes and begins to carefully wipe at Layla's face.

"Mom, what are you doing?"

"These are going to make her feel fresh. She's going to feel all nasty when she wakes up. I'm hoping this will help."

"Let her be, son," Dad tells me. "You know once she sets her mind to something, there's no stopping her."

I nod, knowing he's right. It warms my heart that my mother wants to take such good care of Layla. I talk with my parents for about fifteen minutes or so. "Here's a bag of clothes. When she wakes up, there are some toiletries as well. We stopped by your place on the way here. I had to sweet talk those police officers to let me in," she says with a grin. "I'm not sure how soon until they will let her shower, but when she does, she's going to feel better having her own things."

"Thank you, Momma," I say, standing and walking to where she stands on the opposite side of the bed, giving her a hug.

"We love you both. There's a room ready for the two of you whenever you need it. And the offer stands if you want to go get some sleep. I won't leave her side."

"Thanks, but I'm not leaving."

"We didn't think you would," Dad says from behind me.

"Call us when our girl wakes up. I'll be back this evening to bring you dinner."

"Mom, you don't have to do that."

"I know I don't have to. I want to. Oh, there are some clean clothes for you in that bag as well."

"Thank you both."

"We love you. Both of you." Six words spoken by my father that just about bring me to my knees. I won the lottery when it comes to parents, and I know without a shadow of a doubt that they're going to shower my girl with all the love and affection she can take once I spring her out of here. Hell, they already are, and she doesn't even know it.

They shut the door softly behind them, and it's just the two of us. I take my seat next to her bed and hold her hand in mine. I've done this a thousand times over the last couple of days. My thumb runs over her ring finger, and I can't help but wonder what my ring will look like on her finger. Taking the box from my pocket, I pull back the lid and look at the ring.

"I bought this for you," I tell her. I don't know if she can hear me, but the doctors tell me to talk to her; they feel like it helps the patients. "Royce went with me. Just like I went with him. Sawyer was in on it," I tell her with a chuckle. "Little did I know that it would turn into a routine for the two of you, but that's okay because I love it. I love that you have a friend in Sawyer and that she's going to be my sister-in-law and by default yours." I pull the ring out of the box, setting the box to the side.

"As soon as I saw this one, I knew it was perfect." Without thinking, I slide the ring on her finger. "Fuck, Lay, seeing my ring on your finger, it does something to me. I wish I could find the words to explain this pounding in my chest or the way that I feel… lighter." Carefully, I bring her hand to my lips and kiss the ring.

"When I walked into the house and saw you, I wanted to kill them, but I also needed to get to you. I've never been so scared in my entire life. It's going to be a while, a long fucking while, baby, before I let you out of my sight. I know they're behind bars, but fuck me, I could have lost you, and he could have—" I swallow hard, not able to speak about what that depraved son of a bitch could have done to her. What the police claim he was planning to do to her.

This time I don't choke back the emotion as I let the tears begin to fall. "I'm so sorry I didn't get there sooner." My voice cracks. "I should have been there to protect you. I let you down, and I'm so sorry. You were protecting my family and me, and, baby, I would have given them the money. It's only money. Nothing is more important than your safety. I wish you would have told me sooner, but I know you were trying to protect me. To protect my family."

Lowering my head to the bed, I keep her hand in mine. I let the tears fall. I've been trying so hard to be strong for her, for my family, but here in this quiet hospital room, I lose the battle I've been fighting. I don't bother to stop them or wipe them away. Instead, I let them fall unchecked as I hold her hand in mine. "Please, baby, wake up for me. I need to see those big blue eyes when I ask you to be my wife."

I'm a blubbering mess, so when I feel her hand move, I think that I imagined it. Lifting my head, I see her eyes are still closed, but her fingers move. *Please, God, let this be the time she stays awake. I just... need her.* "Layla?" I ask. Reaching up, I smooth her hair out of her face. "Wake up for me, beautiful," I say, and to my surprise, her eyes flutter. I rush to turn off the lights in the room and pull the blinds. "There, it's dark. Show me those baby blues," I whisper as I hover over her, waiting with bated breath to see her look at me.

Her lids flutter a few more times, and then she's looking up at me. "Hey, baby," I say, choking up. "I missed you." I've told her this every time she's woken up.

She tries to speak but grimaces. "Let me get you some water," I say, reaching for the ice-cold jug I insist on keeping for when she wakes up. I pour her a glass and bend the straw, bringing it to her lips. "Slow," I tell her when she drinks greedily. I pull the straw away, giving her a minute. "More?" She nods, causing her to grimace again. We repeat the process a few more times until she shakes her head that she's had enough.

"I-I'm sorry," she croaks.

"You have nothing to be sorry for. Layla, you were the victim in all of this." Lifting her hand, I place it on my cheek. "I could have lost you."

"W-Wh—" She swallows hard. "What's that?"

"What?"

"My finger?"

"Oh." I smile at her. "I forgot about that."

"What is it?" she asks, her voice weak.

"That's your engagement ring. I wanted to see what it would look like on your finger."

"You still want me?" she asks.

"I want you forever, Layla." I bring her hand to my lips.

"But your family, and the company. This can't be good for either."

"My family loves you as much as I do. They've all been here several times each day to check on you. They're all worried."

"They don't hate me?"

"No, baby. They all love you, almost as much as me." I wink at her. My eyes are dry and gritty from lack of sleep, but my heart, my heart is full and bursting with love for this woman.

Before she can reply, the doctor comes in. This is one I haven't seen yet. "What a nice surprise, Ms. Massey, I'm Dr. Higgins. How are you feeling?" the doctor asks as she comes further into the room.

Massey. We really need to change that. I'll get on that as soon as I break her out of this place.

CHAPTER
Layla
THIRTY ONE

HOW AM I feeling? I repeat the doctor's question in my head. I feel like I've been hit by a truck, so that's what I tell her. Her kind smile tells me she understands.

"It's almost time for more pain medicine," she assures me. "I just need to ask you some questions. Can you tell me your name?"

"Layla Massey."

"And this gentleman?" The doctor points to Owen.

"My boyfriend. I think," I add.

The doctor's brow furrows, and she opens her mouth, but Owen beats her to it. "Fiancé." He offers the doctor his hand. "Owen Riggins, future husband."

The doctor chuckles and looks at me, and I shrug and raise my hand to show her my ring. "Congratulations," she tells me. "But it says here that you're already engaged?" The doctor gives Owen a pointed look.

"He didn't ask me yet," I tell her.

Owen laughs. Leaning over me, he places a feather-soft kiss to my forehead. "Semantics, baby." He then turns his attention to the doctor. "That's the only way they would let me stay here, and no way was I leaving her."

She nods and smiles at him before getting back to business. "Layla. How many fingers am I holding up?" The doctor raises her hands, and she has three fingers raised.

"Three."

The doctor nods and goes on to ask me more questions.

"Headache?"

"Yes."

"Nausea?"

"Not really, not right now."

"Good. Welcome back." Dr. Higgins smiles. "I'll send the nurse in for more pain meds. We're going to want to monitor you for another day or so now that you're awake, and then we'll see what we can do to get you home." She types out a note on the tablet she has in her hand. "The police are going to want to talk to you as well. It's procedure. I'll hold them off to give you all some more time. I'm sure you want to see the rest of your family. I'm told you've had quite the rotating door of visitors."

"Thank you," Owen and I say at the same time.

"I'll also get you something to eat. We're going to start with liquids, broth, Jell-O, and if you hold that down okay, we'll graduate you."

I nod, and she leaves the room. As soon as the door closes, Owen drops to his knees beside the bed. "What are you doing?" I ask him. The way he's looking at me sends my heart into a flutter. Then it registers that he's on his knees. His eyes glance at the ring on my finger and back to my face. The flutter turns into a bass drum that I'm sure the entire hospital can hear as I realize what's happening.

"This isn't how I wanted to do this, but it's where we are, and I'm going with it. Life is precious, and none of us know how much time we have left." He takes my hand and places a kiss on the big-ass sparkling diamond on my finger.

"Layla, you limped into my life and stole my heart. Piece by piece, you chipped away at my armor until you had yourself firmly rooted in here." He taps over his heart with his free hand. "I want every day with you. I want you to be an official member of the Riggins family. I want to make babies with you, and live our happily ever after."

My cheeks heat as hot tears begin to fall. "I was so afraid I would lose you. That you wouldn't be able to see past what they did, putting me on the internet."

"That's not on you, Layla. That's on them. And the police have it all taken down. You were a minor in many of the videos," he says, his voice tight. "It's all down. No one is looking at you. No one but me."

I let his words sink in. It's as if the elephant of fear sitting on my shoulders is gone. It's all gone. The videos, the pictures, my mother and her sidekick. I'm safe, and I have Owen and his brothers to thank for that. If they hadn't shown up when they did, well, I don't even want to think about what could have happened. "You still want that? I mean, you still want me?" I need to hear him say it.

"Fuck, yes, I want you. All of you. Your heart, your body, your mind, your soul." He stops and shakes his head. He slides the ring off my finger, and I fight back the urge to cry. He kisses my finger and smiles up at me. His blue eyes are filled with so much love, I can feel it radiating off him. "Layla Massey, will you do me the incredible honor of being my wife?"

I don't say anything as I stare at the man who changed my world. He brought me to life and showed me what it's like to have a family and to love and be loved freely.

"Layla?" he asks, his voice wavering.

"Yes," I whisper. "Yes, I'll marry you," I say, my voice stronger. He exhales and slides the ring back on my finger, kissing it before standing to kiss me.

"I know it's not an elaborate proposal, but I couldn't wait a second longer to know that you're going to be mine forever." The smile that pulls at my lip causes pain from the cuts, but it doesn't stop me.

Forever.

I get to spend forever with him.

The door opens. "Hi," a young girl says. "I have some food for you." She places a tray on the table and moves the table over to the bed. "Looks like you don't get the good stuff yet," the young girl says. "Broth, Jell-O, and applesauce." Lifting the lid, my meager dinner is waiting for me. "Once you've eaten, the nurse will be in to give you some more medicine for the pain," she says, reading from her piece of paper. She pulls the small plastic cover off the broth, and the smell hits me, causing my stomach to roll.

"O-wen, I'm going." I barely have the words out before he's springing into action and places a small pink tub under my mouth as I vomit the water I just took in.

"I'll go get the doctor." The girl sounds scared to death and runs out of the room as if her ass is on fire.

Barely any time has passed and Dr. Higgins appears again. "Layla," she says. "Tell me, what are you feeling?"

"I feel okay, no change, but the smell." I push the table away from me. "It hit me, and I couldn't seem to hold it in."

She nods. "Okay. We're going to draw some blood and run some tests."

"Thank you, Doctor," Owen says, the worry evident in his voice. She nods and leaves the room. "You want the Jell-O or applesauce?" he asks.

"Either. I need this taste out of my mouth."

He picks up the applesauce container and begins to feed me.

"I can do it on my own," I tell him.

"I'm sure you can, but you can also let me take care of my fiancée." He winks.

I don't argue with him. It's nice to know that I have him to lean on. I've just taken the last bite when two uniformed police officers knock on the door. They ask me about what I remember, and I tell them everything. It's all still very vivid in my mind. They assure me that my mother and Don are going away for a very long time and that they will be in touch. They pass the nurse, who is there to ask me about my pain.

I feel the pain of the beatings they gave me, and the bone-deep exhaustion of the stress of the entire situation. I fear that when I close my eyes at night, it's all going to play like a highlight reel over and over again in my mind. My eyes trail to Owen, and that fear that threatens to cripple me loosens.

I know that this man, the man who has stolen my heart, and asked to keep it forever will be there for me every step of the way. He's proven that time and time again.

He's never given up on me. He *won't* give up on me.

"Dr. Higgins wants to hold off on pain meds until we get your bloodwork back," she explains as she draws two vials of blood. "Here are two Tylenol. Hopefully, this will help a little."

"It's fine. It's not unbearable at the moment."

"She put a stat order on this, so we should have the results soon."

"I'm going to call everyone and let them know you're awake." Owen kisses my temple and grabs his phone from the small table by the bed. I listen as he tells his parents, and asks them to call everyone except Marshall, who he would call himself.

"Why Marshall?" I ask him.

"He feels guilty. He heard you on the phone with your mom at the office, and he's beating himself up over the fact that he let you leave."

"I wouldn't have let him drive me. This isn't on him."

"I know that, but he's struggling."

"Dial the phone," I tell him, holding out my hand. Doing as I ask, he dials Marshall's number and hands me the phone.

"Hey, brother," he greets solemnly.

"Marshall," I greet him.

"L-Layla?"

"It's me," I assure him.

"Oh, thank God," he breathes. "How are you?"

"Well, I'd be better, but I need something from you first."

"Anything."

"I need you to tell me that you know this wasn't your fault."

"Fucking Owen," he mutters, making me laugh.

"Marshall, my mother is crazy. She would have found a way to get to me. She's been recording me for years, and I had no idea." The thought of what she did to me, how she exploited me like that, it causes bile to rise in my throat. I just have to keep reminding myself that it's over, and she can't hurt me anymore. I can finally start my life looking forward instead of over my shoulder.

"I'm so sorry, Layla."

"You want to make it up to me?"

"You know I do."

"Okay, I'm going to need a glass of that ice, you know the small chunks like they have at Sonic?"

"Are you kidding?" he asks.

"No. The ice chips here are bigger, and I'm on all liquids for a while. So, I'm going to need a big glass of that ice." I grin and wink at Owen.

"I'm on my way," he says, and I can hear him putting his shoes on.

"Thank you. Please drive safe."

"You got it, sis," he says, his voice cracking.

I hand the phone back to Owen, and he leans in for another kiss. "You did a good thing."

"I don't want him blaming himself. He's not to blame. If anything, he helped you know there was something to be worried about. At least, I assume that's why all of you were there. I think it was all of you. That part is a little fuzzy."

"We were all there," he tells me.

"I'm sorry your family got involved with my crazy."

"Your family." I hear a female voice. Turning my head, I see Lena and Stanley standing there smiling, both of them with tears in their eyes. "Your family got involved with the crazy lady who is nothing but an incubator for you. We love you, Layla." Lena comes to me and gives me a gentle hug.

"My turn," Stanley tells his wife. She steps away, wiping her eyes, giving Stanley room to hug me as well. "Good to see you awake, darlin.'"

"How did you get here so fast?" Owen asks them.

"This one had a feeling."

"A feeling?" I ask.

"Yep. I don't know how, but she's always been able to sense when something is happening with one of our kids. She said we needed to head over. We were already almost here when you called," he tells Owen.

Owen nods, and when Lena asks about what the doctors are saying, he goes on to tell them what the doctor said. "She got sick," he tells them. "So they took some blood."

"Oh." Lena's face lights up. "I'm sure it's nothing."

"Knock, knock," Sawyer says, walking into the room, Royce behind her.

"I think there's a limit for the room," Owen tells them.

"Tough," Lena tells him. "We're her family, and we're not causing a ruckus."

Owen and his dad share a look, both shaking their heads, a smile playing on their lips. I hate that they're seeing me like this, but even so, I can't help but smile at them. It hurts to move my lips, but I can't seem to help it. They're all here for me, and they've accepted me into their lives, into their family regardless of the shit my mother pulled.

"I heard there's a party?" Grant says, entering the room, Conrad right behind him.

"Where's Marshall?" Stanley asks.

"He's on his way," I tell him. "I asked him to do me a favor." Stanley nods, and understanding crosses his face. I guess it's no secret Marshall has been blaming himself. Speaking of the devil,

Marshall comes rushing into the room. He rushes to my side and hands me the giant cup of ice. "Thank you." I smile at him the best I can with a busted lip.

"How are you?" he asks.

"Better now that I have this." I hold up the cup. Owen takes it from me and pours some of the ice into a small cup that I can hold easier, and hands me the smaller cup.

"Thank you."

He leans in and kisses my temple. "Love you, Lay."

"Oh my God!" Sawyer shrieks. "What is that?" She's moving and doesn't stop until she reaches the bed and takes my hand gently in hers.

"Did we not tell you? We're engaged." Owen grins.

There is a chorus of congratulations, and each of them hug both Owen and me. We spend the next hour or so just talking about anything and nothing at all. They're distracting me from the pain that seems to be getting stronger as time passes by. That makes me wonder what the test results are going to say. What else could be wrong with me that they missed?

"You hurting?" Owen asks. He's so in tune with me.

"Yeah."

"I'll call the doctor," he says as the door opens.

"I'm not even going to scold you about the rules you're breaking right now." The doctor smiles at each member of my family. "However, I have some results for Layla, so I'm going to have to ask you to leave," she tells them.

"No," I speak up. "They can stay. They're my family," I say, choking up at my admission. "You can speak in front of them," I say once I have my emotions under control.

"Are you sure?"

"Definitely."

Dr. Higgins nods. "Okay, well, we did some bloodwork, and I was able to determine why you were vomiting."

"Okay?"

"Congratulations, Layla. You're pregnant."

"What?" I breathe, my hands automatically going to my stomach.

"You're pregnant. I have ordered an ultrasound to make sure everything is okay with the baby."

"Baby?" I whisper.

"When?" Owen asks her.

"They should be up soon."

"Thank you, Doctor," Owen says.

She nods. "The obstetrician on call will be in to speak with you after the ultrasound."

I nod, still unable to process what she just told me. She leaves the room, and it's eerily silent. I look up to Owen, and he's smiling. Not just smiling, his teeth are shining brightly through his beard, his eyes are squinted, and there are tears shining in his blue orbs. He bends so that our mouths are just a breath apart.

"We're having a baby," he says reverently.

"I'm so sorry. I don't know how I let this happen. I promise you I didn't do it to trap you. I-I'm so sorry."

"Layla." He shakes his head, grinning. "I already asked you to marry me, and you said yes, remember?" I nod. "We have to build a new house."

"What? We have a house."

"I can't ask you to live there. Not after—" His jaw hardens. I take a minute to process what he's saying. Can I live there? Yes. Yes, I want to live there. It's my first home, and yes that's where I was attacked, but it's also where we've made our life. Owen loves that house, and so do I. I don't want to move.

"I love that house. That's my first real home. The first place I ever really felt like I belonged."

"Babe, I don't—" He starts, but I talk over him.

"No. Owen Riggins, you are not selling that house. I want this baby to grow up there. I want the life you promised me when you gave me this ring." I wiggle my fingers in front of him. "I mean it."

"Okay." He nods, but I know I'm going to have a fight on my hands. I can see the concern written all over his face. I know we both have healing to do emotionally, and me physically. However, with Owen by my side, I'll get through it. We both will. Together.

"What if the baby's not okay?" I ask him.

"Oh, sweetheart." Lena comes to my side. "I'm sure everything is fine. You getting sick was a good sign. Regardless of what happens, you have us in your corner."

"All of us," Marshall speaks up.

I nod, hot tears pricking my eyes.

"Damn you, Owen. You just had to beat me to the first Riggins grandkid, didn't you? I'm the oldest, remember?" Royce asks. He's smiling wide, so I know he's trying to lighten the mood.

"You need some pointers, big brother?" Owen asks him. The room erupts into laughter, and I know that everything is going to be okay. I can feel it in the lightness of my heart, and the love in this room. Piece by piece, we're going to figure it out, and everything is going to be okay.

EPILOGUE
Owen

I T'S BEEN THREE months since the worst day of my life. Little did I know forty-eight hours later, would be the best day of my life. My fiancée is resilient. She has a few bad dreams here and there, but she put up one hell of a fight to keep our house. We compromised on a remodel. New furniture, paint, flooring. Anything that won't make the house match the one in our nightmares. The counseling also helped. Layla and I both sought the medical attention we needed to help us get past the hurt, the anger, and the pain that surrounded that night.

We both have them.

I can't tell you how many nights I've woken in a cold sweat reaching for her. All it takes is to feel her body next to mine, my hand over our son growing in her belly for me to calm.

That's right. We're having a little boy. We found out three days ago. We haven't told anyone, not wanting to take away from the excitement of this weekend. My big brother is getting married to the love of his life. Sawyer is going to be my sister, and I couldn't be happier for either of them.

"How's she doing?" Marshall asks from beside me.

"She's good, brother." I pull my eyes from my fiancée, who is talking to our mother and the bride. "You have to let it go, Marshall. It's going to eat at you."

He nods. "I know. I'm doing better. I just worry, you know? About both of you and the baby."

"My son is just fine."

"Son?"

"Shit." I chuckle. "Don't tell anyone. We were keeping quiet until after the wedding. Not wanting to take the spotlight away from Royce and Sawyer."

"What about me?" Royce asks, sneaking up behind me.

"Nothing." I try to evade him.

"You always were a shit liar, O." Grant laughs as he and Conrad join our little circle.

"Marsh knows," Conrad calls him out. "I can see it in your eyes."

"Mum's the word." Marshall makes a show of zipping his lips and throwing away the key like we used to do as kids.

"It's my wedding day. You can't keep secrets from me," Royce comments.

"I'll tell you soon enough," I tell him. My eyes are glued to Layla and Sawyer as they walk toward us.

"This looks like a whole heap of trouble," Sawyer says, sliding up next to Royce. He pulls her in tight.

"Hello, wife," he whispers, but we all hear him.

"What's going on?" Layla asks.

I offer her my hand and pull her into my side. One hand is around her waist while the other rests over our son. "Nothing."

"Bullshit," Royce grumbles. "O has a secret, and he's not giving it up."

"And Marshall knows," Conrad adds.

I look down at Layla, and her eyes are wide. I give her a subtle nod and shrug. She rolls those baby blues, but the smile that tilts her lips tells me she's not really mad.

That's the thing about Layla. She's lived through what most of us will never endure. She's a glass half-full kind of girl and doesn't sweat the small stuff. We both know life is too short for that.

WHEN I PULL my eyes from Owen, Sawyer is watching me. She tilts her head to the side, and I know my best friend is going to figure it out. I'm surprised I've made it this long. "Wait a minute. You had a doctor's appointment this week." She looks down at my belly, and I know I've been busted. "I'm such a bad friend I forgot to ask."

"No, we wanted to wait until after the wedding. This is your special day," I tell her.

"Fuck that. That's a Riggins you're carrying. We need to know," Royce says.

"You're holding out on me. You know I've been dying to shop," Sawyer says, her hands on her hips. "Come on, woman, the suspense is killing me."

"Are you sure?" I ask her. "This is your wedding day."

"And you're my best friend and future sister-in-law. I'm sure."

"Wait, if you're going to tell them, we need to get Mom and Dad over here," Owen tells me.

"I've got one better." Royce takes off for the DJ, and I watch as he reaches for the mic. "Ladies and gentlemen, can I have your attention?" he says into the mic. "Not only is today the best day of my life, but my brother and his fiancée have some news as well.

Come on up here." He motions for us.

"That's one way to get you to spill the beans." Grant laughs.

Hand in hand, Owen and I make our way to where Royce is standing. A year ago, being the center of attention would have stressed me out. Now, I'm so used to their antics, and I know they are on my team, so I just roll with the antics.

"I love you, brother," Royce says into the mic.

Owen gives him a hug, and Royce steps in front of me. "You too, baby momma." He smirks before handing Owen the mic.

"Well, we didn't want to do this today, but my big brother is impatient."

"So is my wife!" Royce calls out.

"Tell us!" Sawyer yells out.

"Well, Layla and I are happy to announce that baby boy Riggins will be arriving in April." Owen smiles down at me and bends until his lips press to mine.

The crowd erupts around us, and Royce and Sawyer are the first to wrap us in a hug and offer congratulations. Grant, Conrad, and Marshall are next before Lena and Stanley are standing in front of us. The moment is more than I ever dreamed it could be, as my family wraps us in their love.

"A grandson." Lena smiles through her tears. "Two daughters and a grandson, we are blessed. So incredibly blessed." We share hugs with her and Stanley before Owen leads me out to the dance floor.

"The day I met you, I wasn't sure what to think. I could never have imagined that this is where we would end up less than a year later."

"It's the magic." Owen grins.

"Well, the magic, and you, Owen Riggins. Piece by piece you saved me, you gave me love and a family, and every shattered piece of my heart is now whole, all because of you."

"Piece by piece, baby," he says, kissing me softly.

Thank you for taking the time to read Piece by Piece. Are you ready for more of the Riggins brothers? Grant's story is next in Kiss by Kiss.

Never miss a new release:
http://bit.ly/2UW5Xzm

More about Kaylee's books:
http://bit.ly/2CV3hLx

Facebook:
http://bit.ly/2C5DgdF

Instagram:
http://bit.ly/2reBkrV

Reader Group:
http://bit.ly/2o0yWDx

Goodreads:
http://bit.ly/2HodJvx

BookBub:
http://bit.ly/2KulVvH

Website:
www.kayleeryan.com

OTHER WORKS *by* KAYLEE RYAN

With You Series:
Anywhere With You | More With You | Everything With You

Soul Serenade Series:
Emphatic | Assured | Definite | Insistent

Southern Heart Series:
Southern Pleasure | Southern Desire | Southern Attraction | Southern Devotion

Unexpected Arrivals Series:
Unexpected Reality | Unexpected Fight
Unexpected Fall | Unexpected Bond | Unexpected Odds

Standalone Titles:
Tempting Tatum | Unwrapping Tatum | Levitate
Just Say When | I Just Want You
Reminding Avery | Hey, Whiskey | When Sparks Collide
Pull You Through | Beyond the Bases
Remedy | The Difference
Trust the Push

OTHER WORKS by KAYLEE RYAN

Entangled Hearts Duet
Agony | Bliss

Co-written with Lacey Black:
It's Not Over | Just Getting Started | Can't Fight It

Cocky Hero Club:
Lucky Bastard

Riggins Brothers Series:
Play by Play | Layer by Layer
Piece by Piece

ACKNOWLEDGEMENTS

To my family:

I couldn't do this without you. I love you. Thank you for always standing at my side.

Golden Czermak:

It's always a pleasure working with you. Thank you for your talent behind the lens and bringing Owen's story to life.

Kevin Lajeunesse:

Thank you for doing what you do. You brought Owen to life. Best of luck to you in all of your future endeavors.

Tami Integrity Formatting:

Thank you for making the paperbacks beautiful. You're amazing and I cannot thank you enough for all that you do.

Lori Jackson:

You nailed it. You were patient with me, and worked your photoshop magic. Thank you for another amazing cover. It has been my pleasure working with you.

Lacey Black:

You are my sounding board, and I value that so very much. Thank you for always being there, talking me off the ledge and helping me jump from it when necessary. We both now have a Royce to love and share with the world. Great minds and all that. LOL.

My beta team:

Jamie, Stacy, Lauren, Erica, and Franci I would be lost without you. You read my words as much as I do, and I can't tell you what your input and all the time you give means to me. Countless messages and bouncing idea, you ladies keep me sane with the characters are being anything but. Thank you from the bottom of my heart for taking this wild ride with me.

Give Me Books:

With every release, your team works diligently to get my book in the hands of bloggers. I cannot tell you how thankful I am for your services.

Tempting Illustrations:

Thank you for everything. I would be lost without you.

Julie Deaton:

Thank you for giving this book a set of fresh final eyes.

Becky Johnson:

I could not do this without you. Thank you for pushing me, and making me work for it.

Marisa Corvisiero:

Thank you for all that you do. I know I'm not the easiest client. I'm blessed to have you on this journey with me.

Kimberly Ann:

Thank you for organizing and tracking the ARC team. I couldn't do it without you.

Bloggers:

Thank you, doesn't seem like enough. You don't get paid to do what you do. It's from the kindness of your heart and your love of reading that fuels you. Without you, without your pages, your voice, your reviews, spreading the word it would be so much harder if not impossible to get my words in reader's hands. I can't tell you how much your never-ending support means to me. Thank you for being you, thank you for all that you do.

To my Kick Ass Crew:

The name of the group speaks for itself. You ladies truly do KICK ASS! I'm honored to have you on this journey with me. Thank you for reading, sharing, commenting, suggesting, the teasers, the messages all of it. Thank you from the bottom of my heart for all that you do. Your support is everything!

With Love,

Kaylee Ryan
AUTHOR